NASCAR

SECRETS and LEGENDS

SLINGSHOT MOVES
by Anna Schmidt

From the opening green flag at Daytona to the final checkered flag at Homestead, the competition will be fierce for the NASCAR Sprint Cup Series championship.

The **Grosso** family practically has engine oil in their veins. For them racing represents not just a way of life but a tradition that goes back to NASCAR's inception. Like all families, they also have a few skeletons to hide. What happens when someone peeks inside the closet becomes a matter that threatens to destroy them.

The **Murphys** have been supporting drivers in the pits for generations, despite a vendetta with the Grossos that's almost as old as NASCAR itself! But the Murphys have their own secrets... and a few indiscretions that could cost them everything.

The **Branches** are newcomers, and some would say upstarts. But as this affluent Texas family is further enmeshed in the world of NASCAR, they become just as embroiled in the intrigues on and off the track.

The **Motor Media Group** are the PR people responsible for the positive public perception of NASCAR's stars. They are the glue that repairs the damage. And more than anything, they feel the brunt of the backlash....

These NASCAR families have secrets to hide, and reputations to protect. This season will test them all.

Dear Reader,

What a fun book this was for me! I grew up in the heart of NASCAR country—went to college in Bristol, Tennessee, made frequent stops in Charlotte and have two nephews who are the original NASCAR nerd squad in that they can quote every stat of every race and driver going back many seasons! In researching Steve and Heidi's story I had so many wonderful moments—going "home" to Bristol and Charlotte, attending the NASCAR Sprint All-Star Challenge, spending time with the kinds of wonderful people who were the inspiration for the characters in this series, and meeting a neighbor right on my street here in Wisconsin whose company actually sponsors a car on the circuit! This is a series about family in all its many forms, and never was there a more inspired setting for rich family stories than the NASCAR community. Enjoy!

All best,

Anna

//////// NASCAR

SLINGSHOT MOVES

Anna Schmidt

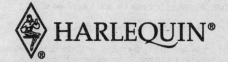
HARLEQUIN®

TORONTO • NEW YORK • LONDON
AMSTERDAM • PARIS • SYDNEY • HAMBURG
STOCKHOLM • ATHENS • TOKYO • MILAN • MADRID
PRAGUE • WARSAW • BUDAPEST • AUCKLAND

ISBN-13: 978-0-373-21788-5
ISBN-10:   0-373-21788-9

SLINGSHOT MOVES

Copyright © 2008 by Harlequin Books S.A.

Jo Horne Schmidt is acknowledged as the author of this work.

NASCAR® and the NASCAR Library Collection are registered trademarks of the National Association for Stock Car Auto Racing, Inc.

Printed in U.S.A.

ANNA SCHMIDT

is a two-time finalist for the coveted RITA® Award from the Romance Writers of America, as well as twice a finalist for the *Romantic Times BOOKreviews* Reviewers' Choice Award. Her most recent *Romantic Times BOOKreviews* Reviewers' Choice nomination was for her 2006 novel *Matchmaker, Matchmaker...,* and her novel *The Doctor's Miracle* was the 2002 *Romantic Times BOOKreviews* Reviewers' Choice Inspirational Category winner. Anna has published a total of eighteen works of historical and contemporary fiction. In 2008 Anna's novels (in addition to this one) include *This Side of Heaven* (Harlequin Everlasting Love), *Seaside Cinderella* (Love Inspired Historical) and *Mistletoe Reunion* (Love Inspired). A transplant from Virginia, she now calls Wisconsin home—escaping the tough winters in Florida.

Readers can contact Anna via her Web site, www.booksbyanna.com, or write to her at P.O. Box 161, Thiensville, WI 53092.

For Roger, Judy, Michael and Jan—you know who you are and what you did for this story—THANK YOU!

REARVIEW MIRROR:

After money scandals and sponsorship troubles caused image problems for Gideon Taney's racing team, he looked to PR agent Sandra Jacobs for help. But the only way to save Gideon's team—and Sandra's agency—was to ally with the man who had destroyed her family.

CHAPTER ONE

"HEIDI, GUESS WHAT?"

Heidi Kramer glanced up from escorting her last patient of the day—a Siamese cat—and its owner out the back door to the parking area and smiled. Steve Grosso—all six feet of him topped with a mop of sun-streaked hair and the bluest eyes this side of a clear summer sky—was standing in the middle of the waiting room of the Ridgemont Animal Clinic.

Heidi took note of the blooming cactus he was holding and grinned. "You've decided to take up gardening?" she joked as she came back toward the reception area, passing the examining room and collecting the chart for the Siamese from the door bin on her way. She made a couple of notes and went behind the front desk to refile the chart.

Steve leaned across the counter, placing the cactus on the desk in front of her. "Better," he hinted.

"You got accepted into the MBA program at the university?" she guessed, her eyes widening with pride. Steve had been talking about going back to school for his master's in business. His job as spotter for his cousin, Kent Grosso, the hottest driver in NASCAR, was more of a freelance position—not one designed to provide long-term financial security. He'd been thinking the higher degree would enhance his chances of getting a more secure job.

"Better," he said again. "Think you and me. Long-term."

"I give up." She laughed, seeing the excitement in his eyes. "Just tell me."

"I got a full-time position with Maximus Motorsports—salary, full benefits, even an office." Everyone in the area knew that Maximus Motorsports was one of the most successful organizations around at producing teams—and drivers—that topped the charts and created some of NASCAR's most recognized names, including that of Kent Grosso.

"Wow," Heidi said. "This is huge news." She put down her files and came around the desk to hug him. "It's terrific news." Her mind raced with the advantages this offered—for both of them. He'd be working right here in town. They could start seriously planning a future together, one they'd talked about off and on—mostly on—for months. "But wait, you love spotting races."

"I can still be a spotter. In fact that's part of the deal."

Heidi squealed with delight and tightened her hold on him. "This is amazing. This is fantastic. This is perfect," she said, punctuating each statement with a kiss. "Congratulations, honey. I am so proud of you."

Two years earlier, they'd met at a computer seminar at the local business college, gone for coffee after class and talked until the clerk in the coffeehouse started mopping the floor and turning out the lights. That night Steve had begun her induction into the world of stock car racing by explaining his role as a spotter.

"Spotters are positioned on the roof above the track with binoculars and a two-way radio to the driver and pit crew," he'd explained.

"Why?"

She'd never forgotten the shocked look on Steve's face. "Because...I've never been asked that before."

"I mean, you get in a car, you've got sideview and rearview mirrors," she'd said and Steve had laughed.

"You've never gotten up close and personal with a race car,

have you?" Then he'd explained about the absence of mirrors and presence of safety features that significantly limited the driver's visual field. "The spotter's job is to guide the driver through anything that happens on the track—a crash, debris on the track, working his way through a pack of cars to the front."

"And you get paid for this?"

He'd grinned. "Not all that much. It's a freelance thing. I get paid by the race."

"So don't quit your day job, right?" she'd said.

Steve had shrugged. "I make enough to get by."

But once they began to dance around the idea of taking things to the next level, Steve had talked a lot about the need to get into something more secure. And now it had practically dropped into his lap. He reached over and retrieved the cactus in its hand-painted clay pot and placed one hand over his heart. "So will you please come to Phoenix," he sang. "You can fly on Kent's jet with me," Steve added, fudging the words to suit his purpose. He flashed the dimpled smile that in all the time they'd been together had never failed to send Heidi's heart into overdrive.

"Phoenix? What about the Talledega race this coming weekend?"

"Front-office job means front work for the team," Steve said, still grinning. He set the cactus on the counter and lifted her in a hug, swinging her around in the open reception area. "Oh, babe, do you know what this means?"

"You're on the payroll?" She returned his hug.

"Big-time," he assured her.

"But this is so out of nowhere—I mean, you didn't say anything about a position opening up."

"That's just it. It's a whole new position," he said, his blue eyes sparkling with excitement.

"Put me down and tell me what happened," she said, taking his hand and leading the way down the hall to her small office.

She was well aware that she was buying time while she digested what this news might mean for the two of them. She was also aware that she was refusing to acknowledge niggling doubts that muttered "red flag" and "caution." A salaried position meant they could afford to talk seriously about a life together—marriage, a family. Wasn't that what they'd both been wanting?

"It was totally out of nowhere," he said happily as he shut the door and plopped onto the small sofa in the corner, pulling her down to sit next to him. "Okay. I get this call from Dawson to stop by the office." Dawson Ritter was the owner of Maximus Motorsports, and because Kent drove for Maximus, technically Dawson had always been Steve's boss as well as Kent's. "And when I arrive, Kent is there with Dawson, grinning at me like the cat that swallowed the canary, but saying nothing."

"You had no idea why they wanted to see you?"

"None. Dawson gets that look he has like the world's falling in around him and tells me he's concerned about how the season is going so far, especially for Kent."

"Well, yeah. Dawson wants Kent to repeat as champ."

"Exactly." Steve stood and started imitating Dawson's habit of pacing. "Then he says, 'Grosso?' I figured he was talking to Kent, but he was looking at me. 'Kent's got this idea that we need a go-between.'"

"Go between what?" Heidi asked.

"That's what I said," Steve replied, shaking his head. "Answer? He's created a new position—team liaison to coordinate things between the front office and the team."

"Wow," Heidi said.

"But that's just part of the position. Dawson wants someone to take on some of the advance work with Kent's public relations rep, Amy Barber."

"She works for Motor Media Group?"

"Yeah. Dawson wants his own person on-site getting things

set up at various venues—races, public appearances, hobnobbing with sponsors—whatever. My role is to help Amy work out any problems before he and the team get there. And I'll get to continue as Kent's spotter."

"So he's sending you to Phoenix for how long? And what about Talledega?"

"I'm heading to Phoenix tomorrow. Kent's scheduled to do the keynote speech for the national meeting of sales reps for Vittle Farms." Vittle Farms, the national leader in the production of organic foods, was Kent's primary sponsor. Their corporate headquarters were located not five miles from Heidi's clinic. "From there Kent and I will go on to 'Bama."

Heidi couldn't help mentally counting the days that he would be away. "That's almost a week," she said softly.

Steve sat back down and took her hands. "Hey, I thought you'd be happy about this. This is what I've—we've—been hoping for. It's the kind of job—and financial security—we can build a future on."

"It's wonderful news," Heidi said, her enthusiasm sounding forced in spite of her best attempts to hide her doubts.

Steve frowned. "But?"

"It sounds like you'll be on the road a lot," she admitted.

"So, come with me," Steve said softly. "It's Phoenix."

Heidi was sorely tempted to chuck her responsibilities and surrender to Steve's plea. They both loved the desert. When they had been in Phoenix the previous November, she and Steve had hiked in the mountains and enjoyed the city with its fascinating mix of Old West and sophisticated contemporary culture. And there on a mountaintop less than a year after first meeting, they had declared their love for each other and started to entertain the idea of marriage and a family.

"I'll even go horseback riding," Steve joked, reminding her of the day they had rented horses in Phoenix. Heidi had been incredulous that this man who grew up around horses was not only nervous, he was terrified of sitting atop a live animal. Heidi, a seasoned rider, had still been laughing about that as they shared a picnic supper and watched the sunset from atop Saddleback Mountain. And then he had said the words she had been longing to hear.

He repeated them now. "Hey, I love you and I want us to build a life together. That life can start today."

"Say it again—that first part," Heidi said as she had that day on the mountain.

Steve leaned in to kiss her. "I love you," he whispered as he kissed the lobe of her ear. "Love you," he said as he trailed kisses along the curve of her neck. "Love you higher than the mountains, deeper than the oceans, forever and a day—"

She kissed him back—once, twice, a dozen times. She lost count.

"So is that a yes?" Steve said when they came up for air.

"It would be wonderful, but you know I can't come," she said, forcing herself back to the reality of her responsibilities. "Clare's out of town and somebody has to mind the office."

Dr. Clare Wilson owned the clinic. Heidi had worked for her for the two and a half years since she'd gotten her license in veterinary medicine. In addition to being her boss and former professor, Clare was also Heidi's mentor, the closest female friend she'd ever had.

"Maybe Clare should stop running around the country organizing protest marches and take care of her business," Steve said, getting up and moving to the other side of Heidi's desk.

Clare was a nationally respected spokesperson for animal rights. "That's not like you, honey. Her advocacy work is important and that was the deal when she took me on here. Besides, you're not the only one working for our future. Clare and I have been talking about my buying into the business over time, becoming a full partner." As soon as the words were out she realized that she'd only made things more complicated. If she became Clare's partner she would have even less time to travel with Steve. "I mean down the road," she added, "after I finally finish paying off my student loans."

Steve ran a hand through his hair. "This partnership thing… well, I mean it's just that my new job gives us the kind of security we had thought maybe we'd need from your work if I went back to school."

"And?" Heidi said. There were isolated moments—occurring lately with more frequency—when it seemed to Heidi as if he often assumed that her career ambitions somehow took second place to his. Admittedly Steve wasn't as single-minded about racing as other members of his family, but there were times— and this was one of them—when she had to remind herself that he was a Grosso. He'd grown up in a world where aside from family, racing came first. "It *is* my profession," Heidi couldn't help reminding him.

"I know. That came out wrong. I'm…disappointed about Phoenix, that's all." He got up again, seemingly at loose ends. Clearly this was not the way he'd pictured her reaction to his news.

She walked over to where he stood by the window and put her arms around him. "I really wish I could go with you," Heidi said.

"It's just with this new job and the season really getting rolling, this might be the one chance we have for a while to steal some time to be together," he said, leaning his forehead against hers. "Lately it's like we're on different schedules and I miss 'us.'"

Us time. Steve had coined the phrase shortly after she began traveling to the races with him. From the start, he had always made sure they had some time to be together away from his responsibilities as Kent's spotter and the often overwhelming world of racing.

Heidi touched his cheek. "I know and I hate it, too. Hey, how about I drive you to the airport?"

"I can take my truck."

"Yeah, but if you do that, what reason would I have to be waiting for you when you get back?" she whispered and kissed him.

IN ALL THE TIME they'd been dating the one thing Steve had never gotten used to was the way Heidi's reaction to any given situation could still throw him off course. He had been so certain she would share his joy in the new opportunity that he'd driven straight to the clinic right after his meeting with Dawson and Kent had ended.

He'd seen her through the front window of the clinic, admiring her professional demeanor as she dealt with her patients and their owners. Garbed in lab coat with glasses perched atop her blond curls was always a turn-on. He'd tried biding his time until the last client left, but this news was too good to keep.

And she had been as thrilled as he'd imagined when he'd first delivered his news. But then as he outlined the details, her eyes had told a different story. In spite of her smile—always heartstoppingly radiant—the sparkle in those baby blues had gradually dimmed with the innate caution and reserve with which, he'd learned early on, she approached life in general.

The other thing he had learned about Heidi Kramer in the time they'd been together was that her childhood had left scars. Her family had moved around—a lot. Constantly starting over in a new school as her father followed his work across the country, she had learned how to protect herself with a veneer that was sometimes hard to penetrate. On the surface, she was all sparkle and quick wit, easily working her way into the very heart of any social gathering. But early friendships she had trusted had withered and died and as an only child with a mother fighting her own demons and a father who was seldom around, Heidi had compensated by finding her way on her own. It explained a lot— her uneasiness around his sometimes over-the-top family as well as her preference for quiet times alone.

Still, he had really thought that she would see the upside of his new position. It meant they could afford to talk seriously about a real future. But then he'd said that dumb thing about her work—always a speed bump with Heidi. The one thing she'd never wavered on was the fact that one day she hoped to have her own clinic, and she was certainly a great vet. If she couldn't have her own place, then partnering with Clare would be the next best thing.

"Is Heidi going to meet you at Talledega?" Steve's cousin Kent asked as the private jet pushed back from the team hangar and out toward the runway.

"She has to work," Steve said as he concentrated on fastening his seat belt.

"She could catch a ride with Tanya," Kent said. Tanya Wells and Kent were newly engaged and caught up in the throes of wanting to share their bliss with every other unattached couple they met.

"She has to work," Steve said again and strained to catch a last glimpse of Heidi standing near the hangar.

STEVE LEFT FOR Phoenix on Wednesday. After his work there he would head straight to the Talledega race in Alabama before returning home on Monday. Seeing him off at the private airport where NASCAR drivers and owners housed their private jets, Heidi had hugged him hard, then waved until the plane was well down the runway. And all the while she was asking herself why his new job felt more like a threat to what they had together than an answer to the future they had begun to plan.

She had no doubt they wanted the same thing—to spend the

rest of their lives together. But all of a sudden she had serious doubts about how they were going to accomplish that without one of them having to make compromises—compromises that might be all right now, but that in the long run they might come to resent having made.

Her parents' experience had taught her that. Her mother had abandoned a promising career as a concert pianist in favor of following her husband's job. But over time her mother's deep sadness and regret over what she had sacrificed had been at the root of the depression she suffered throughout Heidi's youth—a depression that had very nearly destroyed her parents' marriage.

There were two lessons she had learned well in her lonely youth. First, she would one day have a stable home in a community where she knew her neighbors and where her children went to one school. And second, she would build a career in a profession she loved—one that gave her an identity of her own.

After watching Kent's plane lift off, she sighed as she walked back to her car. Sometimes it seemed the closer that she and Steve came to building a life together, the more obstacles they found along the road.

CHAPTER TWO

TRUE TO HER NATURE, Heidi filled the lonely hours of Steve's absence with work. As an only child and ever the new kid in school, she had always found solace in excelling at her work—first with top honors in school and later as the popular new vet in town. She especially enjoyed working late when Steve was away. It made the time pass more quickly and night duty usually meant that an animal had been brought in for the more challenging work of emergency care. Heidi loved that part of her job.

On Friday, just before closing, Chester Honeycutt, the chief executive officer of Vittle Farms—one of the area's largest companies as well as Kent's major sponsor, had pulled up outside the clinic. It was raining hard and she'd held the door open for him as he ran inside carrying his dog, Macho, a feisty soft-coated wheaten terrier that Heidi had treated for routine procedures in the past. She was surprised to see the executive because she knew he'd also been scheduled to be in Phoenix for Kent's appearance at his company's national sales meeting.

Heidi had always admired Chester and his wife. A lot of executives would have chosen to make their home in a larger community like Charlotte, but Chester and Cindy had bought a modest home right in Kannapolis. They had settled in, sent their children to public schools, shopped at local stores and become as familiar a neighbor and resident in the small town as the town barber—or veterinarian. Recently Chester had further cemented his ties to the community by opening a nutrition-research center in the new biotech research park just behind the clinic.

"Heidi, thank goodness you're still here," he said.

Heidi took in the situation at a glance. Macho was bleeding from his head and neck. Chester looked as if he might pass out before the dog did.

"Down here," she instructed, leading the way to the first exam room. "Put him on the table," she said as she pulled on gloves and gathered instruments she would need for the initial examination. "Do you need some water or something?"

Chester shook his head and hovered next to the dog, stroking him gently.

"I've got him," Heidi said as she began cleaning the blood away so she could assess the seriousness of the injury. "What happened?"

Chester sat on the edge of the single chair and watched her work. "I just got home from Phoenix—our daughter's school play is tomorrow, so I came back for that. Anyway, I took Macho out and I didn't see the neighbor kid out walking their Great Dane. Neither did Macho, so when the Great Dane barked, Macho must have been startled. Anyway, he took off after him."

"Trying to live up to your name, were you?" Heidi murmured to the dog.

"The Dane controlled things from the outset. He grabbed Macho by the neck and held him suspended in midair until the neighbor kid and I could sort things out."

"Macho was lucky," Heidi said. "One good shake and the Dane could easily have snapped any smaller dog's neck." She continued her examination. "Some of this is pretty deep. I'll need to put him under while I put in some stitches."

Chester nodded.

"I'd like to keep him overnight just to be sure there are no problems."

Chester nodded again.

"He'll be fine," Heidi assured him. "Why don't you go on home and I'll call you later, after I've stitched him up and made sure there are no further injuries."

"Overnight?" Chester asked uncertainly. He stood and stroked the dog before turning to the open door.

"He's going to be fine," Heidi told him again. "Clare's son will come and spend the night here. That's what we do whenever we have patients who need follow-up after trauma. He'll call me if there's any sign that Macho is in trouble, okay?"

Chester smiled and nodded. "Hey, congratulations to Steve on his promotion. I saw him in Phoenix at the national sales meeting and he was doing a great job coordinating everything. I don't think I've ever seen Kent—or Dawson—so relaxed."

"I'll let him know," Heidi said.

"Call me, okay?"

"I'll call," she promised.

"WHAT WERE YOU THINKING, Macho Man?" she said later as she finished suturing the wound. "A massive dog like that? You should be smarter than to pull such a stunt."

The anesthetized terrier snorted and pumped one front paw as if throwing a punch.

Heidi's dog, Buster—a mostly black with white markings border collie and Labrador mix that she had adopted from the humane society—raised one eyebrow in Macho's direction. *Get over yourself, little guy,* the look plainly said. Buster stifled a yawn and resumed his position curled in the corner, waiting patiently for Heidi to finish up so they could go home.

"Now, Buster, be fair. There's no question that Macho here is brave and tough," Heidi continued, taking note of Buster's editorial comment on the discussion. "That's not the point. But, Macho honey—and I say this with love—even you have to admit that taking on a dog three times your size is dumber than dirt," Heidi said as she snipped the final thread.

Once she had Macho settled for the night and called the Honeycutts to reassure them that their beloved pet would be good as new in a few days, she glanced at the clock and mentally calculated the time difference between Kannapolis, North Carolina, and Phoenix, Arizona. Nine where she was made it six in Phoenix. Or was it seven? She could never keep the time differences straight, especially when she had to factor in daylight saving time. Whatever the time, Steve would soon be on his way to his next assignment—spotting the race in Talledega, Alabama.

Heidi checked on Macho then stretched her back as she walked through the halls of the clinic to the waiting room. Buster ambled across the room and nudged her leg with his wet nose. Dog and owner stood side by side staring out the window as they watched a hard April rain sluice over the redbrick walkways of the restored Cannon Mills shopping area. Her Prius hybrid was the lone car on the deserted street, and all the other colonial style buildings surrounding the tree-lined town center were dark.

"We can't go out in this," she said. Then she grinned down at Buster's upturned face and added, "I wouldn't send a knight out on a dog like this." The corny line always made her smile and lifted her spirits.

But as she returned to the desk to update Macho's file, she couldn't help stopping a moment to consider the large whiteboard that featured scheduled office time for her and for Clare. Steve had a good point. Clare had been traveling a lot recently. On the other hand, Clare had always been more than generous about allowing Heidi to set her schedule so that she could have long weekends off during the NASCAR season whenever possible. It was just that lately a number of high-profile celebrity cases had brought the animal rights issue to the front page as never before. Clare was always in demand, and Heidi understood how important it was to seize the spotlight whenever possible—even if Steve didn't. She might not be as outspoken as Clare was, but the cause of animal rights was no less dear to her heart. She and Clare shared more than a love of animals. They shared a passion for making sure those animals were protected from abuse.

Heidi sighed and absently ruffled Buster's furry head. Her cell phone vibrated against her thigh from its position in the front pocket of her surgical pants. She fished it out and flipped it open.

Spotterman, the screen read. The nickname she'd bestowed on Steve the first night they met had stuck.

"Spotterman?" His laugh had reached his eyes and she had felt the first inkling that this might be something more than just sharing coffee and conversation after a class.

"Yeah. You know, like a superhero."

"We kind of leave that superhero stuff to the drivers," he'd told her.

"Didn't you ever want to be a driver?"

Steve had laughed again. "I don't know anybody in this business who doesn't dream of being the guy behind the wheel. And yeah, I had my shot. But then I was in a pretty bad accident. Truth is, I'm better at spotting than driving."

Gorgeous and modest too, she remembered thinking. "Still, I think it works," she'd said with a sassy tilt of her head.

"Just as long as you don't expect me to wear some kind of spandex costume," he'd joked, and the name had stuck.

Her phone continued to vibrate. "Hey, Spotterman," she said, already feeling the stresses of the day drain away. "How's it going?"

"Other than the fact that I'm missing you and miserable?" he replied. He sounded tired and she could tell that he intended this as his usual lighthearted banter, but given his obvious disappointment when she'd chosen work over Phoenix, it sounded a little too close to blame.

"Sorry," she said.

Neither of them spoke for a beat.

"No, I'm sorry," Steve replied. He took a long breath. "It's just been a day."

"Talk to me," Heidi said and in that instant all was right between them.

She heard Steve's release of breath—release of tension. She imagined his slow grin reaching the corners of his tanned face and crinkling the laugh lines around his eyes.

"Where are you?" she asked.

"Talledega. Just got in an hour ago."

"With Kent?"

"No, I came on ahead. Dawson's worried about the team."

"You flew commercial?"

Steve chuckled. "Yeah. A definite step down."

"How was it?"

"The flight was fine—no screaming babies, actually had an entire row of three seats to myself. All good omens, and then we landed."

"And?"

He sighed. "The usual. Neil's bent out of shape about something and won't say what. Dawson's really starting to lose patience with him and Kent's understandably worried about his focus." Neil Sanchez had a reputation as one of the best crew chiefs in the business. As the linchpin that held the team together, especially before and during a race, Heidi understood that the team needed a crew chief they could count on. But lately Neil had been causing more problems than he'd been solving. "It's beginning to take a toll on everybody," Steve said. "But enough about me. What's happening there?"

Heidi told him about Chester and Macho, embellishing the facts slightly just to hear the music of his laughter. "He said you were doing a terrific job," she added.

"That's nice. You and Buster heading home now?" Steve asked.

"As soon as the rain lets up and Clare's son gets here to watch for any posttrauma signs that might crop up with Macho."

"I did get out for a walk in Phoenix while Kent was doing his thing," he said. "The desert was in full bloom."

"And to think, before I came along you didn't know a cactus even had flowers."

"No question my knowledge of plants and animals has been greatly enriched since you came into my life." He cleared his throat. "They had one of those wedding chapel places at the resort where we stayed."

"You mean like in Vegas?" Heidi gulped back laughter remembering the trip they'd taken to Sin City. "Was Elvis performing the ceremony or was it like that drive-through place we saw last year?" A year earlier, Heidi and Steve had doubled over in laughter at the gaudiness of some of what they'd seen in Vegas.

"No, this one was really nice—beautiful desert setting." He paused, then added, "Maybe you should check it out when we're out here in the fall for the race. A spring wedding might be nice."

Heidi swallowed hard, aware that the conversation had taken a new turn. "Okay, Spotterman," she said. "Didn't see that one coming."

"Yeah, you did," he said. "Honey, I need you with me."

"I know. I miss you, too."

"This isn't just about missing you, Heidi. I want us to be together. I want us to be a family. I want us to—"

"Steven Grosso, don't you dare propose to me over a cell phone," Heidi said, and then laughed to soften the reprimand. "You are not getting off that easily, mister. I want the whole down-on-your-knee package."

"Got it."

"I love you," Heidi said softly.

"Me, too," he answered.

"I know you love you as well, but—"

His laughter warmed her and made the rain seem more cozy than lonely. "I love you, Dr. Kramer. Got to go. Take it slow on the lake road. It'll be slippery with all that rain."

"Once a spotter, always a spotter," she joked.

STEVE CONTINUED to cradle his cell in one hand even after he'd flipped the lid closed, severing his connection to Heidi. The symbolism of the action had not escaped him. In fact, ever since she'd told him she couldn't make the trip he'd thought of nothing but his connection to Heidi.

This wasn't the first time he'd hinted at a proposal. It also wasn't the first time she'd dodged the hint, and if he was truthful with himself her hesitation was the reason he had postponed a serious proposal. So where did that leave them? From the moment he'd first seen her racing down the hall, late for the business seminar, Steve had been hooked. Then when they'd gone for coffee afterward, at first her manner of focusing her entire attention on him had been disconcerting. He was far more used to being in the background and letting others take their turn in the spotlight that followed the legendary Grosso racing family everywhere. But over time he had come to understand that shyness was something they had in common. By focusing on him, Heidi was taking the spotlight off herself.

Recently they had danced around the idea of marriage as they watched friends and family members—some of whom had been together a lot less time than Steve and Heidi—set dates to tie the knot.

"On the other hand," Heidi had announced one evening while they were watching a favorite television program, "just because Kent and Tanya are engaged, that's no reason that we should feel any pressure. I mean, we should seriously consider whether or not it's the right time for both of us, and with how busy we both are right now and with everything we need to work through—to be sure."

Steve teased her constantly about her habit of starting a conversation in the middle and delivering impossibly complex sentences on the thread of a single breath. He called it avoiding the pit stop, hinting that she refused to take a breath much as a driver might refuse to go in for a final pit stop even though the car was dangerously low on fuel.

Sitting alone now at a corner table in yet another hotel dining room that was a carbon copy of a hundred other places in other cities, Steve frowned as he picked at his dinner. It was Heidi's comment about "everything we have to work through" that had gotten to him.

"Earth to Grosso."

Steve glanced up, surprised to see his cousin standing next to him. "You're here already?" He shook off the reminiscing to focus on the issue at hand. "Everything go okay in Phoenix after I left?"

"Yeah." Kent Grosso was six foot three and solid muscle. His rock-star looks and easy smile guaranteed that even women who had no idea who he was couldn't help glancing his way. Kent was oblivious to it all. He was what was known in the business as a "driver's driver"—high praise used in racing circles to refer to a driver who understood this was a sport, not a life. Kent prepared well for every event, did his best, and when it was over, he was just one of the guys. Even those who competed against him week after week respected him, liked him. Kent was no prima donna, in spite of his rising fame and recent success.

Steve pushed his plate aside and indicated the empty chair across from him.

Kent sat and leaned back. "I talked to Tanya. She said Heidi's not going to make it for the race."

"I told you, she has to work. Clare's off doing her soapbox thing."

"Again?"

Steve shrugged. "Be sure to thank Tanya for asking her."

Kent nodded, then leaned forward, his voice low. "Did you talk to Neil?" he asked. He was frowning and Steve understood why.

"Not yet. I did meet with the rest of the team and they're all set."

"Are you saying that I got here before Neil did?" Kent rarely raised his voice, but when it came to his crew chief the fuse of his temper was getting shorter.

The waitress stopped and refilled Steve's coffee. When Kent nodded as she lifted the pot in his direction, she went to get an extra cup. "He's in town," Steve assured Kent. Steve had been trying to connect with Neil since he'd gotten off the plane. But the crew chief wasn't answering calls or picking up messages. He'd checked in at the hotel, according to the front desk, but no one had seen him since. "I thought you were playing golf in the morning and then coming."

"I canceled it. So Neil headed straight for a bar, right?"

Steve glanced away. "Probably," he admitted. "I'll go track him down and make sure he's sober and in the shop within the hour."

"Half hour," Kent said, biting off the words as he stood and strode away.

"He's not usually wound this tight," he said to the waitress who had returned with the cup and coffee. To Steve's relief she obviously had no idea who Kent was. The last thing they needed was a rumor circulating that Kent Grosso had been upset two days before a major race. Steve paid his bill with cash, adding a generous tip. The waitress thanked him then turned her attention to another table as they both got back to work.

"DID STEVE GET BACK YET?" Clare Wilson asked as she settled into the booth across from Heidi on Monday morning and pushed aside the menu. Clare was not a fan of racing. She understood little of the intricacies of the sport and cared less. But she liked Steve, mostly because he was the antithesis of her stereotype of anyone associated with NASCAR.

"He had to stay on after Talledega. Kent had some last-minute appearances," Heidi said, and studied her menu as if there might be a life-changing exam on it within the hour. "Tell me about the march in Atlanta," she said without looking up.

Clare reached over and gently pulled the oversize laminated sheet from Heidi's fingers. "The march was fine. Okay, what's going on with you?"

"Nothing," Heidi lied.

"Look, honey, I may not be the world's fastest study, but you just buried your nose in a menu you've known by heart since two days after the place opened. And you changed the subject to keep from talking about Golden Boy, so something is up. You don't want to tell me, that's fine, but don't kid yourself."

Heidi stared out the window.

Clare sighed and made an attempt to humor her. "Just because I put on my big-sister hat especially for you today…" She adjusted the tilt of the tangerine-colored wide-brimmed straw hat.

Heidi looked back at Clare. "I wasn't aware that your hats had assigned purposes." She felt herself relax, knowing Clare wouldn't push to have her reveal the problem.

"Well, they do, and from where I'm sitting it's just pure dumb luck that I grabbed this one to wear today."

"Your big-sister hat," Heidi repeated.

"It'd be a shame to waste it," Clare mused then turned her attention to the waitress and ordered for both of them.

While Clare defined every detail of the order—eggs scrambled but not runny, bagel warmed but not toasted, coffee poured after she had added the creamer—Heidi could not seem to stop staring at the hat. She'd never had a big sister—or a sibling of any kind. She'd never had a really good friend—until Clare came along.

It wasn't just the absence of lasting friendships that had shaped Heidi's outlook. As an only child she had never known the kind of closeness others took for granted. Of course, Steve was also an only child, but he'd practically grown up with his cousins, and no one had expected him to pack up and move on with no say in the matter time and again.

Heidi had lived all over the continental United States, and if it hadn't been for college, would have eventually spent time living in Alaska as well. That's where her mom and dad had finally landed—and stayed.

"So, Alabama," Clare was saying now. She had turned her attention back to Heidi after the waitress who had served them numerous times before had sighed heavily, taken Clare's detailed instructions and left. "Sorry you had to miss that one."

"He wants to marry me," Heidi said and immediately wished she hadn't.

"Well, that's an interesting response." Clare leaned closer as if about to share a secret. "This is not news, honey. The two of you have been on the marriage track practically from the day you met. Are you suggesting that half the population of this part of North Carolina doesn't know that?"

Heidi sighed and leaned closer as she lowered her voice. "I'm suggesting that it's an impossible situation."

"Right. He adores you and under ordinary circumstances, you blossom like springtime the minute his name is mentioned. I can see disaster written all over that one."

A few minutes later, the waitress delivered their breakfasts and Clare checked her eggs and the bagel then gave the waitress a beaming smile. "Perfecto," she said, and turned her attention back to Heidi. "Do you honestly believe that Steve's proposing is a problem?"

"He hasn't proposed yet," Heidi replied as she smeared orange marmalade on her dry bagel. "Not officially anyway."

"Details," Clare said with a dismissive wave of her fork. "So, clue me in. What is your problem?"

Heidi flinched. Why did it have to be her problem? It was just as disastrous for Steve. "You wouldn't understand." How could Clare possibly understand? She had lived her entire life in Kannapolis. She knew everyone and everyone knew her. She had the perfect marriage and two incredibly well-adjusted and popular kids, not to mention three of the most exotic cats known to exist.

Clare put down her fork and reached across the table. She placed her hand over Heidi's. "Make me understand," she said, all trace of sarcasm gone.

It was hard to break old habits. Heidi had long ago given up confiding in anyone because chances were that person wouldn't be there the next time she needed a friend and Heidi would have to start all over again. But Clare had been there, first mentoring her through vet school, then making a place for her to practice at the clinic. More to the point, she was here now.

"I love him," she began and saw Clare smother a smile. "Okay, that's the obvious part. The not so obvious part is that lately it's more like we're headed in different directions, directions that just can't work for building a solid marriage or a family life."

"Explain," Clare demanded as she resumed wolfing down her breakfast.

"He's starting to really build his career with the team. When we talked about his idea of watching for an opening in the front office I thought it would mean that he would be home more—here, not on the road. Then Mr. Ritter creates this new position and Steve just takes it—without even discussing it with me."

"Maybe he thought you'd see it the way he does," Clare said.

"How do you know how he sees it?"

"I don't, but a wild guess would be that securing a stable job with a reputable company is a huge first step toward securing a future with you."

"Okay, good guess. But what's the first assignment? He has to head to Phoenix to coordinate Kent's schedule at his sponsor's national sales meeting."

"But he's always worked in racing, honey. His entire family, except for his dad, is in racing. It's in the genes. And forgive me for reminding you, but you really seemed to enjoy running all over the country with him these last couple of seasons."

"I know and you're right. But then he was just Kent's spotter. He was only working during race weekend. Before this came along, he was thinking about getting into teaching, maybe going back to school for his MBA."

"One absentminded professor in the family is enough," Clare said, referring to Steve's father, Larry. "I can't see Steve following in Larry's footsteps. He seems close to Kent's parents. You told me that, even before his mom died, he and Kent were more like brothers than cousins."

"That's not the point. Spotting for Kent is very different from being Dawson Ritter's personal troubleshooter. Being part of management involves being available round-the-clock, traveling with the team, getting there early and leaving late. It becomes a lifestyle. Take this weekend. As a spotter, he would have left on Friday at the earliest and been back by Sunday night. But Dawson wanted him with Kent in Phoenix for the sponsors' meeting on Wednesday and then Talledega and then—"

Clare's eyes widened as if a light had just come on. "Oh, I get it. You're afraid that if you marry Steve you'll be right back to the life you hated as a kid."

"We'd be on the road for a good chunk of every week from February through November," Heidi said. She glanced out the window and blinked away a tear of frustration. "I mean, what would happen if we had kids?"

"What do other racing families do? *When* you have kids, you will take them with you or leave them with family or friends, like me, here," Clare explained.

"No. It's my childhood all over again and I swore that there was no way I would ever allow my kids to go through that." She attacked her food and Clare had the good sense to give her a moment to calm down.

"Okay, what else?" Clare asked. "It's not just his job."

Heidi sighed. "This is going to sound really self-centered," she warned.

"Try me," Clare said.

"I worked hard to get my vet's license. You know what that meant—means—to me. But with Steve taking this new position, what does that mean for my career? Am I supposed to be part-time or freelance?"

Clare smiled. "That's up to you."

"And just what do you think would happen to Steve and me if I gave up the work I love so I could follow him around like some gypsy for most of the year?" Blinking wasn't working and the tears started to spill over.

Clare handed her a tissue. "Oh, Heidi, sweetie, there's got to be a solution. I mean his working for Maximus is exactly the kind of secure future you both need, right?"

"Yeah. Job security, great benefits, plus he's going to be so good at it. He's already brimming over with new ideas. What if he's found his niche? I can't ask him to give that up."

"No," Clare said slowly as she took a long swallow of her coffee. "But why do you think this has to be an either-or-type arrangement—his career or yours?"

"Because how am I supposed to build my career and support his, which requires being on the road so much?"

Clare leaned back and studied Heidi for a long moment.

"Oh, I know I sound like some spoiled little brat," Heidi said. "It's all about me, right?"

"Look, I wasn't going to bring this up because I knew the idea was to let you get your student loans paid off before we seriously got into the details of it." Clare had Heidi's full attention. "What if we were to fast-track the partnership idea?" Clare grinned. "Get it? Fast track?"

Heidi blinked, her mouth open. "Are you serious?"

Clare laughed. "Well, yeah. I mean what's a few months between friends. While you get those loans paid off we can at least be drawing up the paperwork."

"You are serious."

"Well, don't act so surprised. You know I had this in mind when I hired you. Look, there's going to come a time when I want to do even more with the animal rights movement. At the same time you're going to need time to go with Steve to as many NASCAR events as possible. Sounds like a win-win to me."

"I…need some time to think about this."

"Fair enough. When will you make the last school loan payment?"

"September," Heidi said, mentally calculating the months. "But wait a minute. My income is the salary you pay me. If I become your partner, how will I have money to invest in a partnership?"

"Details. We'll let the legal beagles figure it out," Clare assured her. "In the meantime, are you in?"

"Yes…maybe…but…"

Clare rolled her eyes. "All right, think it over. In the meantime, as long as I'm on a roll solving your problems, let's talk about this idea you have that bringing up kids in a racing environment will somehow warp them for life."

Heidi sighed. "I do sound like it's all about me, don't I? I mean, how many people would kill for what I have—a man who loves me beyond reason and who I adore?"

"What if you talked to Steve's aunt? She raised two terrific kids."

"Patsy? She's nice and all but she's Kent's mom and, well, she's never really known any life other than racing. She'd have to take Steve's side. Besides, the women in that family intimidate me—not intentionally but they are so strong."

"Come off that. You're strong, too. You just need to think this through. There has got to be a way the two of you can be together the way you were meant to be."

"Without sacrificing who we are in the bargain?" Heidi said. "This homebody fell in love with a man who lives and breathes racing."

"Don't sell him short, Heidi. My guess is that he's well aware of the challenges you're both facing here. You'll work it out together."

CHAPTER THREE

STEVE FELT as if he was pushing Kent's luxurious private jet toward home. In the end it had turned out to be a good week's work. The sales reps for Vittle Farms were thrilled with Kent's stopover at their national meeting. Furthermore, Neil was back on track, which meant Kent was happy. And the extra post-race appearances in Alabama had brought forward two more potential endorsement opportunities. Dawson was going to be very pleased. As the plane droned on, passing from sunset into darkness, Steve tried to concentrate on the spreadsheet he'd opened on his laptop. He recorded the statistics he charted for every race, but his concentration was shot.

He couldn't wait to see Heidi, to feel her arms circle his neck, her nose and mouth nuzzle against his ear. Anticipating her whispered words of homecoming kept him on edge at the same time that the vision of her running to meet him comforted and soothed him. He'd never in his life felt this way about anyone. At thirty-one, he was old enough to recognize love when he found it, and even though it sounded corny, Heidi Kramer was the sun around which his world revolved. Sharing his life with her was everything—the only thing that mattered. Everything else was nothing but a means to that end.

That was the way his father had felt about his mother. Larry and Libby Grosso's love for each other had been the stuff of fairy tales. And realizing what he felt for Heidi, Steve had a fresh respect for how his mother's death just three years earlier had to have been even more devastating for Larry Grosso than anyone could begin to imagine. No wonder the man wandered around much of the time in an absentminded fog.

He closed his eyes and imagined himself married to Heidi, the two of them living in the cozy cottage on the outskirts of Kannapolis that Heidi had rented. The modest little house was set on an acre of land she'd naturalized with wildflowers. Plenty of room for expansion once they had kids. Maybe they should just buy the place. He pictured the gate of the picket fence. She'd once told him that it was that gate that had told her this was home before she'd ever walked through the front door. He could almost smell the sweetness of the twin magnolias that guarded the cobbled front walk. He imagined coming home to her after work each day. She would be watching for him, the lace curtain that covered the bay window fluttering as she dropped it back into place and ran to him.

In his fantasy she would race down the walk and leap into his arms, wrapping those long legs of hers around his hips and locking her fingers in his hair as she kissed him repeatedly. He would kiss her back and laugh with the pure joy of discovering all over again that a woman like Heidi loved him. Then he would set her on her feet, take her hand and lead her to the porch swing he'd given her for her birthday. Yeah, someday after they were finally married there would be days and days—years and years—like that.

As the plane neared Charlotte, Steve focused on the blue satin ring box safely stowed inside his computer bag. His dad had given him the ring shortly after they'd buried his mom.

"She'd want you to have it," Larry had said. "So do I. Find yourself a woman as good as your mother was and you'll be set for life, son."

Lately he had taken to carrying the ring with him, for he had no doubt that he and Heidi would one day become engaged. Once she agreed to be his wife, they would work out the details—his job, her career, how to bring up the kids. He just wanted to find the perfect moment and he wasn't about to have that moment arrive and catch him without the ring. If there was one thing he knew from racing, it was that your one chance might come when you least expected it. You had to be ready.

HEIDI HAD BEEN WATCHING television when Steve had called to let her know that he was finally on his way to catch the flight home. "Kent's appearances ran on longer than usual, so it'll be past midnight before we get back," he'd said. "I'll get a ride to my place with Kent and see you in the morning for breakfast."

They'd maintained separate residences in spite of their growing love for each other. After an intense live-in relationship during her college days when the man had left her for someone she thought was her good friend, Heidi was gun-shy about commitment. Steve wasn't anything like that other man, but especially because they would be traveling a lot to races, Heidi thought it best to establish some ground rules up front. The fact that Steve had accepted her terms—and never pressured her to let him move in—had gone a long way toward building the trust and love she held for him now.

But on this night Heidi had heard something in his voice, something that told her he felt things shifting between them just as she did. So she'd driven to the private airport and parked her car next to Kent's then leaned against the hood, scanning the skies for sight of the small private jet.

In spite of the volume of air traffic and the dark sky, it wasn't hard to spot the plane with its signature color scheme. It was painted in the trademark bright blue with the No. 427 in bright red alongside the distinctive Vittle Farms corporate logo on the tail. Heidi watched as the pilot taxied over to the hangar, cut the engine and lowered the stairs. Steve was the first person off the plane.

He said something over his shoulder, then started striding across the tarmac toward the row of cars parked near the hangar. He stopped when he saw Heidi, then grinned, put down his duffel and eased his computer bag off his shoulder as he held out his arms to her.

She ran to him and between kisses whispered, "Didn't mean to be so flip about that proposal thing."

"I know," he said and held her close for a soul-wrenching kiss that made her very glad he was holding on to her. She definitely couldn't have managed to stay upright on her own.

"Well, thank heavens you're here, Heidi," Kent said, stopping next to them and ignoring the fact that they were taking the art of French kissing to a whole new level. "I mean, we hardly needed fuel with this clown peddling like a hamster in a cage all the way back. I mean—"

"Get lost," Steve muttered, coming up for air before plunging in again.

"Well, you are so welcome, cous. I get you back here in record time and in one piece and that's the thanks I get."

"Oh, Kent, give them some peace." Kent's fiancée, Tanya Wells, hurried across the tarmac, her hands filled with shopping bags and her ever-present camera bag slung over one shoulder. "Take these, honey," she said, thrusting the shopping bags into his hands, "while I get the rest."

"Stuff for the wedding," Kent explained, holding up the bags. "Not that you guys care," he added as he started for his car.

"Ignore him," Tanya said as she paused next to them with yet another load of shopping bags. "Do you two want to get something to eat?"

"Not tonight," Heidi and Steve replied in unison.

"Didn't think so." Tanya grinned.

STEVE RELAYED the inside story of the Talledega race as they drove back to Heidi's house where Steve had left his truck.

"But you got things worked out with Neil?" Heidi asked once Buster had greeted them both and Steve had settled onto the sofa with his feet up.

Steve shrugged. "For now. His personal life is a mess and it's really starting to spill over into the shop. If you ask me, we may need to think about making a change, but Dawson's understandably reluctant to do that in the middle of the season. Besides, Neil's always been considered one of the best crew chiefs in the business."

"You'll work it out," Heidi assured him as she served up bowls of popcorn and large ice-filled glasses of diet soda for each of them. She curled onto the couch next to him. "Can we talk about us?"

"We can always talk about us," he said, but his eyes were wary as if expecting something painful.

"Okay," Heidi said as she sat cross-legged, facing him on the sofa. "We love each other, right?"

"Right," Steve said, taking his time to chew the popcorn as he studied her.

"So there has got to be some way that we can be together without…you know?"

"Hey, I realize we've got stuff to work out, but—"

"It's not *stuff*. It's more complicated than that."

For a moment neither of them said anything, then Steve took her hand in his. "I had an idea," he said quietly. "I'm not sure you'll go along with it, but hear me out before you say anything, okay?"

"I'm listening." She forced her clenched fingers to relax and smiled up at Steve. "You've got the green flag," she said.

"Okay, well, I've been thinking about this—"

"You mentioned that."

"A lot," he added. "It took a while but I think I see where you might be coming from…I mean, why you might think this won't work."

"*This* being you and me in a marriage," Heidi said, and when Steve frowned she held up her hands defensively. "Just trying to clarify," she muttered.

Steve took a deep breath and started again. "I was thinking about what you told me about how things were when you were growing up. Always having to start over—new town, new school, new friends."

Heidi nodded.

"It finally dawned on me that you think that being on tour will be like reliving that," he said.

"Well, I'm not fourteen anymore," she said, "but maybe, yeah, a little like that and especially if we have children."

Steve nodded. "So the challenge is to figure out how I can make you see that it's not at all like that."

"Maybe not exactly," Heidi said, "but—"

"No. It's nothing like what you knew as a kid. I can't explain it, but I know it's not. Practically everyone I know was raised in a racing family, living that life—travel and all—and nobody feels that way, not the ones who end up racing, building the cars or working on a team, and not the women who live on the tour and raise the kids and—"

"And what about those children?" Heidi argued. "What about their schooling and building friendships and—"

"Okay. I'll give you that. A lot of kids today are homeschooled and that's so they can be on the road during the season, but even for those who aren't, there are ways."

"I don't know, Steve." Heidi felt misery surround her. She wanted so much to hear what he was saying and believe in a solution, but she knew how it felt. He didn't.

"Honey, I know you're trying to understand and I love you for that."

"But? Hey, I'm also an only child. I get this."

"But you've enjoyed the best of all worlds—going to NASCAR events with your uncle and then Kent sometimes, but always having that traditional home to come back to, where your mom and dad lived the settled lives of a college professor and his wife."

"So we come from different places."

"You don't get it. If you haven't lived that life—"

"And unless you try the life I'm talking about, you can't fully appreciate what I'm telling you either," Steve said quietly. "I'm asking you to consider trying something, Heidi. Just try it, okay?"

"What?"

"I want you to commit to going to every race with me for the month of May, with the exception of Richmond because I know you're working that weekend." He held up his hand to stem her protest. "I'd like to point out that two of those weekends are races right here in town—you'd be available should something come up at the clinic."

"Oh, babe, I know I've missed some races but—"

"I'm asking you to take this time to really look at how the NASCAR community works. Hang out in the motor home lot, spend our free time there."

"Hanging out with your family at the speedway?"

He nodded. "The Grossos have two or three motor homes at every race, depending on whether Nana and Milo go. Alan Cargill lets them have his whenever they want it." Heidi had met Alan, the owner of Cargill Motors—and Dean Grosso's boss— several times before.

"What good would that do? Spotters don't travel in motor homes or live in the drivers' and owners' lot. You stay in hotels," she reminded him.

"I just want you to see what it's like. Frankly, I'd love it if you'd agree to move into the motor home with Nana and Milo. If not them, then Patsy and Dean have room."

"You've talked to them?"

"Not yet, but—"

"I don't know, Steve. Don't get me wrong. Your family is… fun, generous—"

"Outspoken, overwhelming, chaotic," he added. "It's how we do the family thing. I'm not asking you to change and become like that. I just want you to really look at life on the road—the kids, the spouses, the home life. See for yourself how it works."

Heidi made a detailed study of her fingernails. Over the time she and Steve had been together, she had naturally been included in any number of family events. But those had all been large multigenerational gatherings where it was easy to get lost in the background. Steve was actually suggesting that she move in with his great-grandmother or aunt as if she were a member of the family.

"They scare me," she admitted softly.

Steve burst into laughter and pulled her into his arms. "Baby, they scare me and I've known them my whole life. But they like you and they think I am one lucky guy to have found you. Believe me, the Grosso women are your biggest fans."

"And if nothing changes?" Heidi asked, her voice shaking slightly.

"Then we'll find another way. On the track you get around obstacles any number of ways. We can do this."

Heidi drew in a shaky breath. "You're doing this for me, aren't you? Everything—it's all for me?" she whispered. In her whole life no one had ever put the focus so squarely on her. It was thrilling on one level, but also a little intimidating.

Steve pulled her more tightly against his chest. "Oh, sweetheart, don't you know that I would walk through fire for you."

Steve kissed her. "No pressure. Just promise me you'll give the idea some thought, okay?"

After Steve left, Heidi had trouble going to bed, much less getting any sleep. She had a lot to think about. And as if the whole idea of spending race weekends with the Grosses wasn't enough, there was Clare's partnership proposal. *Fast track,* Clare had called it, and fast track seemed to apply to what Steve was doing as well. He'd taken this new job and now he was ready to move their relationship to the next stage. At least he understood the need to give her options—travel to a month's worth of races and focus on the lifestyle. Gather her facts. He knew her well enough to know that almost from the time she'd taken charge of making her own decisions, Heidi had developed the habit of carefully considering every side of an issue.

She sat at the kitchen table eating vanilla ice cream straight from the container. Buster sat at her side, his large brown eyes patiently following each spoonful from container to mouth.

"Here," she said, dropping the cardboard cover at his feet. "Enjoy." She scraped the bottom of the carton while Buster slurped the excess from the cover. She crushed the carton and tossed it in the garbage, then pulled a legal pad and pen across the table. "Okay, let's figure this thing out," she muttered, and started making two lists, one labeled Partnership Pros and Cons, and the other labeled Life on the Road—Grosso Style.

HEIDI WAS NOT AT ALL fooled by the fact that Steve's aunt Patsy called her out of the blue two days after Steve had laid out his idea for her to spend time with the family. Patsy Grosso practically begged her to come help make the dozens of Italian cookies that were a traditional part of the annual Memorial Day feast.

"I'm not much of a cook," Heidi admitted, when what she really wanted to say was, "Did Steve ask you to call?"

Patsy responded with her signature laugh—deep, throaty and

warm. "Honey, the only true cook in this family is Juliana. The rest of us are just kitchen elves. So what do you say? Will you rescue me?"

"Okay. Sure," Heidi replied. "Can I bring anything?"

"Just your sense of humor," Patsy said. "See you at the farm." *The farm* was how everyone referred to the Grosso place.

The Grossos had been racing royalty for generations in the Charlotte area. Milo, the vibrant ninety-two-year-old patriarch of the family, had started the dynasty. When his son and daughter-in-law had died in a flash flood while hiking in the mountains, Milo had taken in his grandsons, Larry and Dean, and raised them as his own. While Steve's father, Larry, had pursued a career in academia, his uncle Dean had become one of the most respected drivers on the tour. And now Dean's son, Kent, was keeping the tradition of Grosso wins alive as the current season's defending champion and the most recognizable face of Maximus Motorsports.

As soon as Patsy hung up, Heidi called Steve at Maximus. "Nice move," she said when he answered.

"Hi to you, too," he said with a chuckle.

"Your aunt Patsy called."

"Really?"

"Don't play dumb with me, Steve Grosso. When was the last time I was invited to help cook for a Grosso extravaganza?"

Steve cleared his throat, stalling for time.

"That would be never," Heidi continued. "In fact, when was the last time I was at the farm other than as your date?"

"Uh…"

"That would also be never. I have always been a welcomed *guest* and now suddenly I'm a member of the kitchen staff, which practically labels me as a member of the family."

"I swear I didn't put Patsy up to it," he protested.

"You just dropped a hint maybe?"

Steve chuckled again. "Well, I might have said that since Tanya couldn't help out, why didn't they see if you could fill in."

Heidi didn't know whether to be insulted or flattered.

"You said you'd go, right?" Steve asked.

"I did. But get one thing straight, Spotterman, you better not have put them up to using this as a chance to put pressure on me."

"Would I do that?" he asked.

"Yes."

"Okay, that's fair. But I didn't. I just thought that, well, hanging out with them might help you see they don't bite."

Heidi groaned. This thing had disaster written all over it. "Will you find some reason to stop by, just in case I need rescuing?"

"Honey, they're just two women like any other women."

"No. They are two incredible women and they are incredible beyond the fact that they are the matriarchs of the famous Grosso family. I am so out of my league there."

"You women are amazing," Steve said. "I mean, don't you get it that *you* intimidate them? You're a doctor, for heaven's sake."

"Animal doctor," Heidi corrected.

"Whatever. They think you're pretty awesome."

VILLA GROSSO was the name inscribed in the twin stone pillars that marked the entrance to the Grosso farm. Patriarch Milo Grosso was determined that the village of Concord just down the road from Kannapolis would become known as Grosso Land, marked by the landmarks of his—and his family's—rise to glory in the world of racing.

Once past the pillars, there was a tree-lined gravel road that wound for a quarter of a mile bordering a creek. Steve had once told Heidi that he and Kent had caught frogs in that creek when they were boys. The image of a young Steve splashing barefoot around the rocks and cascading water as he and Kent chased frogs made Heidi breathe a little easier as she neared the house. Then the road curved and the house came in sight.

It was a rambling white clapboard-sided structure with symmetrical columns supporting a balcony porch. The upper porch mirrored the main porch as both wrapped their way around three sides of the home. Heidi was well aware that through the years Milo Grosso and his beloved second wife, Juliana, had made several additions to the home and its property—not the least imposing of which was the ten-car garage and workshop she passed just after making the curve onto the circular driveway.

Even though she had been here many times with Steve, this was the first time she'd come on her own. "You're like family," Steve had promised her. Of course, Heidi was well aware that *family* was a relative term when it came to the elder Grossos. It extended to include numerous racing associates and their families as well as an assortment of neighbors and friends. Steve's great-grandmother was a renowned cook and hostess, her Italian feasts a legend among the racing community. It was preliminary preparation for such a feast that brought Heidi to the farm now.

As Heidi took the final curve on the long driveway, she remembered the compliment and felt her confidence revive— slightly. She pulled around to the side of the house and parked her hybrid next to Patsy's SUV. Down in the pasture she saw Milo leaning against a fence as a hired man exercised one of the family's pampered Tennessee walking horses. Three large dogs set up a racket, barking and running toward the car. Heidi was glad she'd opted to leave Buster at the clinic with Clare.

"Settle," Milo yelled and the dogs turned on a dime and returned to stand with him. He shaded his eyes with the back of one hand as he squinted up at her. Heidi waved.

"Who's that?" Milo called.

"Heidi," she called back.

"Steve with you?"

"No, he'll be by later."

Milo gave a wave and turned back to watching the horse. Heidi couldn't help thinking she'd be far more comfortable standing next to Milo observing the horse than donning an apron and helping make cookies.

"Heidi?" Juliana Grosso pushed open the screen door that led through a mudroom, past the laundry room and into the massive kitchen of the house. "Well, bless your heart for coming all the way out here to lend us a hand."

Juliana was an inch taller than Heidi and about fifty pounds heavier, but no one could argue with the fact that at age seventy-seven, she was still a striking woman. Her silver-gray hair was teased into her trademark bouffant loose twist, forty years out of fashion but perfectly suited to the matriarch of one of America's best-known racing families.

As soon as Heidi hit the top step of the wide screened porch off the kitchen, Juliana enfolded her in her arms, then stepped back. Her long lacquered nails pressed the front of the bibbed apron she wore over a floral cotton dress. The dress had seen in-numerable washings, but it showed her still-voluptuous curves to perfection. Heidi had always thought Juliana looked more like the torch singer she'd once been than a great-grandmother.

"Come on inside and we'll get you outfitted with an apron to protect that pretty pink blouse."

"I was so pleased when Patsy called, Juliana," Heidi said politely. "I mean—"

"Now, darlin', you are about as close to being family as it gets without a walk down the aisle, so don't you think it's about time we got together—just us women?"

Leave it to this plainspoken woman to cut to the chase.

"Well, even so, I—"

"And call me Nana. It's about time for that as well. After all, Steve, Kent and Sophia—not to mention just about every other young person in town—already calls me that." She let out a laugh that ended in a snort. "Even relative strangers have sometimes taken to calling me Nana although I find that just rude and disrespectful, don't you?"

She didn't wait for an answer but led the way inside and down the hall to the kitchen/breakfast room/family room that formed the heart of the large house. "Look who I found out there on the driveway," she announced.

Patsy Grosso looked up from rolling out dough on a marble slab. "Well, thank goodness," she said. "Reinforcements at last. Nana's about to work me to death here."

Heidi had always liked Steve's aunt Patsy. She was married to the more volatile Dean Grosso and had raised two children— Kent, following in his father's footsteps and the newest heart- throb of NASCAR, and Sophia, director of nursing for a nursing home and rehabilitation center and recently romantically involved with racing's bad boy, Justin Murphy.

Of course, half the town knew that the Murphys and the Grossos had a long history of animosity. To say that the Grossos and Murphys did not care for one another was putting it mildly. Still, it was amazing to see the way they all stuck together. Sophia was no outcast in spite of the obvious fact that her father—and other members of the family—clearly did not care for Justin. Heidi admired Sophia for the way she had stood her ground. She and Justin were in love and she expected her family—and his— to come to terms with that. Heidi suspected that Sophia had gotten a lot of that strength from her mother.

Patsy Grosso was a practical no-nonsense woman whose life revolved around her family. Their happiness was her happiness. Today she was dressed in her customary tailored jeans with a red-checkered shirt tucked into the waist. She'd tied a denim bandanna over her short brown curls to keep them in place.

Nana handed Heidi an apron. "Just put your purse down over there."

Heidi did as Nana instructed, tying on the apron as she went to the closest of the sinks to wash her hands. Juliana Grosso was a serious cook, and the kitchen she had talked Milo into remodeling for her as a present for their thirtieth wedding anniversary showed it. The dream of any gourmet cook was anchored by two wet zones, both with sinks, disposals and dishwashers. One was located near the massive stainless commercial refrigerator in the area used for food preparation. The other was closer to two large round tables that took up most of both the dining and breakfast areas. It came in handy for clearing after one of Juliana's famous feasts.

Between the wet zones was what Heidi had heard Juliana refer to as the hot zone. It featured a restaurant stove with multiple burners and ovens plus an indoor grill, microwave and convection oven. To either side were deep green granite counters, with pullout chopping boards stowed underneath. Mounted above the counters were cherrywood cabinets and drawers for storing utensils, appliances and pots and pans. Along back of one counter was a spice cabinet with each drawer carefully labeled, often filled with spices Heidi had never heard of. In the center of the entire space was a granite-topped island with recessed shelving underneath to hold Juliana's cookbook collection, and a wire rack above that held an assortment of highly polished copper cookware.

"What are you making?" Heidi asked as she dried her hands on a paper towel and moved around the island to stand next to Patsy.

"A mess," Patsy said with a grin as she patched a hole in the dough with her finger and then handed Heidi a rolling pin. "See what you can do. It's supposed to be paper thin. Right now it's more like cardboard thick."

Cautiously Heidi began to roll the dough.

"She's a natural," Nana announced, watching her. "Here, grind these nuts." She handed Patsy a hand grinder and a bowl of shelled pecans.

"What's this dough for?" Heidi asked.

Juliana struck the pose of an opera singer and sang out the names of the cookies on their menu for the day. "Today we shall create crostoli," she sang out. "Torta de Bernardone *et*—" she pulled Patsy into the circle of her performance and together they gave the big finish "—Fiche e Datteri Affectali."

"But first we start with some basic nut rolls," Patsy said in her normal voice as she resumed grinding the nuts and nodded toward the pastry Heidi was rolling.

"Of course, we could add Italian wedding cookies to the list," Nana added with a bump of her hip against Heidi's backside. "A kind of practice lap, don't you know."

Heidi felt her cheeks flush. "Did Steve say something?" She couldn't help wondering if the entire family was aware that Steve was ready to propose and that she was the one holding back.

Patsy gave a yelp of laughter. "Honey, get serious. Do you know that you were the first girl Steve ever brought to the farm for a family gathering?"

"That's right," Nana said as she took the rolling pin from Heidi, made two quick passes over the pastry and then set the pin aside. "Oh, he'd bring some girl by now and then, pop in and then leave right away. I remember saying to Milo that very day he brought you and stayed the whole day that you were the one for our Stevie."

"So what's the holdup?" Patsy asked, coming directly to the point as usual.

"There's no…that is, well, I've been busy at work and now

he's got this job in the front office and that means more travel-ing and…"

"Traveling for him. You haven't been on the road," Nana said bluntly as she cut the large pastry into four smaller rectangles and indicated with a jerk of her head that Heidi should bring her a bowl of ingredients from the side counter. "Not this season. You've missed…what? Three or four races already and we're not even to the halfway mark."

"Three," Heidi said softly as she tried to repress the shot of indignation she felt, and failed. "I do have a job as well as student loans to repay."

She hated that the tightness in her voice brought conversation to an abrupt halt. This was what she had feared. She wasn't like these women—easy and open. And she did not miss the thinly dis-guised looks of concern that Patsy and Nana exchanged. Finally, after Nana had pinched the last of the nut rolls closed, she reached for four jelly-roll pans and carefully laid one roll on each. "Heidi, sweetie, get me four dish towels from that third drawer on the right. Cover each roll and set the trays over there on the side."

It appeared that the two older women had decided to drop the subject of wedding prospects for Steve and Heidi, but that did nothing to relieve the tension in the warm kitchen. Yet Heidi understood that it was tension brought on by concern. These women were Steve's family, and didn't she hope one day they might think of her as family as well?

"It's more than the job and the finances," Heidi admitted. Once again the kitchen went still, but this time the air hummed with anticipation rather than tension. "I'm not sure how much you know about my background."

"Steve has mentioned that you moved around a lot," Nana said as if testing the waters.

"That's got to have been tough," Patsy added. "I mean, for a kid to have to start fresh not once or twice but over and over."

Heidi nodded and leaned against the island as she watched Patsy wash out the nut grinder while Nana mixed another batch of dough.

"How did you do it?" she found herself asking Patsy. "I mean, raise Kent and Sophia, moving from place to place practically every week for two-thirds of the year?"

Patsy glanced up. "Dean and I did it together, honey. It was the life we wanted—for us and for the kids. It's all either one of us ever knew. My dad drove hauler for several teams while I was growing up." She glanced at Nana for confirmation. "It's been a good life."

Nana wiped the dough from her fingers with a damp cloth. "I think I can see where you're coming from, Heidi." She dried her hands and put her arm around Heidi's shoulders. "Come here a minute, darlin'. I want to show you something." She led the way to the breakfast area and opened the glass-paneled door of an antique maple sideboard. Inside, the shelves were crowded with turtles—ceramic turtles, carved boxwood turtles, glass turtles, turtles made from seashells. All sizes and colors.

"Everybody thinks I collect these guys because I consider them lucky—and I do. But the real reason I like having them around is they remind me of us—Milo and me, Patsy and Dean, the kids. You see, the racing life is a little like being a turtle. Wherever we go we carry *home* with us."

Patsy had come over to join them. "Home, neighborhood, friendships—it's a community, Heidi. It's different from the life you knew, moving from place to place, meeting new people all the time. Not the same at all really because—"

"The faces don't change," Nana finished, then she chuckled. "Though heaven knows there are times you wish they would."

All three women laughed and Heidi relaxed. Steve was right. They were just women—good, caring women.

Just before shutting the glass cabinet doors, Nana took one polished stone turtle the size of a marble and handed it to Heidi. "Put this in your pocket while you think on this, honey. It might help."

"Thank you," Heidi said softly as she tucked the turtle into the pocket of her jeans. "Steve has this idea that if I traveled with the family, staying with one of you and seeing how it really is, then I might change my mind."

"Why, that's a wonderful idea," Patsy exclaimed. "Isn't it a wonderful idea, Nana?"

"Ought to be," Nana said with a wink. "I suggested it to him."

"What would be wonderful," Milo thundered as he swung open the screen door, hung his straw hat on a hook by the door and hobbled into the kitchen, "would be if a fella could get himself something cold to drink."

"Milo Grosso, you've lived in this house for over fifty years now. It's high time you figured out where the refrigerator is," Nana said as she led the women back to work.

Milo grinned and gave his wife a soft whack on the bottom as he walked the length of the kitchen and pulled open the refrigerator door. "I might just be able to manage that if some woman didn't keep changing things around," he muttered.

He filled four glasses with ice and lemonade and distributed them. "What are you three dollies up to?" he asked, eyeing the rising nut rolls.

"Now, what does it look like we're up to?" Nana demanded with a huff of exasperation.

"Baking for the troops overseas?" He reached for a piece of the soft dough and his wife smacked at his hand.

"Close. In case you're getting daft in your old age, mister, race week will be here before you know it."

Milo chuckled and took up residence on one of the high bar stools that lined one side of the center island. "I'm ninety-two years old, woman, and you're no spring chicken yourself. What is it, eighty this next birthday?" He winked at Heidi.

"I am seventy-seven, you old coot," Juliana replied evenly, "and thinking hard about finding myself a younger man." She brushed by him on her way to the stove and kissed the top of his balding head. Patsy grinned at Heidi, and Heidi felt even more at home.

Home.

She fingered the smooth stone of the turtle in her pocket. Could it work? It was certainly worth a try.

CHAPTER FOUR

THE AFTERNOON FLEW by as the sweet smells of cookies warm from the oven scented the air and a parade of Grosso family members, as well as friends from town or neighbors, showed up at the farm for one reason or another. Some came to talk business with Milo as he worked side by side with the women, manning the ovens as tray after tray of cookies went in and came out. Others came on their way to or from somewhere else just to say hello before "heading on down the road."

Heidi had to admit that it was all like a huge block party, but she also reminded herself that they were at the farm—in Concord—just a few miles from her own cottage and the animal clinic in Kannapolis. Things were bound to be different on the road.

"I came to rescue my woman," Steve announced as he hugged his great-grandmother and then his aunt Patsy.

"Who says your 'woman' needs rescuing?" Heidi replied with a wink at the other women.

Nana and Patsy hooted with delight. "That's our girl!"

Steve feigned shock. "You've corrupted her in a single afternoon?"

Nana stuffed a warm cookie in his mouth. "Never underestimate the power of three women to change the world while you men are out tinkering with some fool car."

Steve took a minute to chew the cookie, his eyes glowing with hope as he glanced at Heidi.

"That's right," she said, aligning herself physically and in every other way with Patsy and Juliana. "Nana here has invited me to stay with her and Milo in Alan's motor home from now through race week." She paused dramatically, then added, "And I've accepted."

"As long as you don't park that hybrid thing next to my motor home," Milo bellowed as he slammed the oven door and placed the last tray of cookies on the counter with a clatter. "I've got a reputation to uphold, girlie."

Steve grinned and reached for Heidi. He picked her up and swung her around. "Thanks, babe. You won't regret this. You'll see that—"

"Now, you just stop that right now, Steve Grosso," Patsy demanded. "Your Nana and I spent the better part of the afternoon easing her into giving it a try. You start pressuring her and she's likely to back out altogether."

Steve put Heidi down. "I'm just saying how happy this makes me."

"Done and done," Nana told him. "Now back off, mister."

"Yes, ma'am."

"You two staying for supper?" Nana asked as she washed the last pan and handed it to Steve to dry.

Heidi glanced at Steve. "If it's okay with Steve, I'd like that," she said.

"Oh, honey, do not give a man that kind of power," Patsy warned, "or for sure he'll expect it forever, right, Nana?"

"Absolutely. I can see we have more work to do—and you just stop rolling those baby blues of yours, Stevie," she ordered. She put her arm around Heidi's waist. "Watch this," she whispered, then turned her attention to Steve. "Heidi is staying for supper, Steve. Will you be staying or going?"

"Staying," Steve assured her. "Now, how about you give my girl a break so I can take her down to the stables and show her the new colt."

"As long as that's all you plan to show her," Patsy muttered, to which Nana burst into laughter, and both Heidi and Steve blushed scarlet as he hustled her out of the fragrant warmth of the kitchen.

SUPPER AT THE Grosso farm was always an open-ended affair with Nana and Patsy playing hostess as family members, as well as some members of the teams that supported both Kent and his father, Dean, stopped by and stayed for the meal at the large round dining-room table. When no more chairs could be squeezed into the circle, the overflow settled at the breakfast table or the bar between the kitchen and family room.

All comers understood that food would be on the table promptly at six and the last guest was expected to be gone no later than nine on a weeknight so Milo could get to bed. These were Nana's rules and you broke them at your own risk.

The meal itself was served family style and on this night it was an Italian feast with dishes of heaping pasta, a variety of white and red sauces and platters of hot garlic bread moving around the table in what appeared to be a constant circle. Conversation was lively and punctuated with outbursts of laughter and occasional exclamations of surprise as someone shared the latest gossip.

After supper some guests gravitated toward the fifty-two-inch flat-screen television mounted over the fireplace in the family room to watch the news, while others pitched in to clear and wash up. Heidi had noticed on other such evenings that the open-floor plan of the house never made it seem as if there was any real separation of the sexes. Snatches of some lively discussion among those in the family room could just as easily elicit a response from someone in the kitchen as not, and guests and family members alike moved back and forth between the kitchen and family room, completely at home. Even so, Heidi was surprised when Kent wandered into the kitchen and called her aside just as a pickup truck Heidi didn't remember seeing before pulled into the driveway.

"Hey, Heidi, I was wondering if you'd mind having a look at a friend's dog," Kent said.

"Sure. Tell your friend to just stop by the clinic tomorrow and I'll—"

Kent glanced toward the back door. "Well, see, when Steve told me you'd be over here tonight, I was sorta hoping you might have some time now. He's outside there—my friend, Roger, with his dog, Duke."

"Anybody home?" a slim young man with short-cropped hair dressed in khakis and a polo shirt called as he tapped at the back door.

"Is that Roger?" Nana called. "Come on in and fix yourself a plate."

"No, thank you, ma'am. I just stopped by for a minute."

Kent stepped forward to welcome the newcomer. "Heidi Kramer, this is Roger Clark."

"Hello. I think I've seen you at some of the races."

"Roger's in charge of programming for the NARS," Tanya said, giving their friend a hug. The National Automobile Racing Services, or NARS, was well respected for services such as child care and a fitness center that they made available to drivers and their families during race events.

"I understand you want me to check out your dog," Heidi said.

"If it wouldn't be too much trouble," Roger said, already edging toward the door. "He's out here in the truck."

Heidi dried her hands on a dish towel. "Sure. Let me take a look." She was aware that conversation in both the family room and the kitchen had dropped to a low hum and knew the others were listening in. So, as she followed Kent and Roger out the door, it was disconcerting but hardly surprising to find Steve, Tanya and the rest of the supper crowd trailing along.

The others formed a semicircle along both sides of the truck bed as Roger lowered the back so Heidi could have a better look. Duke was a giant schnauzer, a black-coated gentle giant who got to his feet, stretched, yawned and ambled forward. He licked Roger's face and then sniffed at Heidi.

"He's got these bumps on his face," Roger explained, stepping back to give Heidi more room for her examination.

"Hey there, big fella," she crooned as she gently scratched the dog's soft ears and worked her hand around until she was cradling his face. She could feel Steve's eyes on her and knew if she glanced up she would see such pride and love reflected in that look that it would make her heart skip a beat.

Duke shuddered with the pleasure of her touch and nuzzled her fingers. "Let's see what we've got going on here," she murmured, and lifted the dog's chin so she could examine it from all angles. She smothered a smile.

"How old is Duke?" she asked.

Roger leaned in closer. "He just turned two," he said. "And he's always been in the best of health. Still seems to be, but—"

"Makes sense," Heidi said as she ruffled Duke's furry head and then turned to face Roger. "Your dog is a teenager—at least in human years."

Roger blinked.

"He has a case of acne," she said softly.

"Pimples?" Kent said, and smothered a smile.

"Pimples!" Dean Grosso hooted. "Well, don't that beat all? On a dog?" He moved around to the end of the truck to see for himself. "Look at that, Patsy," he said, holding Duke's face still and fingering one prominent blemish.

"Pimples?" Kent said again, and this time he started to laugh and once he did, so did everyone else. He rested his arm around Heidi's shoulder. "Thanks, Doc," he said finally. "Now Roger here can finally stop worrying."

"Heidi's coming to the race with us this weekend," Nana announced, "just in case any of the rest of you have any 'sick' pets."

"Heidi's always at the races, Nana," Kent said then glanced at Steve. "I mean, those she can drive to—at least most of the time."

"You're not listening, Kent," Milo said. "What your Nana just said is that Heidi's coming 'with us.' As I get it, she'll also be coming to every race in May 'with us.' Is any of this getting through?"

"Well, that's good," Kent said, glancing at Steve for confirmation. "Right?"

Patsy sighed. "I'll explain it to you and your dad later. Right now I've been on my feet most of the day and I'm ready for a hot bath and an evening of mindless television." She kissed Milo's cheek and hugged. "You coming, Dean?" she called, as she headed back toward the house.

"I'll be along directly," he replied.

Kent turned to Steve. "Tanya and I thought we'd catch a movie. You and Heidi want to come?"

"We'll take a rain check," Steve replied, and then glanced at Heidi. "Unless you want to go," he added with a sheepish grin at his great-grandmother.

"I have a full day at the clinic tomorrow," Heidi said. "A rain check sounds like a good idea."

"Roger?" Kent said, including his friend in the invitation.

"Sure," Roger replied, clearly relieved now that Duke had been declared healthy. "I'll meet you there?" He climbed into the cab of his truck and revved the engine.

"Now look here, Roger," Milo said, leaning against the door of the cab and frowning. "Once you get to that movie house, don't you go trying to pass that dog of yours off as underage—he's a teenager now and that means he pays full price." Then his weathered face split into a grin as he pounded the side of the truck. "Pimples," he hooted as Roger took off in a spray of gravel. "Don't that beat all."

"WELL, THIS IS a definite mood swing for the better," Clare said when she walked into the clinic the following morning and heard Heidi humming. "Things must have gone well yesterday."

Heidi grinned. "Yeah. Thanks for covering things here. Oh, Clare, it was better than I could have ever hoped. Nana is unbelievably giving on so many levels."

"Nana? Twenty-four hours ago, you were struggling to form the word *Juliana*."

"Exactly. Of course, we're still a long way from working it all out, but somehow after yesterday, I feel…"

"Hopeful?"

Heidi nodded.

"So what's the miracle cure for this heartache you've been suffering for lo these many weeks?"

"Okay, here's the deal. In the past whenever I've gone to a race, I've always stayed in a hotel or the home of some friend or relative of Steve's."

Clare nodded as she went about her work, checking lab results and updating charts. "And that's been a mistake?"

"In a way. Steve came up with the idea—actually Nana's idea—that I need to live the life they live on the road. That means living in their motor home—at least for the next several weekends. What do you think?"

"Okay, I guess, but I don't see how that's going to ease your concerns about the idea of living the gypsy life you had as a kid." She headed down the hall and into her office with Heidi following.

"That's just it. Patsy says that it's like moving an entire neighborhood week to week during the season. You don't start over with all new people, because it's the same people."

"So for the next several weeks you're going to be gone more days then." Clare sat at her desk and started recording payments and billing on the computer.

"I checked the schedule to be sure you didn't have any rallies or marches coming up in May," Heidi said, tempering her own enthusiasm after seeing that Clare's mind was obviously on something more serious than Heidi's good news. "Hey, what's going on?"

Clare looked directly at her for the first time all morning. "It's nothing. Don't mind me. I'm just in a mood."

"But you're okay with the plan?"

Clare gave her a blank stare.

"For me to go with the Grosso family to the next several races, stay with them for the whole weekend," Heidi reminded her.

"Sure," Clare said. "I'll be here, and heaven knows business is slow enough that we don't both need to be here," she added. She came around the desk and hugged Heidi. "I'm happy things seem to be working out for you, honey." Then she shrugged into her lab coat and headed for her first appointment.

Heidi watched her go, then stepped around the desk so that she could see the computer screen. Over the last several weeks things had been slow, but Heidi had chalked it up to the normal ebb and flow of business. She studied the entries on the flow-chart compared to the same time last year and saw that the drop in business was more significant than she had realized.

A new clinic had recently opened in Concord—not ten miles away. The new place offered grooming services in addition to medical care, and that clearly was having an impact. "One-stop shopping," the place advertised. Heidi felt a twinge of guilt that she had been so focused on her personal life, when it was evident that Clare had more serious matters to worry about.

"Hey, anything I can do to help you?" Heidi asked later that morning when she found Clare nibbling a salad at her desk as she frowned at the computer screen.

"Eventually. Just gathering all the facts, ma'am," Clare

replied, pinching the bridge of her nose as she squeezed her eyes closed and then opened them again.

"Come on. You need a break before you go blind staring at that screen."

"Shall we hang out the Gone Fishing shingle?"

Heidi laughed. "I was thinking of something more like Stop and Smell the Roses. Like a walk around the village?"

"Sounds heavenly." Clare pocketed her cell phone and forwarded the clinic phone to voice mail. The voice mail would give instructions in case someone had an emergency while they were away. Clare paused before the hall tree that sat in the corner near the door and held a display of hats in a variety of styles and colors. "I think this one," she said, pulling down a black baseball cap. "Matches my mood."

"Well, then I should maybe wear this one," Heidi said as she took down the wide-brimmed tangerine straw that Clare had been wearing when they'd had breakfast together a few days earlier. She put it on at an angle and struck a pose. "My heavens, it works. I feel big-sister vibes just pouring through me."

Clare laughed, which, of course, had been exactly what Heidi was after. They locked arms and headed out into the spring sunshine.

CLARE'S OBVIOUS WORRIES about the business had made Heidi more conscientious than ever about following through with patients, calling their owners to see if they had questions after an appointment, putting together packets of information related to whatever the cause for treatment had been. On Wednesday she spent her downtime putting together a comprehensive chart of information on pets she had treated for more serious conditions over the last few weeks, animals that might develop complications and need extra care while she was gone.

On their walk Clare had admitted that the new competition

was indeed taking a greater toll than she had expected. She talked about the need to find some way to enhance their appeal without having to spend big bucks to do that. At the same time she rejected Heidi's suggestion of an advertising campaign as too expensive and risky. The idea of offering grooming services had been rejected as well. "Copycat," Clare had said. "Yuck. We need original, innovative."

Heidi's heart had warmed at Clare's use of the plural "we." It had not escaped her notice that ever since Clare had talked about moving forward with the partnership, more and more Clare talked as if Heidi and she were already partners. But ever since they'd returned from their walk, with Heidi unable to offer anything more than "Something will turn up," Clare had grown increasingly tense and depressed.

The day before she and Steve were to leave for Darlington and her first experience living in Nana and Milo's motor home, Heidi hesitated before knocking on Clare's office door. She'd just sent their the last patient—a corgi with a cough—and his owner on their way.

"Come on in," Clare called. She was just finishing punching in a series of sums on her calculator and held up a finger while she jotted down a note to herself. "All set to head out?" she asked, leaning back in her desk chair and indicating that Heidi should make herself comfortable as well.

Heidi nodded, but did not sit down. Steve would be waiting for her at home. "I updated all the charts for patients I saw this week and made notes in case anything comes up." She handed Clare a copy of the information sheets she'd worked up for each of her patients. "I don't anticipate any problems. Everything was pretty routine, but just in case," she added as Clare flipped through the pages and set them aside.

"I'm sure it'll be fine," Clare replied. She stretched and folded her arms behind her head as she smiled at Heidi. "So this is the big test, right? Living with the family. Your own unique NASCAR experience. Are you nervous?"

"Not really," Heidi said, then admitted, "Maybe a little."

"I'd be beside myself. Milo Grosso has always terrified me. Something about those eyes."

Heidi felt relieved that Clare seemed more like her old self. "He's ninety-two and three inches shorter than you are," she replied with a laugh. "In a fair fight my money would be on you."

Clare shrugged. "You know the gossip as well as I do. What you see is not always what you get with folks like the Grosso gang."

Heidi knew that Clare was referring to the rumors—now legend—that the death of veteran driver Connor Murphy in a motorcycle accident had been no accident. According to the locals, after Connor had bragged about adding ether to his gasoline, allowing him to beat Milo for the season's championship, a witness had reported seeing Milo's pickup tailing the cycle as Connor started up the steep curvy mountain road. And while Milo had an airtight alibi for that night, his past career with the FBI had people speculating that if he didn't do the deed, he had friends who did. Nothing had ever been proven, but Connor's untimely and unsolved death had resulted in decades of bad blood between the two families. This, plus Troy Murphy's hit-and-run accident, deepened the feud. Both had certainly become the backdrop for Sophia's star-crossed romance with Justin.

"You watch way too much television," Heidi told Clare with a laugh as she gathered her things. "I'll see you Monday morning," she said, and headed for the door.

"Have fun," Clare called as she pulled one of the files toward her and frowned.

CHAPTER FIVE

BY THE TIME Heidi reached home Steve had dinner almost ready.

"Hi, honey, I'm home," she called as if they were characters in a television sitcom.

Buster bounded into the kitchen. "Hey there, big guy," Steve said, ruffling the dog's coat as he tried to control Buster's exuberant greeting.

"Down, Buster," Heidi instructed, coming into the kitchen and dropping the mail on the counter. "Smells great." She stood on tiptoe and kissed Steve, pushing the dog out from between them.

"The chili or me?" he joked as he pulled her into his arms for a real kiss.

"Both," she said. "I am starving."

"Rough day?"

Heidi washed her hands at the kitchen sink then started to gather the makings of a salad from the refrigerator. "It's Clare. I think business must be down more than I thought. I knew we'd been through a couple of slow months, but the way she's acting, I don't know. She's really worried."

"I know you don't like my saying this, honey, but maybe if Clare didn't go flying all over the country at the drop of a hat and paid more attention to her business—"

Heidi shot him a look as she tossed a Caesar salad with more energy than necessary.

"I know," Steve said as he rescued a piece of romaine lettuce that had gone flying across the counter and popped it into her mouth. "I'm just saying—"

"This is not about her work in animal rights. It's about the clinic. It's about finding a way to bring new business through the door. I mean, right now how she can even think about taking on a partner is beyond me." She was in the process of drowning the salad with the dressing that was her specialty when Steve took the carafe from her and recapped it.

"Don't jump to conclusions unless you can see the whole track. You and Clare aren't partners yet and there may be things she's facing that—"

Heidi's eyes widened and she pressed her fist to her mouth. "What if she not only has to back away from offering me the partnership, what if she has to let me go? I mean, that would explain the way she's been beating herself up emotionally. It would—"

"Let's eat," he said, taking the salad to the table and setting it in place along with the loaf of Nana's Italian bread that he'd brought with him. He got butter from the refrigerator while Heidi filled their glasses with iced tea.

"We have to think of something, Steve. Something new and fresh," Heidi continued as she dished up bowls of chili and then sat opposite him, "We can't just copy the other guy."

"What's this 'we' business?" Steve asked as he blew on a spoonful of chili.

"Clare and me—the business."

"Maybe the reason she suggested partnering now is that is she needs your investment."

"What investment? I owe money. I don't have money."

"Good point," he admitted and placed his hand over hers. "Honey, this is a bump in the road and we are not going to be able to fix it overnight. Let's just enjoy our dinner and then head for Darlington, okay? Once we're on the road I promise we'll talk about business or anything else until you've run out of things to say or you fall asleep, whichever comes first."

Heidi smiled and felt a loosening of the knot of anxiety she'd been carrying around ever since she'd left the clinic. "You know, I'm likely to be asleep within the first half hour," she said, "especially after eating."

"That's the plan," Steve said as he placed a thick slice of Nana's bread slathered with butter on her plate. "Now, eat up."

IT CERTAINLY WASN'T the first time that Heidi had been inside the luxurious motor coach that Milo and Nana called home on the road. It was just that looking at it from the standpoint of sharing it with two larger-than-life people plus Buster for the next forty-eight hours made it seem like tight quarters in spite of its size.

"Did you eat?" Nana asked as she greeted them with open arms and a smile. They assured her they had. "Well, Heidi, let's get you settled. Steve, the guys have all gone over to Kent's hauler—a card game, I imagine. Milo said to tell you they'd save you a place at the table."

Steve hesitated.

"Go on," Heidi said. "I'm fine."

Steve kissed Heidi's cheek. "I'll take Buster with me and catch up with you later, okay?"

Heidi nodded, swallowing the urge to cling to him and state the obvious—that they should probably both rethink this whole idea. Instead, she waved as he and Buster sped away on the golf cart painted to match the subdued brown and tan exterior of the motor home.

"You've seen the place before, of course," Nana said as she led the way inside. "Living room slash guest room." She pointed to the white leather sofa and matching love seat that occupied the area right behind the driver's seat. The matching passenger seat could be turned forward or back depending on whether the coach was in motion or the chair was needed as part of the seating arrangement.

"Dining area slash kitchen," she added with a wave toward the minireproduction of the kitchen at the farm and the booth-style table and benches across from it.

She opened a narrow closet. "I cleared this out for you. It's here next to the powder room. Towels are there on the top shelf. I'll make sure Milo is out of the main bath when you want to take a shower or change." She indicated the full bath beyond the bedroom she shared with her husband.

"It's fine. Thank you," Heidi murmured and knew that she sounded stiff and formal.

Nana spun around and frowned. "Oh, now, sweetie, do not tell me that all that good progress we made the other day at the farm has gone the way of the bathwater."

Heidi could not help smiling. "No. I mean, I really appreciate this, but it's just that it struck me that having a third person in here—a stranger, not to mention one with a dog. Well, you and Milo…"

"Are you kidding? Milo's talked of nothing else but 'bringing you up to speed,' as he likes to say. The man will talk your ear off if you give him half a chance. I'll try to rescue you if it gets too bad. As for Buster, we love having him. Good company for me when everybody's off doing their thing."

Heidi smiled. "Milo's stories are always fascinating."

Nana rolled her eyes. "You marry Steve and be around to hear them for the next decade or so and see how *fascinating* you find them." She pulled fresh towels from the closet and hung them in the bathroom. "And as for you being a stranger, you need to get past that. You're family—and I don't intend to keep having to tell you that, understood?"

"Yes, ma'am," Heidi said, but it was pleasure not embarrassment that she was feeling. "It won't take me a minute to unpack. I travel pretty light."

By the time the men got back from their card game, it was past Milo's bedtime, so Nana, Steve and Heidi sat up talking until Nana covered a yawn and declared she was too old to keep up with "you young people."

"It is late," Steve said, putting his arm around Heidi as they sat close together on the couch.

"You aren't fooling me for a minute, Steve Grosso," Nana said, wagging a finger at him. "You've been hoping for the last half hour I'd nod off or go to bed. I'm not *that* old."

Steve grinned and stood up to kiss Nana good-night. "Smart lady," he said. "Thanks—for everything."

Nana turned to Heidi. "Glad to have you here, Heidi—feels right." Not seeming to expect a response, she eased open the bedroom door and slipped inside.

"Does it?" Steve asked as he sat back down on the sofa and pulled her into his arms. "Feel right, I mean?"

"This does," she whispered, kissing his jaw.

"Okay, got it. Too soon to tell."

THE FOLLOWING MORNING, Heidi was awake at dawn. She got up, brushed her teeth in the tiny powder room, dressed and had the coffee going by the time she heard stirrings in the bedroom at the back of the motor home.

"You're up with the rooster," Milo said as he opened the bedroom door and then ducked back inside. Heidi could hear him talking to Juliana and wondered if he'd forgotten she was staying with them.

"Did you sleep well?" Nana asked as she hurried into the kitchen, tightening the belt of her terry cloth robe and immediately pulling things from the refrigerator. "That sofa bed is supposed to be the best, but it's still a pullout no matter what fancy name they give the thing."

"It was fine," Heidi declared. "I was thinking that after breakfast I would get the outside tables and chairs out of the storage bay and set up the portico area. I think I remember how you like it."

"Oh, sweetie, there is nothing sacred about the way I do things. You set it up however seems best to you. A change is always nice."

"Anybody up?" Steve called half an hour later as he pulled open the coach door.

"We're all up," Milo announced, emerging from the bedroom fully dressed and freshly shaved. "Aren't you due at the spotters' meeting about now?"

"I've got a few minutes," Steve replied, pouring himself a mug of coffee as he cast questioning glances in Heidi's direction.

"Well, clearly she made it through the night," Nana said as she nudged him out of her way. "So you can stop your worrying."

Steve grinned and Heidi marveled at Nana's unique ability to assess a situation for what it was without a word being spoken.

"Okay then. That's all I wanted to know," Steve said, kissing Heidi on the forehead and then dumping the remains of his coffee in the sink. "I've got a meeting."

"Yeah, like I said," Milo grumbled.

While Steve was at his meeting, Heidi set up the folding picnic table and benches with multiple lawn chairs around next to the motor home. Beneath the patio furniture was a field of artificial turf bordered by a low white picket fence. The entire side panel of the huge motor home lifted to form a protective covering from the elements.

"Looks like we're ready for anything," Heidi observed, standing back to check her work as Nana emerged from the coach carrying a stack of colorful plastic plates with matching cloth napkins.

"Yep. Rain, sun, sleet or wind—any plague Mother Nature sends our way," Nana agreed. Next she and Heidi unloaded several coolers filled with food that Juliana had brought with her to supplement the stock of staples the coach driver always made sure were available. Heidi filled one cooler with ice and cans of beer and soda while Juliana set up the grill. As Steve drove up with Milo next to him the two women were sitting across the table from one another, soda cans between them and their heads bent close together in conversation.

"We're back," Milo announced as Steve swung the golf cart around and parked it next to the entrance to the motor home.

"Just like a man to think just because we didn't bring out the brass band that we didn't notice," Nana said to Heidi.

Steve reached inside the cooler and retrieved a can of soda and tossed it to Milo, then got another for himself. He popped the key and took a long swallow. "You two ladies seem to have settled in," he said, straddling the picnic table bench closest to Heidi.

"She's a prize. Don't know how we got this all set up before she came along," Nana announced as she stood and stretched. "Milo, go inside and lie down. You're going to want to watch the practice laps and—"

"Woman, I am perfectly capable of knowing when I need a nap," Milo grumbled, but he did as she suggested and headed inside.

Nana smiled as she watched him go and then turned her attention back to Heidi and Steve. "Well, I'm going to call on the neighbors and catch up on the gossip. See you two later?"

"How are you doing?" Steve asked as soon as his great-grandmother had left.

"Fine," Heidi assured him. "Really."

Steve grinned with relief and drained the rest of his soda. "Want to take a walk with me over to the garage area? I need to check on something."

"Sure."

At the gate leading to the area where the trucks used to carry the race cars and then serve as command centers for each team were parked, they were stopped by security. It didn't matter that Steve was wearing the uniform of the Kent Grosso team—black slacks, a blue knit polo shirt with the "Flying V" Vittle Farms logo over the left pocket or that the security guards greeted him by name. Anyone expecting to get past these guys had better have credentials—the right credentials. A hard-to-come-by "hot" pass if the cars were active on the track or a "cold" pass if the cars were in the garage area and being worked on by the teams, getting them ready to pass inspection.

Once inside, Heidi and Steve headed down the long row of oversize eighteen-wheeled trucks where race cars—instantly identifiable to any fan by their trademark color scheme and sponsor logos—were in the process of being unloaded. The haulers formed a fruit salad of polished metal ranging from bright mango gold to lime green to vivid strawberry red and beyond. A novice to NASCAR might think they were all brand-new, but Heidi knew better. One of the facets of racing that had always impressed her was the enormous pride every member of every team took in maintaining the equipment. A person could practically eat off the floor of the garage bays assigned to each team across the lot.

As they approached Kent's unique vivid blue hauler with its distinctive tomato-red accents, Steve quickened his stride and Heidi hurried to keep up. They were now in what constituted the backstage area for a NASCAR event and everyone was focused on the business of getting the cars unloaded, inspected and ready for the afternoon's schedule of practice and qualifying laps. She might have just as easily been walking down the corridors of some giant corporate offices or the assembly line of a multimillion-dollar industry. If anyone doubted that NASCAR was big business, all they needed to do was observe what happened in the garage area on the day before a big race.

When they reached Kent's hauler, one of the team members pointed across the way to the long row of garages when Steve asked if anyone had seen Neil Sanchez.

"I'll be right back," he told Heidi.

Heidi watched the team unload Kent's car and walk it from the hauler over to the garage bay assigned to Kent's team. Over the next day and a half the car would be tested and fine-tuned to give Kent the best possible chance of winning. At the very least the goal was to have Kent finish high enough in the standings to increase his point total in the quest to repeat as NASCAR Sprint Cup Series champion. All around Heidi other teams were performing similar tasks. In some cases a member of the team had climbed the ladder mounted on the side of the hauler to set up a viewing perch of the track.

"Hey there, Heidi!"

Heidi glanced up in search of the voice calling her name. Kent's sister, Sophia, stood on top of his team's hauler, a piece of bright blue metal piping in one hand. Apparently she had decided to make herself useful by setting up the topside viewing stand for her brother's team. Sophia had Patsy's flawless complexion and no-nonsense personality. Heidi had always admired Sophia, seeing her as another woman dedicated to her career and at the same time hoping to someday have a solid marriage and a house filled with children.

"Hey, I thought you were working this weekend," Heidi said as she climbed the ladder on the side of the huge truck and joined Sophia on top.

Sophia grinned. "One of the perks of managing a nursing home full of nurses is that I get to make the schedule. Here, give me a hand with this."

Heidi couldn't help wondering why Sophia was here with her

brother's team instead of just three large trucks away where Justin Murphy's hauler was parked.

Sophia followed her glance toward Justin's camp as she handed Heidi a piece of the blue metal railing. "Justin had to go to a meeting with his sponsor so I thought I'd give Kent a hand."

Heidi blushed. "I didn't mean…you certainly don't need to explain…"

Sophia smiled. "Hey, you've been hanging around this family long enough to know the story. Don't try to pretend you don't know all the intrigue surrounding the star-crossed romance of a Grosso with a Murphy." She placed the back of one hand on her forehead in a theatrical gesture of distress.

Heidi couldn't help laughing.

"Steve told me the two of you met with both families. Pretty brave move given the history. So how's that going?"

"Ever try to walk on eggshells without breaking them?" Sophia asked.

"Got it." She couldn't help admiring Sophia's attitude—positive and upbeat as if she had no doubt that she and Justin would clear every hurdle. It struck her that Sophia was certainly a poster child for growing up in the NASCAR life. And she certainly seemed to have turned out okay—better than okay. Heidi fitted the predrilled rod into its hole and picked up another piece.

"Thank goodness for Mom," Sophia continued, her tone chatty. "At least Justin and I can count on her to point out to the Neanderthals of this family that a fifty-year feud is a little much, even for the Grosso clan and the Murphys."

Heidi grabbed the last piece of the railing and slid it into place while Sophia dragged two bright blue Adirondack chairs into position. Sophia plopped down in one of the chairs and untwisted the cap of a bottle of water. "Pull up a chair," she invited. "Our work here is done."

Heidi couldn't help feeling pleased at the way Sophia was talking so openly about her situation—as if they were friends. In the time she'd been with Steve her interactions with most of the family had been of the large-gathering variety. Conversations with individual members of the family had always been more along the lines of social chitchat—brief and general. But now here she was, alone with Kent's sister, and Sophia was treating her as if they'd been friends for years.

Heidi sat down and flipped open the cooler that served as a shared ottoman. She pulled out a bottle of water for herself. Following Sophia's lead, she leaned back, propped her feet on the closed cooler and turned her face to the warmth of the sun.

"How's it going? The grand experiment?" Sophia asked.

Heidi hesitated. "It's—they're lovely people," she began.

Sophia snorted as she choked on a long swallow of water. "That good, huh?"

They were quiet again and then Heidi said, "Can I ask you something?"

"Sure."

"Well, you probably know that the issue here is that I have serious reservations about raising our children—I mean, if Steve and I married..."

"*When* Steve and you marry," Sophia corrected. "Continue."

"So, what do you think? I mean, you grew up on tour. What was it like for you, as a young girl and a teenager?"

Sophia stretched and folded her hands behind her head as she gazed out over the action going on all around them. "Well, look around you. Doesn't all this remind you of a small town kind of coming to life in the morning? Imagine that we're here in the downtown area, the 'shops' are opening up for the day."

Heidi had to admit she'd never thought of it that way. She closed her eyes and listened to the activity below them.

"And over there," Sophia continued, pointing to the fenced-off area where luxurious motor homes lined up in rows forming a grid of streets, "that's the ''hood.' "

Of course. There were the streets with the "houses," and parked outside each home was either a golf cart, motor scooter or both for getting around town and the "hood," as Sophia called it.

Sophia waved her hand toward two blue tent-shaped awnings. "Child care there and then over there—" she turned and pointed to a large white motor home "—fitness center. We even have our own supermarket and over there, the suburbs," she added, grinning as she pointed to the distant area where a few lucky fans could rent camping spots in the infield. "Home sweet home," she said.

"But growing up on tour?" Heidi asked again.

"It was the best," Sophia admitted. "Like being on vacation with your best friends most of the year."

"What about school?"

Sophia shrugged. "We all went to public school in Concord, although these days homeschooling is all the rage. Like Nana always says, if it takes a village to raise a good kid, you're not going to find a better one anywhere than this."

Heidi was beginning to see that she might have a point. "On the other hand," she said, "when you and Kent were growing up…well, Patsy didn't…I mean, it's different from today. You have a career. I have a career."

Sophia nodded. "I guess the trick is to find a way to have it all—challenging but not impossible. Speaking of you and that cousin of mine, there's Mr. Nice Guy now," Sophia said, nudging her and pointing to where Steve had emerged from the garage and was obviously looking for her. "Hey, cous, up here," she called.

Steve glanced up and when he saw Heidi, he broke into a grin that smoothed the worry frown lines Heidi had been seeing much too often over the last couple of weeks. "What are you two women up to?"

"We're working," Heidi called back.

"Come up and see for yourself," Sophia yelled, tossing him a bottle of ice-cold water that he caught with one hand.

"Not right now. I promised Nana we'd be back in time for lunch. You coming?"

"Nope. Got a date with a driver," Sophia said. She turned and gave Heidi a light hug. "See you later, Heidi—and hey, welcome to the neighborhood."

CHAPTER SIX

"THANK HEAVENS you're back," Nana said, rushing forward. Steve assumed that this greeting was aimed at him, but Heidi was the one that Nana grabbed by the arm and started pulling down the lane to a motor home parked three doors away.

"Sybil?" she called as she entered the motor home without knocking. "I've brought the doctor. Now where's Henrietta?"

"But, Juliana—Nana—I'm not a people doctor," Steve heard Heidi say in a low voice as they followed his amazingly agile great-grandmother into a home on wheels that was considerably smaller than Milo's. The place was decorated in a jungle motif complete with leopard print–covered furnishings, lush plants and a working fountain that resembled a miniwaterfall. Then Nana came to an abrupt halt, and Steve had to smother a smile as Heidi found herself face-to-face with Henrietta, a large gold and blue umbrella cockatoo. The bird looked directly at Heidi and bobbed her colorful head in welcome.

"Hello."

"Hello, Henrietta," Heidi replied.

"Sybil, this is Dr. Kramer. Heidi, this is Sybil Marshall, her husband, Chuck, heads up the NARS. He's Roger Clark's boss," Nana explained. "Heidi just worked on Roger's dog last week," she explained for Sybil's benefit.

"How you doing, Miz Marshall?" Steve asked as he removed his cap. "What's the problem with Henrietta?" he added sympathetically.

"Oh, Stevie, darlin', she's been off her feed for more than a week now and she's losing her feathers—more every day." Sybil wiped her eyes with the corner of her oversize hand-embroidered shirt.

"Now don't you worry," Steve said, moving forward and putting his arm around Heidi's shoulders. "Dr. Kramer is the best vet around. How about you let her take a look?"

Heidi stretched out her arm and the woman nodded and allowed the cockatoo to come to her. Then they all followed Heidi into the kitchen area—the closest flat surface available for an examination. As always, Heidi's focus on the animal was total.

The large bird shuddered and attempted to flap the wings that Heidi held secure. "Shh," Heidi whispered. "You're all right, Henrietta. You're going to be just fine."

Steve couldn't help noticing that even though Heidi's words were directed at the parrot, they had a calming effect on Sybil as well. And given Sybil's inclination toward the dramatic, that was some accomplishment.

"Mrs. Marshall," Heidi said finally.

"Sybil, please." She took a seat on the bench next to where Heidi held Henrietta, gentling her with a light touch. "It's bad, right?"

"Henrietta has a case of what is known as feather picking. See these areas where the feathers are either missing or broken off?"

"I thought she was just molting."

"Could I ask you a couple of questions? I'm not placing blame, just trying to come up with the best remedy," Heidi hastened to add.

"Anything," Sybil replied.

Heidi probed into the bird's routine and how it might have been altered.

"Oh, it's all my fault," Sybil moaned. "You see, I grew up in racing, traveling to every race, and then when I married Chuck…well, he traveled but I stayed home."

Heidi glanced around the claustrophobic motor home and Sybil followed her look as she continued her explanation. "Chuck surprised me with this for our wedding anniversary last February. Said he knew how much I missed being a real part of the community, so now that the kids are grown and gone we'd be spending this season on the road together."

Heidi nodded. "And before that, Henrietta was at home in familiar surroundings with you and your children while your husband traveled to and from the races?"

Sybil nodded.

"Henrietta's whole routine has changed in these last few months," Heidi said gently. "This is all new to her."

Sybil stifled a sob and looked miserable. "So I should take her home?"

Heidi placed her hand on the woman's shoulder. "Let's talk about the medical treatment first," Heidi said. "There are options. We could start by putting a collar on her to prevent her from picking, but since the cause of her affliction is stress, we don't want to do anything that will add to that stress."

"Stress?" Steve swallowed a smile, but the look he gave Heidi shouted, *You're kidding, right? It's a bird.*

Heidi ignored him and turned her attention back to Henrietta. "Umbrella cockatoos are affectionate and gregarious by nature," she continued. "From what you've told me about the changes you've made since you and Mr. Marshall decided to spend race weekends on the road, Henrietta has had to adjust to new surroundings, and chances are she's been spending a lot of time alone."

"Well, we do have people in or we go out, but not everybody takes to her, you know, and—"

"She's lonely and a little frightened, Sybil," Heidi said gently. "She's homesick, not necessarily for your regular house, but for a more normal routine. The remedy for that is for you to spend more time with her, let her be outside where people pass by during the day, and make sure to cover her cage at night so she's on a regular sleep-wake schedule. As for the medical solution, we can spray a bit of bitter apple on the areas she seems to have targeted for picking. It doesn't always work," she warned, "but I'd rather start with something simple."

As Steve watched Heidi work with the bird and deliver her diagnosis, all the while soothing a nearly hysterical Sybil, it occurred to him that he was seeing a side of Heidi he hadn't really considered before. Up until now she had been his girlfriend. More recently she had become the woman he wanted to marry. Now he saw that the way she handled the distressed parrot—not to mention Sybil—was almost like gentling a frightened child. Heidi was going to be an incredible mother.

Of course he had thought about them having kids one day, but the thought had always been in the abstract—a logical aftermath of getting married. And of course there were her reservations about how their kids would be raised, maybe even doubts about the wisdom of having kids at all. Sometimes when he thought about how her vagabond childhood had left her with so many fears and reservations, he was at a loss to know how he could show her that things didn't have to be that way. Maybe after this weekend—

"Steve," Nana shouted as if he were hard of hearing. "Pay attention. Heidi needs you to get her some of that bitter apple stuff. I think there's a bottle in the cabinet under the sink in our place."

"On my way," Steve said as he put on his team cap and headed for the door.

NANA STOOD at the door of Sybil's motor home and watched as Steve took off across the compound. "That boy gets more like his daddy all the time," she said with a soft chuckle. "A dreamer, that one."

Heidi smiled to herself as she continued to assure Sybil that she would be around all weekend and would be happy to check on Henrietta's progress. But she was thinking about Steve. Yes, the man was a dreamer, but with an undercoating of reality. He saw all the possibilities in life and rarely seemed to consider the improbability of a situation. In the face of all her doubts and fears it was Steve who usually came up with solutions. For Steve the question was *how* a thing could be done—not *whether* it could be done. It was one more trait that made him one of the best spotters in auto racing. But more to the point, it was one of the reasons she had fallen in love with him.

Nana insisted that Sybil and Henrietta come to the Grosso motor home for lunch as a first step toward acclimating Henrietta to her new neighborhood. As usual, the place was a magnet for family, team members and friends. Patsy and Tanya arrived with their contributions to the spread of food, and the conversation soon turned to Tanya and Kent's wedding plans, while the Grosso men discussed preparations for the afternoon's practice laps.

"Want to come watch the practice?" Steve asked as he grabbed another apple turnover for the road and headed for the golf cart.

"No. You go on. I'll stay here. Tanya and Patsy are going into town, shopping for the wedding. They asked me to come along." She couldn't help sounding pleased at being included.

Steve kissed her and grinned. "You're getting the hang of this thing, aren't you?"

"That's the plan, right?"

Later that evening after supper, the race cars came out—not the track cars, but miniature remote-controlled versions. Several drivers gathered in the streets of the owners' and drivers' lot and lined up their entry at the starting line. Others gathered along the edges of the makeshift track to cheer for their favorites.

"You're going down, son," Dean announced as he placed his car next to Kent's.

"Not likely. I got a new hot driver," Kent replied, handing his control over to Tanya.

The crowd cheered and Tanya grinned and took a bow.

"Two can play that game," Dean shouted. "Heidi, come on," he called.

Heidi laughed. "I'm a rookie," she said. "You want someone more experienced. Steve can do it."

"Nope. I've seen that boy drive and I'll take my chances with you."

Heidi looked up quickly to see how his uncle's words had affected Steve. She was sure she was the only one who saw the hurt look that skittered across his eyes before he grinned. "Come on, Heidi. I'll spot for you."

She took the control and Steve stood behind her, his arms lightly around her waist, his mouth close to her ear.

The other drivers lined up their cars and took their places. Heidi considered the field of six miniature cars. Tanya had the pole position and Heidi's car was on the outside.

"Gentlemen—and ladies," Milo intoned, "start your engines."

"Okay," Steve instructed, "Milo's car is the pace car. You'll follow it around once and then when he peels off, that's your signal to go."

Heidi's attention was riveted on the remote as she memorized each control. She was glad that one of Steve's favorite pastimes was playing the arcade games at the huge mall near the speedway outside Charlotte. They had spent many an evening there competing for top points and she'd gotten good enough at the necessary eye and hand coordination to at least give Steve a competitive game.

"Be ready," Steve whispered as they came around the track the first time. "Okay, pace car off, go!"

Heidi pushed every button on the panel and her car careened crazily along the track.

"You've got time," Steve said. "The No. 427 car's laying back."

Heidi glanced over and saw Tanya preparing to make her move. "Now?" Heidi shouted excitedly over her shoulder.

"Crash on turn three—stay high. Stay high," Steve said calmly.

Heidi managed to push the right controls to carry her car around the crash that had eliminated three of the other cars. It was down to Tanya and her and the other remaining car as Milo crowed gleefully and brought out his pace car once again.

"Lay back. Behind the No. 443 car," Steve advised.

"The No. 443 is not in the lead," Heidi protested and gave an apologetic glance to the driver to her left.

"That's okay. Stay on his bumper."

Heidi did not see the point especially since Tanya's car was running parallel to the No. 443 car and would easily shoot forward and into the lead once Milo pulled the pace car off.

"Stay with me," Steve murmured, his voice calm and steady as if he had read her mind. She noticed him nudge the driver of the No. 443 car, saw Steve make a gesture and the man nodded and grinned.

Milo pulled the pace car off and the No. 443 car and Tanya's car shot forward with Heidi right on their bumpers.

"Be ready to go low and inside," Steve said.

Heidi stared hard at the track, watching Tanya's car and the No. 443 car jockeying for position and concentrating on staying right with them, her thumb fairly itching to make the pass.

"Go! Go! Go!" Steve ordered, his voice never rising above a normal business tone.

Heidi pressed the control and as she shot into the lead she realized the No. 443 car had moved higher on the turn, effectively blocking Tanya from making her move. Tanya was forced to drop low and go around the No. 443 car and in that moment lost the lead—and the race.

Dean shouted with joy as if he'd just won the NASCAR Sprint Cup Series. He raced over and grabbed Heidi in a bear hug, swinging her around. "Slingshot move," he shouted. "Did you see that, Kent?" he yelled. "Slingshot—and from a rookie."

"Rookie with the best spotter in the business giving her the moves," Kent replied as he wrapped one arm around Steve's shoulders.

"Fair is fair," Milo declared and presented Dean with a small gold trophy.

"What's a slingshot move?" Heidi asked Steve later after everyone had gone home and Juliana and Milo had retired for the night.

They were sitting outside next to a small portable fire pit that Steve had set up following the race. Nana and Patsy had provided a victory feast of s'mores and coffee before the night air grew damp and chilly. Everyone else had taken the cooler weather as their cue to head back to their own motor homes, but Steve and Heidi had donned hooded sweatshirts and pulled their chairs closer to the fire, reluctant to call it a night.

"A slingshot move is when one driver rides the draft of the car or cars ahead of him and then pulls out and passes. It has to be quick and perfectly executed or he loses the momentum of the draft, but if he—or she—can pull it off, it works almost every time."

"Is that something you advise Kent to use in a close race?"

Steve grinned. "Too risky. It's really an all-or-nothing move and you don't want to try it unless you've got everything to gain and pretty much nothing to lose."

"Like tonight?"

Steve laughed. "I figured Tanya wouldn't expect it."

"The other guys let it come down to us, didn't they?" Heidi guessed. "I mean, come on, four NASCAR drivers against two women?"

"Hey, the crash was legit. They were overdriving their equipment. No way they were going to make that turn driving the way they were, but yeah, I expect they would have pulled back and let you two gals go at it."

He leaned over and kissed her.

"You miss driving, don't you?" she said.

His eyebrows lifted in surprise, but he didn't move away. "Yeah, well, you always think about it. It's like any athlete, as a kid you dream about making the big league and when you realize you don't have the right stuff—or the right stuff any longer— then that's a coming-of-age thing, I guess. You either accept that it's never going to happen and move on or you let life pass you by while you keep living on might-have-beens."

Heidi rested her head on Steve's shoulder as they both stared into the fire. "I love you, Steve Grosso," she whispered and felt his arm tighten around her.

ON RACE DAY the atmosphere was decidedly more tense and charged with anticipation than it had been the evening before. Right after breakfast everyone gathered at the media center for the traditional ecumenical church service. Heidi sat between Steve and Milo in a row filled with members of the Grosso family and their teams. The men left right after the service and did not return throughout the day.

As the start of the race grew closer, the tension mounted. Wives and girlfriends of the drivers—including Patsy, Sophia and Tanya—headed for the pits for a final kiss before the race. Meanwhile the family motor home lot grew strangely quiet. Conversation was hushed as if in respect for the reality that a race—any race—held the potential for serious injury. Only the occasional shrieks of children playing in the child-care area run by the NARS interrupted the sudden stillness of the compound.

During prerace ceremonies, Heidi helped Nana set out snacks and beverages on the kitchen counter. Eventually Tanya, Patsy and even Sophia made their way back to the motor home. Heidi could feel the tension as each of the three women glanced at the television screen and away, then prepared themselves a plate of snacks as they waited for the familiar call.

"Gentlemen, start your engines," the announcer intoned, and in unison the field of forty-three customized stock cars fired their vehicles to life. The sound was amazing as it ricocheted around the speedway and over the infield in a singular roar that was as perfectly on pitch as the Mormon Tabernacle Choir holding an opening note.

Heidi watched the women move around, staking out their positions, settling into their preferred seats—Patsy on the love seat while Nana curled into a corner of the larger sofa. Tanya chose the single swivel armchair by the door. Sophia paced the length of the motor home like a panther in a cage. Occasionally she would cut her eyes to the screen. Heidi realized that she was here because these women were her family regardless of their feelings about her relationship with Justin. Heidi could not help thinking of her own mother—of the times when Heidi had wanted to turn to her with some hurt or joy. But most days her mother had been too caught up in her own problems to give Heidi the level of intimacy and unspoken support that seemed to come so effortlessly to these women.

She glanced up at the television and saw what she had seen dozens of times from her usual position in the stands—the field of cars following the pace car as they swerved slightly from side to side to warm up their tires and gain traction before the flag dropped. And as soon as that green flag dropped it was as if the women had also received the signal releasing them from the constraints of holding their position. Patsy sat forward while Sophia hugged her knees to her chest. Tanya folded her legs under her in the large chair. Only Nana remained as she had been, seated in the corner of the sofa fingering her glass of iced tea.

"Come sit over here, Heidi," Nana said, indicating the vacant spot next to her.

Heidi got up from the place she'd taken at the small dining table and sat on the sofa. She couldn't help wondering if this might become her designated place among this unique club of women. She imagined them spending the weekends of February through November watching as the men they loved raced for the glory of a national championship.

"Hey, give Justin some space," Sophia shouted, gesturing wildly at the screen.

Nana reached over and laid a calming hand on her great-granddaughter's shoulder. "Rubbin' is racin'," she reminded her.

"Rubbin's one thing," Sophia huffed as Justin Murphy took the turn on the inside and moved past the offending car. "That was payback for last week."

Before Nana could say more, there was a crash sending multiple cars careening into the wall on turn three. Every woman in the room leaned closer to the television as if they might be able to do something about the mayhem. In fact, Heidi realized they were looking for the cars they each cared most about—Kent's, Dean's and, in Sophia's case, Justin's.

When all three drivers cleared the crash site without incident, the women relaxed and returned to their normal positions, adding their own color commentary to that of the television announcers. As the hours passed and it became clear that Dean had taken a commanding lead, the joy in the room was surprisingly subdued. And as the laps dwindled with little chance for anyone to catch him, Patsy sighed.

"You should go," Nana said.

Patsy nodded and left the motor home.

Heidi glanced at each of the three remaining women, who all seemed to understand. "Dean's going to win, right?" she said, looking at Nana for confirmation.

"Big-time," Sophia said, getting up to get herself a bottle of water.

"I don't understand. Shouldn't that be a good thing? I mean, Patsy seems so—"

"Mom's been trying to get Dad to retire, to make this his last season. She wants him to do well, but when he wins…well, he gets this idea that maybe this is his year to win it all."

"She's just worried," Nana added. "I know when Milo was racing, the older he got, the more years that passed without him getting injured or killed, the harder it was for me to watch. In a way, it felt like we were living on borrowed time and testing fate every time he got behind the wheel. Patsy's feeling that."

"But Dean loves racing—it's all he knows—has ever known," Tanya protested.

"She loves him," Nana said. "Same way you love Kent, and Heidi loves Steve." She cast a glance at her great-granddaughter and added, "And Sophia loves Justin. You're all young and a little bit invincible—or so you think. Right now it's who they are. It's part of what makes them the men you love. But in time—"

The four of them turned their attention to the television as the camera found Dean—one arm pumped high in victory and the other holding Patsy at his side. Patsy was smiling up at him, her eyes glistening with tears, and who could have guessed they were not tears of happiness?

CHAPTER SEVEN

STEVE COULD NOT help noticing that Heidi was unusually quiet on the drive back to Kannapolis after the race. He had tried several topics of conversation—Sybil's cockatoo among them—and Heidi had smiled and made a comment. But she had done nothing to sustain the conversation. He should be used to this by now, but from where he sat it seemed everything had gone so well. So why this reserve? Why was she pulling away yet again?

"Okay, what are you thinking about so hard?" Steve asked finally. "I can practically hear the wheels turning all the way over here."

"Oh, you know, mumble jumble."

Mumble jumble was Heidi's unique expression for when she had a lot on her mind. On those occasions he could feel her pulling away from him, closing herself off until she figured out the answer to whatever was on her mind. "I've got a couple of hours," Steve said, indicating the road ahead. "Maybe I can help straighten out the jumble."

Heidi sighed, started to say something and then sighed again. "Well, for starters," she managed to say finally, "I was thinking that other than the accommodations, this weekend wasn't all that different from any other we've been on over the last couple of years."

"I thought that was kind of the plan," Steve said. "Are you

saying Nana's motor home wasn't up to the standards of the local budget hotel?"

"You know better," she answered and he heard the slightest hint of exasperation in her tone. He knew this was a surefire indication that whatever this was, she'd been thinking about it for some time. He was just damned if he could figure out which way this conversation might be headed.

Now it was his time to sigh. He ran one hand through his hair and glanced her way. "Don't let me mess this up by asking stupid questions," he said. "Just talk to me."

She curled one leg underneath the other and twisted in the seat so that she was nearly facing him. Her seat belt was stretched and would be useless if they had an accident, but he said nothing. "Here's the deal," she said, her words rushed as if she needed to get them out before they disappeared. "Your family is amazing—warm, welcoming, caring people."

Steve laughed, thinking about the harsh words that had flown after the race between Kent and Neil. "Not everyone would agree with that assessment, but go on."

"I expected there to be moments—certainly at the beginning, if not throughout the weekend—when I was reminded that I was a virtual stranger, not intentionally, of course, just somebody new, you know?"

Steve glanced from the road to her and back again. "No, I don't know. It's not like this was the first time I brought you home to meet the folks."

"I know, but well, other than the baking session last week, it's really the first time that it's been so obvious that I might actually be moving in the direction of becoming a member of the family."

"You lost me about a mile back," Steve said, shaking his head as he tried to maneuver through a convoy of eighteen-wheelers stretched across both lanes of the interstate. At the moment working his way to the front of that convoy was way easier than navigating his way through this conversation.

Heidi took a deep breath. "I know I'm not making much sense, but, okay, look at it this way. Wasn't there ever a time when you had a friend and you played or studied at their house, saw their parents come and go, even ate meals with them, but then the first time you stayed over it felt different."

"So, staying with my great-grandparents was like going to a slumber party?"

"No! Oh, I'm not explaining this well at all. The bottom line is that I felt right at home after the first half hour and that never changed. Not the whole weekend. I walked into that motor home and before I knew it I was helping Nana with everything for the tailgate—settin' up and washin' up as she would say. For heaven's sake, I was calling the woman Nana and not even stumbling over the word."

Steve chose his next words very carefully. "And is that a good thing?"

"It's awesome," Heidi said. "I mean, it really didn't hit me until we started to drive back. I realized that all the things I'd thought might happen, all the awkward moments I'd prepared myself for, all the lists I'd made of things I might talk about when you weren't around and it was just me with your great-grandparents or the other women… I—I mean, one of the things I was most nervous about was being with the women. They're so close and everything. I was positive that I would be like some fifth wheel."

"You made a list of topics of conversations?" Steve was incredulous. He knew that Heidi was superorganized, thinking through every detail before she made a move, but this seemed a bit over the top—even for her. He couldn't help it. He started to laugh.

"Stop it," she ordered, slapping lightly at his arm, but she was grinning sheepishly.

"I want to see the list," he said.

"You just keep your eyes on the road."

"At least tell me some of the topics."

She went very quiet and when he glanced over he saw that she was trying unsuccessfully to repress her own laughter. "Tomatoes," she finally blurted.

Steve could barely form the word. "Tomatoes?"

"Well, Milo grows these amazing vintage tomatoes and there are so many of them and how on earth does Juliana use them and—"

"You cannot be serious," Steve said. "I assume that's the best one?"

Heidi giggled. "Well, it was at least a topic that might interest both of them. That's not so easy, you know."

"Honey, they've been married since the edge of forever. By now they have a lot of interests in common. So what else was on the list?"

"Now you just want to make fun of me," she accused.

"Well, duh!"

"Okay, I can take it. I also had ice cream on the list."

"Seems to have been a food theme here. Why ice cream?"

"I was going to have them tell me the difference between ice cream and gelato."

Steve shook his head. "And then what?"

"I don't know. I guess I thought if I asked something like that it would lead them to broaden the topic, like maybe Milo would remember gelato he had back in Italy when he was stationed there during the war."

"And you abandoned this list—wisely, I might add— because?"

"I never needed it. Heavens, I could hardly get the sofa bed put away and me dressed in the morning before somebody was at the door ready to share breakfast with Milo and Nana. Before

I knew it I was right in the middle of a multifaceted debate on the merits of a Ford over a Chevy, and do not get them started on the Toyota. And things just went from there. I would wake up, jump in and just let the current carry me."

"And you never felt—"

"I didn't have time to consider what I was feeling. Do you know how many people are in and out of that place in a day? Or how many calls up and down the lane that Patsy and Nana make—as if they hadn't just seen Nellie or Jan in town two days earlier. That's the point. I'm just now starting to digest what happened."

Steve felt warmth spread through his chest. His plan had worked—at least for this weekend.

"You know I've been making a list myself."

She glanced at him. "Really? What's on your list?"

"One, to get a real job. Something that could seriously support a wife and family." He made a gesture of checking off that item. "Done."

"Two?"

"Two was to find a way to help you see that living on the road didn't have to be a bad thing. That maybe it could even be fun."

"Okay. It's only been one weekend, but I can at least see the possibilities."

"So, don't check it off yet?"

"Give it the month," she said. "Anything else on your list?"

"Well, there's your job," he said, reluctant to bring that up when things were going so well.

"Yeah. There's that."

"You know, lately I get the feeling that somehow your way of looking at your career is somehow tied to your past. I mean, I'm not a shrink or anything close to it, but I'm a good listener and lately…well, you've gotten pretty tied up in knots every time something comes close to affecting your position at the clinic."

"I don't," she protested.

"Yeah, you do. Like that day when I wanted you to come to Phoenix? And like this week when it looked like Clare might have to rescind the partnership offer?"

"My career is…it…I've worked hard to get to where I am and—"

"But it's more than that, right? I mean, you have a profession and skills that can go anywhere. You don't need Clare. You don't even need Kannapolis."

"That's what my father told my mother," Heidi blurted. "And she believed him and look what happened. My mother was—is— a gifted pianist. She could have made a career as a concert performer. When she met and married my father she thought that following him from job to job would not affect her career. She could get work and perform anywhere, right?"

Steve wasn't about to answer what was clearly a sarcastic and rhetorical question.

"Wrong," Heidi said bitterly. "Instead she settled for teaching others, offering piano lessons from our house and mourning what might have been. She eventually became so depressed that she had to be medicated and she was incapable of taking care of me—or my father. I will not make the same mistake." She folded her arms and slumped into the seat, staring out the windshield at her past.

"Honey? I'm really sorry about that, but you aren't your mother," he ventured. "And I am not going to expect you to give up the work you love to follow my job, okay?"

She nodded and he could see that she was fighting back tears.

"How about a pit stop?" he said, nodding toward the signs lining up to signal the next exit. "Pretty sure they won't have gelato, but I'll treat for an ice-cream sundae."

She reached over and caressed his cheek. "I'll settle for a chance to stretch my legs and splash a little water on my face," Heidi said, then she uncurled her legs and stretched her arms high over her head, scraping the ceiling of Steve's truck with her knuckles.

At the truck stop they decided to order breakfast instead of ice cream. Heidi picked at her stack of blueberry pancakes while Steve attacked his eggs, toast and grits as if he might have to go without food for days.

"You gonna finish those?" he asked as he sopped up the last of his egg yolk with a piece of toast.

Heidi pushed the plate toward him. "It's going to be interesting at work tomorrow," she said.

"On what level?"

"You know. Clare was pretty distracted before I left on Thursday. I've never seen her quite that down, although to her credit she tried to put on a good show."

"She's worried," Steve said with the assurance of someone who had been there. "It's like Neil. Lately he's been a bear to work with. He's got three alimony checks due, plus his new girlfriend might be in a family way, and then if I had to guess, it's all made worse by his being afraid that somebody else on the team might show him up."

Glad to have the spotlight of their conversation focused elsewhere, Heidi leaned forward. "How so?"

Steve shrugged. "Over the last few weeks Tobey Harris—Neil's assistant—has started to speak up in meetings, offering solutions to problems that Neil had already pegged as nearly unsolvable. Kent took a couple of his ideas and they worked and so Kent jokingly asked Neil why *he* hadn't thought of the solution. Neil went ballistic."

"And so it falls to you to mediate," Heidi said, pulling the plate of pancakes so that it was between them as she took a bite.

"It's a control thing," Steve said. "That's probably what's going on with Clare. She sees business slipping and can't figure out how to fix it. And she's maybe feeling guilty because she's brought up this partnership idea and now she's thinking she'll have to back away from that. Clare's been more than your boss. She's also your friend. Not to mention that she's the reason you went to vet school in the first place."

"So we go back to plan A—postponing the partnership until I pay off the last of my student loans in September."

"I could help with that—paying off the loans. I mean, now that I have this steady salary plus the money I earn spotting."

Heidi ran her finger up and down her water glass as if it were important to clear up the moisture that had condensed there. "I can't let you do that."

"Why on earth not?"

"The loans are my responsibility. Not that I don't appreciate the offer. It's just—"

"Honey, it's okay. Whatever makes you comfortable. Just know the offer is here." Steve forked up the last bite of pancakes and held it out to her.

To his relief Heidi took the pancake and washed it down with the last of her coffee. "Don't mind me. I don't want to spoil what's been a really wonderful weekend by talking about work things."

"Well, there's one 'work thing' I want to talk about. Sybil Marshall was raving about you to everybody she could find to listen to her. Dawson was even talking about it one day when we were all sitting around the hauler lounge. He said that if he heard one more time how fabulous my girlfriend was he was thinking of marrying you himself."

Heidi blushed. "He's already married. Besides, he's old enough to be my father," she protested as Steve paid the bill and they headed back to his truck.

"Ah, but he's also rich enough that you wouldn't need to care," Steve teased.

"I like Anna way too much to be a home wrecker," Heidi said as they climbed back into the cab of his truck.

"Wait a minute, does that mean I need to worry that if you found some rich guy with a wife you didn't care for, you could—"

"Oh, shut up and drive," Heidi said as she leaned across the center console and planted a kiss on his lips.

Steve pulled her closer until the padding of the console pressed against her side. He deepened the kiss, possessively claiming her mouth with his, their tongues dancing in the familiar tango that only they knew.

After a long moment he slid his mouth across her cheekbones and over her ear. "Or we could stay right here, steam up the windows real good and see what happens," he whispered.

The moist heat of his breath against her ear was thrilling. "Or," she whispered as she allowed her mouth and tongue to roam over his neck and jaw, "you could start your engine and get me home so I can catch a couple of hours of sleep before I have to be at work tomorrow."

"My engine's already running," he whispered. "Turns on automatically the minute you're in the area. Marry me, woman. I wonder if there's a justice of the peace around here somewhere."

Heidi sat up and held his face with both palms. "Steven Grosso, if that's your idea of a proposal, your choice of venues is the worst. The parking lot of a truck stop? You cannot be serious."

"I'm always serious when it comes to that topic," Steve said and grinned. "Hey, I've worked hard to find these unique situations. How about when I almost asked you over the phone a couple of weeks back?"

Heidi groaned. "Is it too much to hope that I just might have a proper proposal, one I can tell our grandchildren about one day?"

Steve laughed and pulled away from her as he started the truck. "What's wrong with these stories for the grandchildren?" he asked, checking both ways before pulling onto the road and signaling a left turn onto the ramp to the interstate. When Heidi didn't answer he placed his hand on her knee. "You'll have a proper proposal as soon as I complete my list and as soon as I'm sure," he said, his tone suddenly serious.

Heidi shot him a look of stunned disbelief. "I thought you were sure," she said.

"Sure that you'll say yes," he said and pressed the accelerator to the floor.

WHEN HEIDI AND BUSTER arrived at the clinic the following morning she hoped that sharing the excitement of her first race weekend spent with the Grosso family might brighten Clare's mood. But she quickly realized that Clare's attempts at interest were halfhearted at best.

"Okay, talk to me," she said, coming into Clare's office and closing the door.

To her astonishment Clare buried her face in her hands and burst into tears.

"Are the kids okay?" Heidi asked suddenly, afraid that this was far more than an unplanned downturn in business.

"Fine," Clare replied, her voice muffled behind her hands.

"Jerry?"

Clare's husband had had a recent bout with a stomach virus that had caused him to miss several days of work.

Clare sniffed, wiped her cheeks with the back of one hand and looked up. "Jerry's feeling much better. Back at work."

"So why the meltdown that is totally out of character for you?"

Clare shrugged. "Business. There are things I counted on that never materialized and things I didn't see coming."

"Such as?"

Clare inclined her head toward the street outside her window where there were still a number of vacant storefronts. "I thought this business district would be booming by now and—" She swallowed a fresh round of tears.

"And here I've been prattling on about my weekend," Heidi said. "I'm so sorry."

"Oh, sweetie, don't be sorry about that. I'm thrilled things look like they might work out for you—at least on that front."

Heidi felt a knot of panic tighten her stomach. "Things will work out here as well," she said in a voice that was overly bright and falsely cheerful.

Clare looked up at her and cleared her throat. "We have to talk about the partnership plans. Here you've had this dream of running a clinic practically since the day I met you, and frankly you have a greater gift for that than I'll ever have. Our clients—and patients—adore you."

"Hey, I told you that could wait. We just go back to the original timetable."

"Oh, Heidi, the truth is that if business keeps on the way it is now, I don't know if I can afford to keep this place open." Her eyes were bloodshot with lack of sleep and more than one bout of crying.

All the times when her father had come home and announced that they would be moving—starting over somewhere new—flashed across Heidi's brain. If Clare shut the clinic, Heidi would have to start over. She had worked so hard for this. She had found this town and her little house in the country and this job all on her quest for stability. *No!* she screamed inside. *Not again.*

She drew in a deep breath. Clare was sobbing again, berating herself for the mess she had made of things.

"Come on," Heidi told her. "Stop crying. Let's figure this out together." She found a blank notepad and a pen on Clare's desk and started a list. "What we need is something that will provide a boost to the business, right?"

"Yeah, that would help. Got any new patients you can bring in—or old ones who need more therapy or treatment?"

Maybe, Heidi thought, then wrote two words on the pad. *Duke.*

Henrietta. "I just might," she muttered and realized she'd spoken aloud when Clare leaned toward her and grasped her forearm.

"Really? I mean, even one or two new clients might get things moving in the right direction. They tell a friend and that person comes in and so on. Word of mouth is our best advertising—always has been."

"Now don't get too excited. This is still just internal brainstorming."

"Want to take that brainstorming external?"

"Not just yet. Give me a couple of days, okay?"

"HOW MANY DRIVERS and owners do you guesstimate travel with their pets as well as their families?" Heidi asked Steve later that night.

"Quite a few. Why?"

"I was just thinking. Remember when Roger stopped by Nana's with Duke?"

Steve glanced at her over the top of the sports page of the newspaper and nodded.

"Then there was Henrietta," Heidi mused more to herself than to him.

Steve folded the paper and laid it aside. "Out with it. What's cooking in that gorgeous head of yours, honey?"

"Has NASCAR ever considered providing vet services for the pets that travel with their owners? I mean on-site?"

"I don't know," Steve admitted. "Are you thinking that—"

Heidi held up her hands to stop him from getting ahead of himself—or her. "I'm not sure what I'm thinking. Just trying to make sense of something. I had this idea. I mean, it's like when you get a certain song on your mind and you can't seem to stop hearing it?"

"And where's this 'song' coming from?"

She told him about her conversation with Clare. "I knew she

was worried about the business—or lack thereof—but then she started talking about possibly having to shut down the clinic entirely."

"So you would leave the clinic and set up your own thing with NASCAR?"

"No. It would be part of the clinic in town—a sort of mobile pet care unit. Think about it. A direct tie between the clinic and NASCAR? In this part of the country? I mean, you can't walk two feet without running into a fan. And think about how loyal they are to any product or service linked to NASCAR. Clare and I could move forward with the partnership. But, of course, the problem is one of finances. Setting up a whole new clinic would cost big bucks and—"

"You might be able to get a business loan," Steve suggested, warming to the idea. "Or sponsorship funds. After all, corporations are always looking for new venues to put their brand name in the public eye."

"I keep thinking maybe somehow it could be connected to the NARS. Sophia and I were talking the other day about all the different services they offer—child care, fitness center, chaplains, medical services."

Steve nodded. "That's a great idea. You should probably talk to the folks at NARS before you get too far into this, see if they've ever considered anything like it. Maybe they have and rejected it for some reason."

"But you think there are possibilities?"

"Honey, I think this could be great on so many levels," he said, pulling her into his arms. "I don't want to rush things, but it seems like your first experience living life on the road was a positive one. And well, don't forget that third item on my list—finding some way we could integrate career schedules so that we each have what we want in terms of work and still have a life together."

Heidi snuggled closer in his embrace. "I especially like that 'together' part."

"Me, too," Steve whispered, kissing her.

Heidi wrapped her arms around him and pressed her body closer to his. In Steve's arms her mind sang a new song. *Together. Together. Forever.*

CHAPTER EIGHT

LATER THAT WEEK while Heidi sat down with Roger Clark and other programming staff from National Automobile Racing Services to pitch them her idea for the mobile pet care clinic, Steve had a meeting of his own—with his boss, Dawson Ritter.

"I just want to make sure you're okay with this," he said after laying out the basics of Heidi's idea. "We just want to be sure we cover all the bases. We realize that her project could have some spillover for Kent. I mean, we *are* family and Heidi will be once we're married."

Dawson's heavy eyebrows furrowed as he rocked back in his desk chair and studied Steve. "Mobile animal hospital, you say?"

"That's the concept. Heidi's meeting with some of the folks at NARS now. Of course, they may already have plans of their own in that direction, just haven't gotten around to putting them into action. If so—"

"Haven't heard of any such plans," Dawson mused. "She'd need a place to set up shop at every track."

"I was thinking maybe we'd buy a used motor home and convert it."

Dawson nodded. "The two of you could live in it on the road once you're married. You *are* getting married one of these days, aren't you?"

Steve grinned. "That's the plan."

Dawson stood and offered Steve a warm handshake. "Well, good luck to her. I think it's a splendid idea. Don't see any problem."

Steve left Dawson's office and went back to his desk. He stared at the files he'd been working on before he'd decided to go and talk with Dawson. He drummed his fingers on the desk and eyed his cell phone. Surely she would call him the minute her meeting with Roger was over.

As if he'd willed the thing to ring, it started playing his signature tune—a country-western song about a blond-haired, blue-eyed gal. Steve flipped open the phone and grinned when he saw Heidi's name.

"How did it go?"

"They like the idea," she said, sounding breathless with surprise. "I mean, actually they loved it. Now I just have to talk to Clare. I didn't want to get her hopes up until I'd had a chance to see how the folks at NARS would react. Roger is talking to his boss, Mr. Marshall. Sybil and Henrietta might be a help if he has any reservations," she muttered absentmindedly, and Steve was sure she was making a note to call Sybil.

"Still here," he reminded her.

"Oh, Steve, the staff came up with so many things we need to consider beyond the whole business of how to finance this thing."

"Such as?"

"Fixed fees or donations for treating the animals belonging to members of the NASCAR community *and* they brought up the same thing you did—the possibility of finding some corporate sponsorship."

"I've been trying to tell you that there's a brain behind these good looks," he teased.

"I think this could actually happen," she said. "It's not going to change things right away, but it's a start, right?"

"Congratulations, honey. It's a wonderful idea and you're just the person to put it all together."

"I don't even know where to begin," she said. "I mean, they brought up the fact that I'll need a place to set up shop at every single track. It might be wise to think in terms of starting this program next season and give us time to get everything in place," she said, and her voice drifted in and out of normal volume. *More notes to herself,* Steve thought and grinned. "When will you tell Clare?"

"Soon. Obviously she needs to be involved if we're planning to link the mobile clinic with the one in town." She sighed. "Oh, I don't know what to do. Should I wait?"

"That depends. How do you really feel about the partnership idea?"

"As opposed to not being Clare's partner?"

"As opposed to having your own business separate from Clare."

There was a pause—one Steve waited out.

"I like the idea of the partnership. For one thing, we can save money not having to start from scratch outfitting the mobile unit."

"And for another?"

"I'm bringing something to the partnership, something that pays Clare back for all she's done for me."

Steve groaned. "Honey, that's no way to do business. You've paid her back a dozen times by everything you've already brought to the business—your gifts as a vet, not to mention your people skills, which you have to admit Clare is sometimes sadly lacking. Besides, if Clare needed to, don't you think she would let you go to save her business?"

"She would never—"

"Never think never, Heidi. So what else makes the partnership appealing?"

"You're not going to like this. But Clare and I share a passion for animal rights. A lot of people pay lip service to the cause, but Clare's the first person I've known who is every bit as dedicated to it as I am—maybe even more dedicated."

"That's all well and good, but think business, Heidi. Why this partnership?"

"Because…" She hesitated. "Because in some ways, what I've begun to build with Clare—the business relationship *and* the friendship—feels right. I know that's not very professional, but it's how I feel." She paused. "But you're the business major. If you think I should wait…give this all some more thought?"

Steve sighed. "Nope. If that's how you feel then strike while the iron's hot, as Milo would say. Tell Clare your idea, but remember that this is *your* idea. Clare didn't come up with it, and the price for sharing it with her is a full partnership in the business. If this is what you want, get yourself a lawyer and put this thing together."

"Things are moving so fast," Heidi said, her voice sounding a little breathless but excited. "I mean, we still have to come up with some way of actually mobilizing—moving this thing from event to event."

Steve laughed. "Welcome to NASCAR. You take care of getting things legalized with Clare and let me worry about the logistics of how this will work at the various race tracks. Okay?"

"Here's Clare," Heidi reported in a stage whisper. "Wish me luck."

Steve flicked his phone closed and realized he was still smiling as he made the sign of a huge check mark in the air above his desk. It was all coming together. He opened his computer bag and pulled out the worn blue ring box. "Time to plan that proposal," he said to himself as he pried the cover open.

"Wow! That's beautiful!"

Amy Barber, Kent's publicist from Motor Media Group, was leaning against the door to Steve's office. Motor Media handled publicity and public relations for a number of drivers. As Kent's publicist, Amy now worked together with Steve coordinating Kent's schedule of photo opportunities, speaking engagements and public appearances.

"Sure hope she agrees," Steve said as he snapped the ring box shut and stuffed it back in the inside pocket of the computer bag.

"Ah, you could give her a Cracker Jack prize and she'd say yes. She's head over heels for you." Amy sat down in the lone chair next to Steve's desk. "And speaking of Heidi, Dawson just told me about the mobile animal hospital idea. Awesome!"

Steve grinned. "Yeah, I think so, too."

"You know, there might be a way we could make this work for Kent as well."

"Not following you," Steve said.

"Well, what if Vittle Farms sponsored the clinic? We could build a sort of public service announcement campaign with Kent as the spokesperson."

"What kind of public service ads?"

"The importance of getting pets spayed and properly checked out as well as correctly inoculated and such."

"I don't know," Steve said. "This is Heidi's thing."

Amy shrugged and stood up. "It's just an idea. Run it by her and see what she thinks. It would be great exposure for Kent."

"Like he needs it," Steve joked.

"Hey, easy come easy go. Last year he was the NASCAR Sprint Cup Series champ, but this year? In this business—like everything else—the paying customers have short memories and even shorter attention spans."

"If I didn't know better I'd think you didn't care for our legion of fans."

"Not so. I love each and every one of them, especially those who cheer for Kent and especially those who are brand loyal to Vittle Farms and Kent's other sponsors. But we both know that fan loyalty can be fickle—even in NASCAR."

"The old 'what have you done for me lately' rule?"

Amy stopped smiling, her demeanor once again all business. "You've got it. Run the idea by Heidi and see what she thinks. If it helps, we can even put her in the ads—white lab coat and all. Couldn't hurt business."

"WELL, SHE'S GOT a point there," Heidi agreed when Steve told her about his discussion with Amy. "Although the mobile unit would be for the drivers' and owners' pets—not the general public. On the other hand, people would see the connection to the clinic in town. On the other hand…"

"You can say no," Steve reminded her.

"Did you mention the idea to Kent?"

"Yeah. He likes it. He's been looking for something else he could do—community service or charity. It's important for his image, but it's also because he just wants to do some good. And he's a natural when it comes to doing interviews and that sort of thing."

"Good. Because I'm definitely not a natural," Heidi said. "I'll have to talk the idea over with Roger and Clare. After all, I'm not in this alone." She laughed. "I cannot believe how Clare practically had her lawyer on the phone before I finished telling her about the mobile unit. He's going to have partnership papers ready for signing by the end of the week. I think I must be dreaming."

Steve pulled her into the circle of his arms. "No, you're not. The way I see it this is real life—*our* life. You should have heard Kent going on and on about your idea to Milo when we both stopped by the farm earlier. Then Nana said—"

Heidi leaped away from his embrace and glanced at the kitchen clock. "Oh, shoot, I almost forgot. I promised Nana that I would come over and help her with the plans for the Memorial Day bash."

She grabbed her purse, a notebook and pen and Buster's leash. "Buster, car," she ordered then looked back at Steve. "You coming?"

"Just waiting for my command," he said, grinning at her as he followed Buster out to the car.

"YOU'RE KIDDING," Clare said when Heidi revealed that they had NARS's approval of the idea and desire to see the clinic set up and ready to go for a trial run in time for the NASCAR Sprint Cup Series race in Charlotte. "That's next week."

"Their thinking is to introduce the plan while we're still close to home and then see how it goes. That way if we need something we can just run back here and get it."

"But where will we set up?" Clare asked.

"Well, that's the part they're still working out, that and the contract. For now I think we'll probably be in a tent sort of like the child-care area. Roger said he could loan us a small camper that's not being used right now for storing supplies and equipment. Then he thought he could find an extra awning like the ones they use to create shade in the child-care area. They want to try this out first before they commit to anything in writing."

"Makes sense," Clare agreed and then she grabbed Heidi and hugged her. "You are amazing, lady. I knew it the first time I met you."

Heidi blushed with pleasure, glad to have made a significant contribution to the future of the business and to be back on the familiar and easy ground of the friendship she and Clare had shared. "Just remember, it's not a done deal yet," she warned.

Clare released her and turned to get a legal pad from her desk. "Details," she said, dismissing Heidi's concern with a wave of her hand. "We are going to make this work."

RACE WEEK in Charlotte was pure celebration time for the city and every small community in the surrounding area as fans from all over the country filled every available hotel room and campground spot. Business boomed in every restaurant and shopping mall within a fifty-mile radius—and beyond—of the famed track. Technically the speedway was located in Concord, but everyone talked about going to Charlotte for the race. This was also the home base for many of NASCAR's best-known drivers—past and present—and the shops where the cars were built and the headquarters for the teams owned by that group.

In Kannapolis the town council had taken full advantage of the opportunity to draw the fans and their money by creating a self-guided tour of the historical roots of the sport. Fans enjoyed making their own personal odyssey to see where the sport of auto racing had gotten its start and racing legends had not only lived, but also built their first cars and raced them against each other in the town streets or area dirt tracks. It was like a journey to Mecca for the faithful.

Heidi well remembered the day that Steve had first taken her on the tour.

"It'll give you a real sense of the history of the sport—the way it started," he'd said and then added, "and the way it's changed over the years."

After her first introduction to the roots of auto racing, revisiting each landmark during race week had become a tradition for them. They always began their tour in the beautifully landscaped park just behind the clinic. With its neat brick walkways, colorful flower beds and welcoming park benches, it was a place Heidi visited often during the workweek. But going there during race week with Steve was special.

On that first tour, they had driven from the park to the end of West Avenue. "Welcome to Idiot's Circle," he'd announced as he playfully revved the engine of his truck.

"What a name for a street," she'd said.

"Back in the sixties, this is where the kids gathered. They'd race down one side around the turn here and up the other. A lot of folks think this is where some of those early drivers got so good on the turns."

"You're not planning to try to duplicate that move, are you?"

Steve had laughed. "Not tonight."

They'd driven through the neighborhood where men and women who had worked in the textile mill that had been the main source of employment for the community in those early days had raised their families. "The guy who lived in that house raced for over twenty years—and worked at the mill while he and his wife raised six kids," Steve had told her. It was the moment when Heidi had begun to understand that NASCAR was so much more than just a sport. For these working-class people racing had become an effective remedy for the boredom and monotony of performing the same mill job eight hours a day week in and year out.

She'd also begun to appreciate the role that racing had played for the young people. In a place where in those early years few could imagine the opportunity for college or a life beyond Kannapolis and the mill, racing brought color, excitement and that element of danger mixed with possibility. And when the mill shut down for good with little warning, racing had become the refuge people needed to get through the hard days of no jobs and what appeared to be a bleak future.

"You know, when you and I first took this tour," she said to Steve now as they drove up and down streets with names like V-8, Ford, Chrysler and Dodge, "I seriously underestimated this sport. It's so much more than the trappings and logistics of racing itself, isn't it?"

"Is it?" Steve asked, and she could see by his bemused smile, so like his father's, that he was pleased, like a teacher whose student had finally gotten the lesson.

"You know it is. It certainly makes as much sense as guys in floppy short pants racing up and down a basketball court or hulks in padding and helmets crashing through each other to reach the end zone."

"It's not something I've spent a lot of time thinking about," he said, "but yeah, I guess when you look at it that way."

"Well, that's just it. I mean, my dad lives and breathes college basketball. He's been a diehard West Virginia fan ever since he graduated from there. He wouldn't miss March Madness—Mom and I used to have to plan our schedules around that as well as his job."

"Okay, so what's the connection here?" Steve asked.

"Racing is like that for any number of people. They get the same high from following the fortunes and failures of a certain driver as Dad does from following WVU basketball. He understands the intricacies of college basketball the way NASCAR fans understand the intricacies of racing."

"And?"

"Well, doesn't it just drive you nuts the way people stereotype the sport—and especially the fans?" Heidi asked.

"Honey," Steve said, reaching over to interlock her fingers with his. "That's just people who know nothing about racing. And believe me, most folks aren't losing any sleep over it. Especially not the drivers and owners who are winning—or the sponsors, for that matter. NASCAR fans are the most brand-loyal folks in the world. The sponsors are laughing all the way to the bank."

"I guess when you put it that way." Heidi leaned over and kissed his cheek.

"What was that for?"

"Just happy," she said. "Just happier than I can ever remember being."

They drove the rest of the route ending up back at the park where—as was their tradition—they shared a picnic lunch of tomato and mayo sandwiches that had been a staple for families in the area during the hard times after the mill closed.

"How would you like to join me on spotters' row tomorrow night for the all-star race?" Steve asked as he started on his second sandwich before Heidi had even finished her first half.

Heidi was surprised. Steve had never asked her to watch him

work before. He'd explained that it was vital for him to give the race—even this one that heralded the start of race week but had no point value in the Chase for the NASCAR Sprint Cup—his complete attention. "And frankly, honey," he'd always added, "I find it next to impossible to concentrate on anything but you when you're around."

"You're asking me to come and watch you while you're working?" she asked as she put her sandwich down and gave him her full attention. It wasn't like Steve to make a joke about his work.

"Well, I've gotten to watch you work a couple of times lately and I thought—"

"I'd love it," Heidi hurried to assure him. "I promise I won't get in the way and I'll be quiet as a church mouse, and—"

"Okay then," he said, and he was grinning as he reached for the last chip on her plate. "It's a date."

Heidi had imagined any number of scenarios for Steve to propose to her. As they shared their picnic in the park, it had certainly occurred to her that given her conversion to racing fan after that first tour of the historical landmarks, a proposal in the park would not have been out of the question. Of course, it was a busy place with bus tours of fans eagerly staging photo ops or listening intently as their tour guide regaled them with stories of racing's role in the development of the area.

And then it hit her. Steve planned to propose after the race as they stood together high in the stands, directly above the start/finish line. Perhaps Kent would win, which would only add to the drama. After all, a million dollars in prize money was nothing to sneeze at. Even if he didn't win there would be fireworks—the night sky backlit in a blaze of color as Steve dropped to one knee and… Oh, it was going to be absolutely perfect. And this time she was ready to say yes.

CHAPTER NINE

IN SPITE OF the fact that she lived only a few miles from the track, Heidi planned to spend the weekend in Milo and Juliana's motor home—although the two elder Grossos had opted to remain at home on the farm for most of the week. Several of the motor homes belonging to drivers from out of town would be occupied the entire week. Heidi saw this as a super opportunity to immerse herself in NASCAR road life.

"I have a million things to do for the party Monday," Nana told Heidi. "Would you have time to arrange everything at the track for the festivities? That way I could concentrate on everything that needs doing here."

"Just tell me what to do," Heidi said, suspecting that this sudden decision to give her the motor home to herself meant Nana was in on Steve's plan to propose. She smiled at what she saw as a fairly obvious ruse.

"You know the drill, just make yourself at home, okay? And anything you need just call one of us and we'll bring it when we come for race day."

So instead of driving home right after work on Friday, Heidi and Buster headed in the opposite direction—toward the track and the Grosso motor homes. By the time she'd showered and changed, her phone was ringing—the first of several calls over the next half hour.

First Nana called to make sure she was settling in and had

everything she needed. She'd barely hung up from that when Tanya called to invite Steve and her over to Kent's motor home for a cookout. That call was followed by a call from Patsy.

"Oh, good, I caught you in," Patsy said without the preamble of identifying herself. "I have been meaning to ask you something. You can say no. I appreciate how swamped you are these days."

"How can I help?" Heidi asked, and recognized the feeling of pleasure that swept over her as one of being needed, being able to do something for these people who seemed so incredibly self-sufficient.

"I'm on the committee to organize this charity event for Dover," Patsy said. "One of the committee members came up with this idea that a new twist on the usual might be to have some of the NASCAR families make an appearance on Souvenir Alley with their pets. The thinking is that if fans believe they'll have the opportunity not only to see a favorite driver and his wife and kids, but his dog or monkey or whatever, we might draw a larger turnout and raise more money."

The Dover charity event was one of many activities that the women's auxiliary organized each season to raise money for selected causes. "What a great idea," Heidi exclaimed. "What do you need from me?"

"Couple of things. Have a kind of first-aid station for the animals available just in case something happens—a splinter in a paw or some such."

"Sounds like a good idea. What else?"

Patsy hesitated. "Join the committee?"

Heidi couldn't believe she'd heard that right, so she said nothing.

"It doesn't take a lot of time…I mean, I know how busy you are."

"Oh, Patsy, thank you for thinking of me. I can't imagine what I can offer, but I am thrilled to be asked."

Patsy laughed with relief. "I was hoping you'd say that. And you have plenty to offer. For starters, you can help us plan for the unexpected—a couple thousand walkers and drivers with pets? Sounds like a recipe for problems to me. How about we get together at Kent's party and we can talk over the details."

LATER THAT NIGHT she and Steve joined the other drivers and their wives and girlfriends for the cookout at Kent's. Tanya brought out her camera and snapped pictures while Heidi helped Patsy keep the buffet filled and caught up on the plans for the charity walk in Dover.

"Now, tomorrow, Roger asked me to dogsit for Duke during the race," Patsy told her once she'd given Heidi the schedule of meetings for the coming week. "I think he has a date," she confided with a wink. "Roger, not Duke. Anyway, how about I take Buster as well?"

"Oh, Buster will be fine. Besides, I can run back and make sure he has water and his supper before the race."

Patsy stopped her with a hand on her shoulder. "You should spend this time with Steve," she said. "Let me help."

Was Patsy giving her a hint? Had Steve confided a plan for proposing to his aunt? "Well, that's really nice of you," she said. "If you're sure."

"One dog or two," Patsy said with a shrug. "Doesn't make much difference."

Later, after Steve walked her back to Nana and Milo's motor home, he suggested they sit outside and enjoy the star-filled night. He led her to the portable porch swing that Juliana and Milo usually occupied on a night like this. Buster curled up on the artificial turf at their feet and promptly fell asleep.

"You seemed right at home tonight—at Kent's party," he said.

Heidi guessed where this was headed and reached over to take his hand. "Right at home," she confessed. "We might have been at the farm or my house or Kent's place at the lake. Nana's right. The location may change but the people won't, right?"

He squeezed her fingers. "So, no more doubts?"

"About life on the road?" She thought about it for a long moment. This was a key to their future happiness and demanded complete honesty. "I'm still uncertain about the impact on children," she said and felt his fingers tense. "But, from what I've seen this week and last, what I know for sure now is that we can work it out." She made the sign of a check mark.

Steve cupped his palm around her jaw and drew her to him. "I love you so much," he whispered before kissing her.

It was several moments before either of them said anything with words. Instead, they shared their happiness through touching, kissing, holding. Finally Heidi settled herself on Steve's lap, her head on his shoulder, her hand resting lightly on his neck.

They stayed that way—Steve gently rocking the swing with one foot as he held her—and listened as all around them neighbors and friends up and down the streets of the compound called it a night.

"It is kind of like home," she whispered sleepily. And even though she knew that as a spotter Steve would not have a motor home once they married, she could imagine years of weekends, just like this one. Working, playing, being with friends and family. A life—their life.

FRIDAY MORNING OF race week was just hours away from the dropping of that green flag, the speedway and surrounding area was more like a movie set—everything in place but nothing yet up and running. All of that changed throughout the day as the food and souvenir vendors set up shop in the vast area across the road from the track while thousands of fans poured into the area, checking in to their motel rooms or setting up in designated campgrounds all around the enormous complex.

Golf carts vied with pedestrians, campers, shuttle trams and delivery trucks as they all raced up and down the roads leading around and into the infield of the vast speedway. By midafternoon, traffic was solid on both I-85 and Highway 29. The all-business demeanor of the racing teams stood out in sharp contrast to the celebratory mood of the fans. Kids ogled the merchandise at the stands—huge eighteen-wheeler trucks emblazoned with the likeness and sponsor logos for their favorite driver. Lines formed at the restrooms and concession stands. Vendors hawked their wares and crowds surged in every direction in a seemingly disorganized but still orderly stream on both sides of the local highway.

Heidi had always loved the action of mingling with the fans, and once she'd dropped Buster off with Patsy, she took the opportunity to check out Souvenir Alley while Steve was busy with meetings and checking out last-minute details with the team.

She stopped to watch a young boy and his father as the boy was fitted with a set of headphones and taught the rudiments of setting the handheld scanner so he could listen to his favorite driver communicating with the pit crew or spotter. She imagined Steve teaching their son—or daughter—the same thing. At the next stand a trio of teenage girls debated the vast choices in T-shirt styles and colors, their money clearly burning in their pockets. Heidi pictured her future daughter in the intensely serious and then suddenly laughing faces of the girls.

Steve hasn't even proposed yet and already you've filled the house with teenagers, she thought as she moved on.

She especially enjoyed watching people who were obviously new to the sport—some of them college kids and others young professionals. It was always fun to watch them try to maintain an aura of cool in the face of the dazzling array of activity and excitement that surrounded them. They usually lost the battle early on, surrendering to the sheer excitement of attending their first NASCAR event. Heidi could not help smiling at everyone she passed. And they smiled back, forming the kind of instant connections with each other that were unique to settings where strangers gather in anticipation of a good time.

Heidi stood in the midst of a throng of fans waiting patiently to cross the road and inhaled the festive spirit that surrounded her. She joined in the cheer that went up from the crowds gathered at all four corners of a major intersection when the police stopped all traffic to permit everyone to cross. She caught the last seat on a shuttle tram and settled in for the ride halfway round the exterior of the speedway to the tunnel that would lead her into the infield and back "home."

Every action she took suddenly seemed instilled with a deeper meaning. She took special care as she showered and dressed. After all, this could turn out to be one of the most important nights of her life. Black chino slacks, the blue polo shirt with Kent's team logo embroidered over the left pocket. She had packed her black cross-training shoes since she'd be standing a good part of the evening. The final touch was the red-and-blue-print scarf that she would thread through the loops of her slacks as a belt.

"Wow," Steve said when he called for her an hour later. "Every time I think I've gotten used to just what a knockout you are, you go and KO me all over again."

"I could change," Heidi said. "Wouldn't want to interfere with your concentration, after all."

Steve held out his arms to her and she went to him. "Don't change," he said. "Anything."

"Do I look professional? I mean, like a member of the team?"

"Stop fishing, lady. You know you look like a million dollars. They ought to give *you* the prize money."

"Speaking of which, what are Kent's chances?"

Steve laughed as he took the blue hooded sweatshirt she

would need later and stuffed it into his duffel. "Honey, this race is a free-for-all. You know that."

"Yeah, but wouldn't it be nice if he won? Or your uncle Dean. That would be just as great, of course."

"Ah, but if Kent wins, Dawson's promised everyone on the team a bonus. On the other hand, you know, it's not winner take all. Other teams will end up in the money."

"I also know that the lot of you would do this for nothing," she teased. "By the way, I got hit on today while I was walking around the shopping area," she announced as they started across the compound.

"Doesn't surprise me," Steve said evenly.

Heidi sighed. "Is there not even one jealous bone in that gorgeous body of yours?"

"Only if you decided to hit back," Steve said. "Did you?"

"Do I look that blond to you, Spotterman? I've got everything I want or need in a man walking right here beside me."

Steve took her hand and didn't let go. "Good."

STEVE AND HEIDI had been invited to a prerace party in Dawson Ritter's private suite. Heidi could not help being amused at several executives from Vittle Farms that Dawson had also included. There was no denying that they were a different breed—edgy and tense even in a party setting. But a couple of them were clearly every bit as starstruck as some of the fans she'd seen earlier. When Kent stopped by to meet with key sponsors before heading down to the garage, they tried playing it cool, but pressed forward to meet him and have their picture taken with him.

"Heidi." Chester Honeycutt was making his way toward her.

"Hey, how's Macho doing?"

Chester laughed. "I think he may have learned a valuable lesson. I notice when we're on our walks that he gives larger dogs a wide berth these days. I wanted to tell you what a great idea I think this mobile pet unit is. I understand you came up with that."

Heidi felt a rush of pride. "Thanks. It's been more of a team effort really. I mean, if Roger Clark at the NARS hadn't backed the idea—"

"If you've got time this week, I'd like to bring some of our board members out to the track so they can see what NARS does, including the clinic. We might have some sponsorship interest through our corporate foundation."

Heidi felt a little light-headed. Was the chief executive officer of a national corporation actually suggesting the two of them do business? "I'd like that," she managed to say.

"Great. I'll ask Terry, my administrative assistant, to contact you with the day and time." Chester shook her hand and moved on to the next group of guests.

Amy Barber was also working the crowd, and she cornered Heidi over a plate she offered to share of goat cheese and whole-wheat mini-pita pockets with an assortment of cold veggies and a hot artichoke dip.

"So, Heidi, did Steve tell you about my idea for Kent's public service campaign?" the PR rep asked, then continued without waiting for an answer. "It's going to be terrific for Kent's overall recognition, not to mention fantastic image building for Vittle Farms. Any time we can make the sponsor happy is a bonus."

Heidi liked Amy, but she was uncomfortable in the fast-paced world of public relations. It seemed as if ideas like this one came out of nowhere and in a matter of hours were a "done deal" as Amy was fond of saying.

"I was thinking it would be a great connection to shoot the television spots with you and that adorable dog of yours in the background. Set it all up for Dover." Amy popped the last bite of pita into her mouth. Heidi could see that the woman was already envisioning exactly how this would go, oblivious to the fact that Heidi had not agreed. She was about to mention that Amy might want to take a step back, when Steve came over and took her by the hand.

"Hey, you don't want to miss this. The crew chief race is about to start and believe me, as good as these crew chiefs are at keeping cars on the track, they are terrible drivers," he said. "Come on, I saved you both a seat."

"Not for me," Amy said. "Schmoozing time," she added with a grin as she turned her attention to the group of Vittle Farms execs gathered around the mirrored bar in the corner of the suite.

"Thanks for rescuing me," Heidi said as she and Steve took their seats in the second row of chairs overlooking the track.

Steve's eyebrows lifted in surprise. "I thought you liked Amy."

"I do. She's a wonder, but she can be a little overwhelming sometimes." She turned her attention toward the track. "Enough about that. So, who's the favorite here?"

KENT AND TANYA stayed for the first part of the crew chief race and then headed for the track. Steve and Heidi left shortly before the pre-race was to begin and took the stairway up to the roof of the speedway and Spotters' Row. The sun was just beginning to set, casting a reddish-orange glow on the far side of the track as Steve led the way along the boardwalk to where a track official in traditional black slacks and white, black and yellow shirt waited with a clipboard.

"Steve. You're early—the pre-race is just getting started," he said with a nod in Heidi's direction as he checked Steve's name off on his list.

"Wanted to get a good seat," Steve joked.

"Have a good race."

Heidi could see that several spotters had brought a guest along to watch the race from this primo setting.

Steve headed for a space between a large air-conditioning unit and three massive field lights and set his duffel on the bleacher-style bench just behind the railing bordering the edge of the flat roof.

As he pulled out a headset and scanner for Heidi, he introduced her to two other spotters who had taken up their position in the same small area and were preparing their equipment for the evening's main event. Below them the stands were filled with fans—not as many as would gather a week later for the NASCAR Sprint Cup Series race, but an impressive crowd. On the field, three giant flatbed trucks formed a stage where the drivers and their teams were gathering for the prerace introductions.

Steve handed her the headset and scanner. "Car No. 427," he said with a grin. "In case you forgot."

"I hear that driver has the best spotter in the business," she replied as she programmed her scanner so she'd be able to listen to Steve talk with Kent and Neil during the race.

Steve checked his equipment—headset, binoculars, cell phone—in case he and Neil wanted to discuss a last-minute strategy without the entire field plus a huge number of fans in the stands listening in.

By NASCAR standards the race would be an abbreviated one. "Four segments of twenty laps each with drivers having the option of a pit stop after the first twenty-lap segment," Steve had explained. "Of course that would mean giving up their on-track position."

"And most drivers would wait for the mandatory pit stop after the second twenty-lap segment," Heidi said, parroting the short course Steve had given her the first time she attended the race.

"Very good. Then what?"

Heidi searched her brain, determined to get the complex race format correct. "All remaining cars resume their position on the track to start the third segment. At the end of that segment, they circle under the caution flag, pit under normal race conditions, and how they exit the pit road sets the starting lineup for the fourth and final segment. How am I doing, professor?"

"Perfect. You must have had a terrific teacher."

"Ladies and gentlemen, please rise for our national anthem," the announcer intoned.

The stands went silent as everyone stood and faced the color guard positioned center stage. To the delight of the crowd, one of the world's top rock stars had been invited to sing the anthem. When she reached the line about "rockets' red glare," a wave of cheers from the crowd exploded along with the red fireworks behind the singer.

Heidi glanced at Steve who stood tall, hand over heart, his eyes locked on the flag. She felt her own eyes fill with tears as she took in every magical detail of this night she was certain she would remember for the rest of her life.

As the last note reverberated across the speedway, showers of red, white and blue fireworks shot up from the back of the stage and the crowd went bananas, cheering and remaining on their feet as the introductions of the teams began. Each team was greeted with thunderous applause as they filed off the stage and back to their stations along pit road. As each driver squeezed inside the opening where in a normal car the driver's window would be, the frenzy of the crowd continued to build. Steve put on his headset and nodded to his peers on either side.

Heidi sat on the back of the bleacher, her feet on the seat as Steve and the others moved forward to the railing. She felt the simultaneous roar to life of the engines of the smaller field of twenty-four cars before she registered hearing the incredible ominous rumble. In her ear she heard Kent's voice.

"All right, gang, let's just have some fun tonight."

A voice she recognized as Neil's came back. "Forget fun. Let's win this thing. I need the money." He laughed, but there was little humor in the sound.

"You up there, Spotterman?" Kent said, ignoring his crew chief.

"Right here." Steve smiled at Heidi, knowing she'd heard Kent use the nickname she'd given him.

She gave him the thumbs-up sign.

"Got backup for you," Steve added.

Kent laughed. "The way she drove the mini the other night, I'll take it."

And then Heidi heard a shift in Steve's voice, saw a change in his posture. "Ready to go," he said quietly, his eyes scanning the track. "Pace car's ready. Get set."

Heidi craned her neck to see the cars as they flashed by on the near side of the track, then followed them on the uphill front stretch over the hump of the first turn and on to the downhill of the backstretch.

"No. 466 is coming," she heard Steve say, his voice even and calm.

Heidi cringed as three cars bumped and spun out on turn two. And still the voices of the men remained steady and business-like, as if they were in the boardroom discussing next quarter's marketing plan.

"Stay low," Steve instructed. "Clear."

"Something on the grass," Kent replied.

"Ten-four. Think about that later. Pace car's on."

As the cars lined up double file behind the pace car, Heidi saw one of the convoy of pristine white wreckers enter the track, clear the debris from the spinout and leave.

"Okay, get ready," Steve murmured.

"I just want to go," Kent said impatiently.

"Too damn many cautions," Neil said.

Heidi saw Steve frown, then heard Neil ask, "How's the tire?"

"Feels okay," Kent replied.

Things continued that way through the first three segments.

Then came the mandatory pit stop. Steve had explained to Heidi earlier that coming out of the pit stop in the lead would be critical. She focused on Kent's pit crew stationed about halfway along pit road.

"Go," she whispered, urging the crew to do their work in the split-second timing they were famous for.

"Now," she heard Steve calmly say as Kent's car sped past other cars still being serviced and back onto the track.

Heidi checked the leaderboard. Kent was in fourth place— in the money but still not in the lead. Twenty laps to go. She glanced at Steve. During the pit stop she'd seen him flip open his cell phone and take a call. He'd nodded, then seemed to debate the issue and finally snapped the phone closed and returned it to his pocket.

As the race entered the final five laps, she saw Steve tap a fellow spotter. That spotter said something into his microphone and gave Steve a nod.

"No. 467 car is still laying back."

He stepped closer to the edge of the roof, his eyes fixed on turn four.

"Don't let the beast bite you, boy," she heard Neil say.

Like any driver needs to hear that in the final laps, Heidi thought, and could not help wondering if Neil was deliberately trying to rattle Kent.

"Here he comes outside," Steve said.

"Two to go," Kent replied.

"Clear by three," Steve said, then seconds later, "Clear by a half. At the bumper. Inside corner. Inside. Inside."

Heidi held her breath as she watched Kent maneuver the narrow turn four and head for the final lap.

And then it happened. Rafael O'Bryan's car bumped Kent from behind, making him swerve enough to lose ground as Rafael headed for the straightaway.

"Still in there," Steve said as if nothing had happened. "One to go. You still got time."

Was he nuts? There was only one lap to go. Heidi checked the leaderboard again. By some miracle Kent was now in third place.

"Stay high. You're clear. Inside behind Bart Branch."

Heidi saw the tension in Steve's body, felt him pushing Kent to do what he needed him to do to make this final move.

"Be ready," he said, and it was almost a whisper as he drew out each word. Then, "Now!"

In a flash Kent shot past as the driver of the car whose spotter Steve had signaled moved over, rubbing up against the back bumper of the leader—Rafael—in the split second before the checkered flag signaled the finish.

Had the maneuver given Kent the minuscule lead he needed? The two cars had appeared to cross the finish line dead even.

For what seemed an eternity, there was complete silence, other than the occasional rev of a car's engine. The fans were all on their feet. The leaderboard was blank. Kent's battered Chevy and the Chevy driven by Rafael O'Bryan slowly circled the track. Other spotters who would normally have packed up and headed down the stairway by now, stood riveted to their positions.

Suddenly the leaderboard flashed to life and there at the top was car No. 427. An earsplitting roar went up from the stands, but Heidi was only aware of Kent's shout in her ear that it was "Doughnut time," as he took his victory lap and then sent his car into the trademark spirals of the winner.

Meanwhile Steve grinned and accepted the congratulations of his peers. Heidi waited her turn to get close to Steve. By the time the other spotters and the official had left and she and Steve were alone, the flatbed stage had been brought back on the field. And as at center stage amid fireworks and cheers Kent and his team stepped forward to accept the oversize mock-up of the million-dollar payday, all Heidi could think was, *This is it.*

"Congratulations," she said, holding out her arms to Steve.

He pulled her close to his side as they watched the presentation below. She felt her heart beating in time to the hard beat of the music that blasted through the night.

When Steve turned so that they were facing each other, she thought her heart would pound its way right out of her chest. She waited, willing him to say the words.

"Come on, honey," he said as he grabbed his bag. "Let's get out of here."

CHAPTER TEN

HEIDI WAS DETERMINED not to let Steve see how disappointed she was. He loved her. She was sure of that. He would propose in his own good time, she told herself as they navigated the stairway and the throngs of fans that filled each landing. After all, she was the one who had kept him waiting—with her fears about living a big chunk of the year on the road and her determination to secure her own career. Just because she was ready now didn't mean that—

"You okay?" Steve asked as a couple of overly exuberant fans pushed past her, knocking her sideways into the railing.

"Fine." She heard the tightness in her voice and saw Steve glance at her uncertainly. "I'm fine," she assured him with a smile. "They're just happy because Kent's their driver," she added, pointing to the back of one young man's T-shirt that featured an artist's rendering of the smiling face of Kent Grosso.

"This way," Steve said, taking her elbow and guiding her against the throng and then through a short corridor until they were out on the track.

Kent and the team were still celebrating, signing autographs, answering the shouted questions of reporters and doing the traditional hat dance. Steve and Heidi waited on the fringe of the crowd as Kent patiently put on one team cap after another—each bearing the logo of a different sponsor—and posed for pictures. Then he turned to accept the congratulations of those fans lucky enough to have been invited onto the track, including some of the Vittle Farms executives that Heidi had seen earlier in Dawson Ritter's private suite.

"Steve!" Kent roared, and everyone turned their attention to Steve as Kent made his way through the crowd. When he reached Steve, he threw his arms around his cousin, and Heidi heard Steve say, "Great driving, man," as cameras flashed and clicked all around them.

Then Kent kissed Heidi's cheek and whispered, "I knew you'd bring us luck." In an instant the moment passed and Kent was once again swallowed up in the crowd. Heidi saw Amy Barber take Kent firmly by the elbow and head back toward the stands. There, a private elevator would take them back to Dawson's suite where more of what Steve sometimes referred to as "the money folks" were waiting.

"Come on," Steve said as he took her arm and headed across the infield.

When they'd shown their credentials to the security guard outside the chain-link fencing that surrounded the motor home lot, Heidi automatically turned down the lane that would take them to Milo and Nana's.

"I've got something to show you," Steve said, steering her gently in the opposite direction.

When they passed up Kent's motor home as well as Dean's, Heidi was confused. "Where are we going?" she asked.

"Just down this way," he replied, and he sounded nervous. He stopped in front of an older motor home close to the children's play area. Heidi didn't recall noticing this particular one before. It was smaller than most, but the lights were on inside, casting a golden pattern of light onto the asphalt.

"Who lives here?" Heidi asked as Steve tapped in a code on the keypad and unlocked the door.

"Nobody—yet," he said, and held the door open for her, inviting her to step inside.

The furnishings confirmed her observation that it was an older model. Nothing so grand as Milo's or Kent's, and yet she liked it immediately. There was something almost cozy about the all-white kitchen area and the plantation-style shutters that covered the windows. The furniture was traditional in style, the kind that invited a guest to curl up and feel at home. The tiled floor in the sitting area was covered with an oval braided rug.

"It'll need some refurbishing," Steve said as he followed her through the living area to the kitchen and then past the small bathroom to the bedroom at the very back of the motor home. "But I think it might work—that is if you like it."

Heidi turned and stared up at him. She was speechless. "Work for what?" she managed to say.

Steve grinned.

"Well, for starters, I was thinking it might make a good mobile pet care clinic."

He pointed to some documents laid out on the kitchen table.

"The contract?" Heidi squealed as she turned to the final page and saw the blank spaces waiting for her signature and Clare's.

"Ready for signing subject to everything going well over Memorial Day weekend," Steve declared. "I was thinking that you could set up an exam area outside under the portico and store all your equipment underneath."

"And I could live here during the season—with Buster," Heidi said as she retraced her steps through the motor home and tested out the sofa.

Steve cleared his throat. "Well, actually," he said as he followed her into the living area and knelt next to her, "I was kind of hoping that I could live here with you and Buster. Really have started to hate those hotel rooms."

HE HANDED HER the small blue box.

"Marry me, Heidi," Steve said as she pried open the hinged

lid and ignored the tears of pure wonder and joy that rolled down her cheeks.

"It's perfect," she whispered. "Everything—it's all so perfect," she added, looking around and then at the man on his knees before her.

He took the box from her, removed the ring and set the box on a side table. "Is that a yes?" he asked, holding the ring poised over her left hand.

She slid her finger into the ring and then threw her arms around him. She kissed him so hard that they both tumbled backward onto the floor.

"Yes!" she shouted. "Yes! Yes! Yes!"

"Shh. You'll wake the neighbors," he said, but he was laughing.

"I love you, Steven Grosso," she whispered, and smothered his laughter with another round of kisses.

"MIZ KRAMER? Okay. Mom," Steve said when Heidi handed him the phone after calling her parents to give them the news. "Hope we didn't wake you."

Heidi stood close to him straining to listen in on the conversation from Alaska.

"Congratulations, son," she heard her father boom. "Although we have to say we were getting worried. I mean, when you called us last month to ask our blessing—"

"We've been waiting on pins and needles for this very call," Heidi's mom interrupted. "No news could possibly be happier for us than this."

"Yeah, me, too."

"So when are you two coming to Anchorage?" her dad asked. "No time like summer."

Heidi took the phone from Steve. "Hey, Dad, fair is fair. I chased around all over the country with you guys for years. How about coming down here?"

"We started talking about that very thing right after we got Steve's call," her mom replied. She sounded normal—sincerely happy for Heidi. "I mean, is he the sweetest boy ever, calling to ask your father's permission?"

"He's pretty special," Heidi agreed, her eyes misting over as the emotional roller coaster of the day caught up with her.

"Did you set the date or is that going to take another six months?" her dad teased.

"We've got a lot to talk about," Heidi said, recognizing that for the understatement it was. "Mom, will you come down so we can make plans? I want you to meet Steve's great-grandparents and his dad and—"

"We'll start looking into that tomorrow," her father promised. "In the meantime we've got telephone and e-mail, okay? Now, put Steve back on."

Heidi handed the phone to Steve. He listened and then walked a step away, turning slightly so she couldn't really read his expression. "Yes, sir," he said softly and listened again. "Yes, sir. You can count on that, sir." Pause. "I'll tell her. Good night."

He clicked the phone shut. "Your dad wants you to call your mom every day so she feels a real part of 'this thing,' as he called it."

"And what else? What was all that 'Yes, sir' business?"

Steve grinned. "He told me that other than your mother you are the love of his life and I'm to keep that in mind."

"He threatened you?"

"Not in so many words but—how big is your dad anyway?"

Heidi laughed and threw herself into his arms, covering his face with kisses. "Not to worry, Spotterman. You've got me to protect you now. Let's call your dad. Let's call Nana and Milo. Let's call the immediate world!"

After they had made several more phone calls, they sat up until the first rays of dawn streamed through the white plantation shutters talking about the future they would build together. Heidi started pages of lists, checked the calendar for the rest of the year and into the new year and every once in a while broke into a fit of delighted giggles.

Then while Steve showered and shaved, Heidi returned to the senior Grossos' motor home and gathered supplies for making a pancake breakfast. On her way back she ran into Patsy with Buster and Duke.

"Well?" Patsy said, her eyes twinkling as she glanced at Heidi's left hand.

Heidi dangled the ring in front of Steve's aunt as Buster danced around, thrilled to see his mistress.

"Well, finally," Patsy said, dropping the leashes and hugging her hard. "You two make the perfect couple. We are going to be one busy family once the season ends."

"Maybe Tanya and I should talk about making this a double wedding," Heidi joked.

"Absolutely not. Every woman should have her own wedding memories." Patsy gave her another hard squeeze and released her.

Heidi picked up Buster's leash while Patsy retrieved the leash for Duke. "Come on and walk with me. Roger's over at the fitness center and I'm on my way to drop off Duke—and see if Roger had as good a night as you did." She winked.

As they walked, Heidi filled her in on the details of exactly how the proposal had gone, the calls they'd made together to her parents and Steve's dad, and the way they'd awakened Nana to tell her and Milo the news.

"What did Milo say?"

Heidi lowered her voice to the rougher gravelly sound of the older man. " 'Tell her that this ain't news,' " she rumbled. " 'And tell Steve I said it took him long enough. Two years and counting.' "

Both women laughed, knowing that Milo's gruff exterior hid

a soft heart. "He can be such a curmudgeon," Patsy said as they approached the corner where the motor home Steve had given her was parked. "So how do you like the new place?"

"You knew about that as well?"

Patsy shrugged. "Dean knew somebody who knew somebody who wanted to trade up. Will it work for the mobile unit?"

Heidi nodded. "It's perfect. Come see. I love it." She giggled. "The truth is, I pretty much love everything and everybody," she crowed.

Patsy laughed and hugged her again. "I'll see it later. Got to get Duke back to Roger and catch up on his news. And then my dual contribution to the cause of romance is complete—as are my dog-sitting duties." She turned down the lane that would take her to the fitness center parked just outside the compound fence. "See you later at the farm," she called.

MILO AND JULIANA'S Memorial Day bash was always one of the highlights of race week—at least for the Grosso family and their many friends. By scheduling it a week before the actual Memorial Day Monday, Nana had found she could include many of the out-of-town drivers and owners she enjoyed so much. These were people who understandably were anxious to get back home as soon as possible for their own holiday celebrations following the NASCAR Sprint Cup Series race that was the crowning event of race week in Charlotte and Memorial Day weekend. And because the party came a couple of days after the immediate hoopla, and rehashing of the previous week's race had quieted yet far enough before the following weekend's NASCAR Sprint Cup Series event, the guests were relaxed and definitely in a festive mood.

"This year is going to be special. This year we have so much to celebrate beyond racing," Juliana told Milo over breakfast the morning of the party.

"Like what?" he huffed.

"Kent and Tanya?"

"Old news."

"Steve and Heidi?"

"About time," Milo grunted and drank his coffee. Then he glanced up at his wife. "You aren't thinking of adding Sophia and that Murphy boy to the list, are you?"

Juliana sighed. "Not yet. But you and Dean may as well find some way past that. You saw how determined they are. Coming to us—and the Murphys—the way they did to ask us to give them a chance. That took courage, and I for one admire them for not allowing the past to color what they've found with each other."

"Dean has concerns," Milo said.

"So does Patsy, but at least Patsy has the good sense to know that Justin and Sophia are both adults. They are perfectly capable of making their own decisions—not to mention their own mistakes, if that's what this romance ever turns out to be," she added with a wag of her finger.

"I have the right to worry over my great-granddaughter no matter how old she gets," Milo grumbled.

"You know what I'm saying. And another thing," she said as if the idea had just occurred to her. "I will not stand for any 'incidents' at this party."

Milo's bushy white eyebrows shot up. "You're saying she's bringing him?"

"And why on earth wouldn't she? She's in love with the man. It's a party—a *family* gathering," Juliana snapped. "I would think the two of you could cut her some slack. She spends long, hard hours taking care of other people. It just seems to me that when she needs some tender loving care she should be able to find it right here."

"She's done us proud," Milo admitted. "To be in charge of a whole bunch of nurses and aides at her young age."

Juliana rolled her eyes. "I give up. She will always be that little girl to you, won't she? She'll be walking down the aisle or bringing you great-great-grandchildren to play with and you will persist—"

"You can't stop me from hoping that she'll not be walking down the aisle with that Murphy kid," Milo exclaimed, pounding his fist on the table for emphasis.

"Now you listen to me, old man," Juliana said, placing her hand firmly on top of his. "There's a better than good possibility that Sophia will bring Justin to the party. I don't expect you—or Dean—to be warm and fuzzy, but you will be polite. Understood?"

Milo ran a finger around the rim of his mug, then he glanced up at his wife and grinned. "Anybody ever tell you how sexy you are when you get your dander up, woman?"

"I give up," Juliana said, but she had trouble hiding a pleased smile as she looked out the kitchen window. "Here's Heidi and Steve now," she said, giving Milo one last look of warning, "Behave yourself."

She failed to see Milo's mouthed imitation of her reprimand as she retied her apron and headed out to greet Steve and Heidi.

"I packed up the extras from the fridge at the speedway," Heidi said. She and Steve were unloading several bags of groceries from Steve's truck. Buster ran to greet Milo's dogs and the pack of them took off across the yard.

"I don't know where we're gonna put one more thing," Milo observed, following Juliana out to the back porch. "This woman's got every inch of space filled—even in that oversize monstrosity of a combo refrigerator and freezer she had me buy her. Never thought I would see the day she could fill that thing up, but I shoulda known better."

HEIDI BENT to kiss the old man's cheek—an action that seemed to come as naturally to her as walking straight into the house without knocking. She and Steve had been engaged for less than forty-eight hours but already she could feel her life shifting—in a good way. The undercurrent of nerves she'd felt from the moment Steve had officially proposed she had elected to label as post-engagement jitters.

"Where do you want this soda pop, Nana?" Steve called, indicating several unopened cartons in the back of his truck.

"Put it in those tin washtubs over there under the willow tree—diet in the one on the left and regular in the middle one," Nana instructed. "Then you can go get the ice—and take Milo with you."

Milo adjusted his straw hat as he headed down the porch steps. "Don't ask questions, if you don't want her to put you to work," he advised.

"Come on, Heidi. Patsy and the others should be here soon. Let's get that stuff sorted out and put away and then you can help me set the tables."

By the time Steve and Milo returned an hour later, the yard was filled with round tables covered in red or blue cloths, each surrounded by white folding chairs from which a red, silver or blue balloon bobbed gaily in the light May breeze. On each table was a centerpiece of red geraniums interspersed with blue bachelor buttons and white daisies. At each place was a rolled napkin in the contrasting color to the tablecloth, tied with a silver ribbon.

"Where'd you two go for that ice? Alaska?" Nana shouted as Steve started unloading the bags and dumping the contents into the row of tin washtubs under the tree.

"You're not the only one having a party today, missus," Milo shouted back as he picked up a bag of ice and hauled it to one of the tubs. "Besides, I noticed that third tub was empty—we had to get the beer."

"Don't you go throwing your back out," Nana warned. "I've got no time for that today."

"Should I help?" Heidi asked, glancing from Nana's worried frown to Milo and back again.

"No. Steve will see that he doesn't overdo it. I just wish he'd use his cane like he's supposed to, but he thinks he doesn't need it." She wiped her hands on her apron and surveyed the yard. Her smile was as spectacular as the sun suddenly emerging from behind a cloud. "Looks real nice, Heidi. Festive, don't you think?" She put her arm around Heidi's shoulders and the two of them returned to the kitchen.

"I love your ring," Tanya said a little later as the two of them stood across from Patsy filling deviled eggs.

"It was Steve's mom's, wasn't it?" Patsy said. "She'd be so proud to know he gave it to you," she added.

"What was she like?" Heidi asked shyly. "I've seen pictures, but Steve doesn't talk much about her."

Patsy nodded. "It's been three years now, but I'm sure it's still hard. She was so vibrant and funny and a little like you, come to think of it."

Tanya laughed. "Way to put a damper on the engagement, Patsy. Every girl's just dying to hear that the guy picked her because she reminds him of his mother."

Patsy paused, a scoop of yellow egg filling halfway to its shell. "Oh, Heidi, sweetie, that's not what I meant. Libby was all those things, but well, the truth is that Steve is more like her than you realize—funny but reserved, always there when you need him but never wanting the spotlight, you know?"

"Nice save," Tanya muttered and all three women laughed. "Is Larry coming today?"

Patsy rolled her eyes. "If he remembers to look at his watch," she said. "I swear, what that brother-in-law of mine needs—"

"—is a good woman," Heidi, Tanya and Nana chorused, having heard this declaration from Patsy on any number of occasions.

"Well, he does," Patsy said as she filled the last egg and placed it on the plate. "Okay, Nana, what next?"

CHAPTER ELEVEN

BY NOON the large yard was filled with guests of all ages. On one side of the spacious deck off the back of the house, a trio of musicians—a fiddler, guitarist and bass player—played country-music dance tunes. The rest of the deck had been cleared of all furnishings, leaving the perfect dance floor. Young children raced in and around the tables, ignoring the shouts of parents for them to take their games away from the food area.

Kent and Dean were in charge of an open-pit apple-wood-chip fire where several dozen whole chickens roasted on spits. With Justin nowhere in sight, Sophia had taken charge of managing the games for the older children—races, obstacle courses, tug-of-war. Heidi couldn't help noticing that every game was competitive—and so was just about every child.

"Is that a frown or is the sun in your eyes?" Steve asked, coming up beside her and wrapping his arm around her waist.

"I was just watching the children," she replied.

"And thinking about our little rug rats-to-be?"

She laughed. "I'm thinking about our getting married first. Then we can start planning for a family," she said.

"Sassy," Tanya observed as she clicked their photo.

Once Tanya had moved on to her next subject, Steve said, "Seriously, they look like happy well-adjusted kids to me—for kids raised in racing families," he added.

"Everything's so competitive," she said. "What if—"

He took her by the shoulders and gently turned her toward the front of the house where another group of young people—smaller than those involved in the races and games—had gathered. "Look around," he whispered. "It's all normal, kids who are jocks, kids cheering the jocks, kids playing guitar or teaching the little kids something, kids just hanging out."

And he was right. When Heidi looked at the entire picture, it was what Nana and Patsy had promised—a unique community of friends and neighbors raising their families, going about the work they knew best, and once in a while stopping to enjoy it all at a party like this one. "Wanna dance, Spotterman?" she asked and didn't wait for an answer as she took his hand and pulled him over to the deck where a line dance was forming.

Through the afternoon, the guests kept coming. Lunch was an informal, if traditional, picnic affair of hot dogs and hamburgers hot off the grill, Patsy's potato salad, the deviled eggs that were gone in half the time it had taken to assemble them and Popsicles for dessert. The main meal was scheduled for six. In between there was a rousing game of boccie ball—a must as far as Milo was concerned—followed by the annual softball game, the teams made up of Dean's racing team against Kent's.

"Sophia!" Dean shouted from the pitcher's mound. "Come on, baby. I need a catcher."

So far there still had been no sign of Justin, although Heidi had noticed the way Sophia checked out every arriving vehicle the minute she heard the crunch of gravel on the driveway. Now she glanced at her father and rolled her eyes, but picked up a glove and trudged out to the makeshift field. Dean met her halfway and pulled her close for a pitcher-and-catcher consultation.

"Now, that's a nice gesture," Nana observed.

"He's trying. I'll give him that," Patsy agreed then she turned her attention from the field to Heidi. "While you and Steve were getting engaged the other night, Sophia and her dad had a major argument. They haven't spoken a word to each other since then—until now."

"Justin?" Heidi guessed.

Patsy nodded. "It had to do with something he thought that Justin had tried to pull on Kent last week. I just hope that the only reason he called her over wasn't because he realized he doesn't have a prayer of winning this softball game without her."

"Dean's very competitive," Nana explained. "In case you haven't noticed."

Patsy snorted. "I swear, if it came down to a choice between me and racing, I'm not sure he wouldn't have to take a minute to think about it." She stared hard at her husband on the mound, and her eyes filled with tears. "Coming up on fifty years old and still racing like he was thirty. Stubborn fool."

But in the next moment she had leaped to her feet and was yelling at the umpire—a neighbor and a judge. "That was right across the plate," she yelled. "Clean off those glasses."

Heidi saw Dean grin as he looked at his wife. "Baby, he's not wearing glasses," he called to her.

"Well, here. He can borrow mine," she yelled back, and everyone on the field and along the sidelines—including the judge playing umpire—laughed.

After the game several of the players trooped into the house to take turns showering and changing into the extra set of clothes they'd brought along. Guests with small children set up a napping area on blankets and sleeping bags spread out under the trees on the far side of the house. Nana insisted Milo take a nap.

"I'm not one of your children," he grumbled.

"I'll come with you," Nana said with a wink, and Milo chuckled and headed for the house.

Heidi could not help noticing the way the guests had made themselves completely at home, dispersing now from the formalized activities to go off on their own. A few grabbed fishing rods from the back hallway and headed for the creek. Dean and Patsy led another group down to the stables to saddle the horses and take them out for some exercise. Others gathered in small groups on swings and lawn chairs—lemonade or beer in hand—to visit and relax.

"Come on," Steve said, taking Heidi's hand and pulling her up from a lawn chair. "There's someplace I want to show you."

THEY WALKED hand in hand down the long gravel driveway, past the creek where Steve, Kent and Sophia had played as children and where even now Sophia was wading alone, her jeans rolled to her knees and her head bent in thought.

"Where are we going?" Heidi asked as they stood at the entrance gates and waited for a hay wagon to pass before crossing the road.

"Just up the road a piece," Steve said. "Are you having a good time?"

"I always have a good time at these parties," she replied.

"But this one's different, right?"

"This one is special," she said, taking his hand and weaving her fingers through his. "This one is my first as an almost Grosso."

Steve laughed. "Oh, so that's how we're to mark these things? This time you're 'almost Grosso,' and next year?"

"One hundred percent Grosso," she promised him.

He turned off the main road and headed down a lane lined with a canopy of oak trees. At the end of the lane Heidi could see a wrought-iron gate with a fence running to either side covered in honeysuckle. Steve reached inside the gate and released the catch.

"I never knew this cemetery was here," Heidi said, her voice quieted by respect for her surroundings.

"It's the old town cemetery. Mom's buried here," he added as he led the way through neat rows of headstones to a plain blue marble stone under an apple tree.

Elizabeth "Libby" Grosso
Wife, Mother, Friend
February 16, 1955–May 30, 2005

"She was so young," Heidi said more to herself than to him as she studied the dates and did the math.

"Hard to believe she's already been gone three years," Steve said as he brushed away some dead leaves from the stone. He fingered a rose in a vase filled with a profusion of wild roses and baby's breath. "Dad's been here."

"She died over Memorial Day weekend?"

Steve nodded. "Right after Nana's party—that night. We didn't even know anything was wrong."

"I'm so sorry," Heidi murmured.

"She would have loved you. From the day I turned twenty-one, she started going on about finally getting a daughter once I married. 'Another woman in this family of alpha males is always a good thing,' she used to say…" His voice trailed off.

Heidi tightened her fingers on his, giving him the moment he needed to compose himself. A flutter of breeze brought apple blossoms cascading gently over them and the grave. Steve squeezed her fingers and then found two small stones and handed one to Heidi. Reverently he laid the stone atop a small wall of similar stones circling the grave. Heidi placed her stone next to his and then followed him from the cemetery, neither of them saying a word until they reached the gates to Villa Grosso.

THE IDYLLIC SCENE they'd left behind when they walked to the cemetery had changed dramatically by the time they returned. The atmosphere was heavy with tension. Guests appeared to move with great care, if they moved at all, and all eyes were focused—furtively or directly—on Justin Murphy. Evidently he had just arrived, for he was striding across the yard toward the house with the confidence of someone who had visited the home many times. All of the guests were well aware of the history between Justin's family and the Grossos. But they were equally aware—and perhaps even admired—the way Justin and Sophia had stood their ground with both families that the past was just that—the past.

Sophia had obviously abandoned her vigil by the creek and returned to help Nana. When she came out the back door, she was laughing at some snatch of conversation that had followed her from the kitchen. She turned, saw Justin, and everything about her expression softened. With the grace and elegance of a princess she moved down the back stairs to meet him. Justin's eyes locked on her as if she was a lifeline in this sea of potentially hostile faces.

Kent watched as his sister embraced Justin. Then, ever the gentleman, he stepped forward and offered his rival a handshake. "Glad you could make it," he said.

Justin returned Kent's handshake and nodded to Tanya, who had also joined them. Then he turned his attention back to Sophia. "You look great," Heidi heard him murmur.

"Sophia's been watching the road," Tanya said, addressing Justin directly and in a light teasing voice.

"I had that autograph signing at the mall," Justin explained. "It ran long."

"You're here now and that's all that matters. Come say hello to Mom and Nana," Sophia suggested as she led Justin up the back-porch steps.

Once they were inside, Heidi noticed that it was almost as if everyone had released a breath held too long. Conversations were resumed and the air was ripe with the sound of laughter and music and the smell of the apple-wood fire where the chickens slowly rotated on spits. By the time Sophia and Justin came outside again, everyone seemed to have relaxed. Justin walked over to the washtubs and fished out beers for himself and Sophia, and the two of them talked quietly and intimately as they leaned against a large willow tree.

Kent headed in their direction.

"Hey, Kent," Steve called. "Maybe leave well enough alone?" he suggested.

"I'm doing this for Sophia," Kent said. "I don't know what she sees in the guy, but as long as he's with her, he's welcome here." He took four cold beers—two in each hand—and with Tanya following, approached Sophia and Justin. "How about a refill?" he called, holding up the beers.

"No, thanks," Justin answered, taking Sophia's arm and obviously intending to move to a new location—away from Kent. "Let's dance," he said to Sophia.

"What's your problem?" Kent asked. Justin froze, then turned around. In a single stride he was standing toe-to-toe with Kent. Steve moved a step closer as well, but Kent waved him off.

"Don't go there, okay?" Justin said evenly. "It's a party, right?" Again he turned his attention to Sophia, ignoring the other guests. "Hey, do I get my dance or what?"

"Got my dancing shoes on," Sophia said as she followed Justin across the yard. Just then the musicians struck up a fast-paced tune and the leader invited everyone onto the deck for a square dance.

"You want to tell me what that was about?" Tanya asked Kent.

"Nothing important. Just jealous that we're the team that walked away with the million-dollar check last night." He shrugged. "I don't think he liked that maneuver Steve had me pull in the final lap. Can't think why he took it out on me. I already told him after the race that it was Steve's idea."

"And of course you never question my ideas," Steve said, laughing.

"Not when they end up getting me across the finish line ahead of the rest of the pack," Kent replied. He wrapped his arm around Tanya's shoulders. "Your dad's here," he told Steve as he led Tanya toward the dance floor.

Steve glanced across the yard to where Larry Grosso was talking quietly to Dean, who kept shooting lethal glances at Justin and looked ready to explode. "Looks like he could use our help."

"You go," Heidi said. "I'll see if I can help in the kitchen." She kissed him on the cheek and, as she climbed the porch steps, she shot a quick glance toward where Sophia was dancing with Justin. They were both laughing as they wove their way through the steps of the dance, changing partners and then coming back to each other. The way Justin looked at Sophia was the same as the look she had seen a thousand times in Steve's eyes when he looked at her. It was the look of love.

BY DUSK, a fresh group of invited guests had arrived and the yard and house were alive with people munching on appetizers, enjoying the music and looking forward to dinner and the special laser light show that capped off the evening.

"Any fool can set off fireworks," Milo had decided several years earlier. "Let's have some of those hotshots at the shop stage one of those light shows." Juliana had loved the idea—and so had their guests—and the light show had become a much-anticipated treat.

The evening guests included executives and their wives and children from a variety of sponsors for Dean and Kent. Among them were several people from Vittle Farms, including Chester Honeycutt and his wife. Nana had also included Clare and her family on the guest list. The minute the guests from Vittle Farms arrived, Heidi saw Clare's smile stiffen. Heidi excused herself and moved closer to her friend and business partner.

In the excitement of Steve's proposal and the gift of the home for the mobile unit, Heidi had completely forgotten about Chester

Honeycutt's request to tour the facility—perhaps with the idea of offering funding for the clinic. She was just about to tell Clare about the idea, when something in the way Clare was looking at Chester Honeycutt stopped her.

"Having a good time?" she asked casually.

"Sure," Clare said as her eyes kept track of Chester Honeycutt.

"Clare," Heidi said, taking her friend's arm, "what's going on?"

"Did you see today's news?" She didn't wait for Heidi's response. "Vittle Farms has acquired Vitality—the so-called 'natural' cosmetics company."

"They make excellent products," Heidi said, recalling that Tanya had suggested one of their lipsticks for Patsy when the women had gone shopping together in Darlington.

Clare focused her attention on Heidi. "Oh, come on, Heidi, you know as well as I do that there have been rumors for years about the company using animals for testing." She shuddered. "It's inhumane what some companies—"

"Some companies," Heidi repeated. "I mean, do you have proof that Vitality—"

"Not definitive," Clare admitted. "But when those kinds of rumors persist for as long as they have with Vitality, well... Oh, sweetie, I'm sorry. This is a party and here I am getting all caught up in business." She made an exaggerated gesture of stepping down from a platform. "Officially off my soapbox," she assured Heidi and headed off to where her husband was talking with Roger Clark.

Heidi watched her go. She wasn't fooled for a minute. She had no doubt that this would be the first topic of discussion once they reached the clinic the following morning.

The large bell hanging outside the back door of the farmhouse sounded. "Ladies and gentlemen," Milo boomed over the microphone he'd confiscated from the leader of the band, "take your places. Dinner is about to be served."

Heidi hurried back to the kitchen where all the members of

the Grosso family had formed a line. Each carried a large dish filled with some delicacy that Nana had created for the evening menu. With Nana in the lead, they marched out the back door and wound their way among the tables on their way to the buffet as Milo introduced each member of the family.

"The wondrous Juliana," he boomed, "hostess extraordinaire and my own bombshell beauty."

The guests cheered and whistled as Juliana sashayed among them with an exaggerated swing of her generous hips.

"Dr. Larry Grosso—our professor—could never get that boy away from the books long enough to teach him racing."

Larry grinned at his grandfather and then concentrated on getting his dish of pasta to the table without tripping or allowing the contents to spill over the sides of the large shallow bowl.

"Dean Grosso," Milo boomed with obvious pride. "Best damn driver in the business—and not a bad judge of women either."

Everyone chuckled as Dean waited for Patsy to come alongside of him.

"The lovely Patsy Clark Grosso," Milo said, his change in tone a clear indication of the esteem and respect he held for Dean's wife. "I don't know how we Grosso men keep doing it, but we do find the finest women in the world. And speaking of that—" He paused dramatically as Kent and Tanya stepped to the edge of the porch, followed by Steve and Heidi. "Looks like these boys are following in our footsteps and looks like we'll be celebrating not one but two new additions to the Grosso family this year. My great-grandson Kent, and his lady, Tanya Wells, and my other great-grandson, Steve, and his lady, Heidi Kramer—a doctor in the family at last."

More cheers and whistles as the four of them crossed the yard and deposited salads and platters of antipasto on the buffet.

Heidi glanced back as the applause died and saw Sophia standing hesitantly at the back door with Justin. Milo was about to hand the microphone back to the band leader, when Nana caught his attention and nodded toward the back door.

"And last, but never least," Milo said as he walked to the door, opened it and offered Sophia his hand, "my great-grand-daughter, Sophia, who is beautiful and strong and more like her Nana every day, and her…escort, a rising star in racing, Justin Murphy."

It was a momentous breakthrough for the old man and everyone knew it as Milo accompanied Sophia and Justin to the buffet, then turned and shouted, "Well, what are y'all waitin' for? Let's eat."

AS FAR AS HEIDI WAS CONCERNED, race week had flown by at warp speed. Having decided that this would be a good opportunity to "test-drive" the mobile clinic in Charlotte and again on the road in Dover before signing the final contract, the NARS team urged Heidi and Clare to do whatever it might take to get the unit in place by Thursday. There was also the matter of working out the logistics of just how the day-to-day functioning of the business was going to work now that the clinic was expanding services and Heidi and Clare had officially joined forces.

"Why don't you handle the mobile unit and I'll handle the clinic here," Clare suggested.

"For now that seems to make the most sense," Heidi agreed. "Do we need to add a clause to the partnership agreement?"

"I don't think we need anything official—unless you want it," Clare said.

Heidi hesitated. *Never a good idea to go into business with friends,* her father had warned her when she'd told him about the mobile unit and her partnership with Clare.

"I mean, unless you think there might be a need to spell things out in such detail," Clare said, sounding hurt.

This is Clare, Heidi reminded herself. They had a legal agreement. That should be enough. "No," Heidi said before she could change her mind.

"Great. Okay then. Let's take a look at the inventory we have here and see what can be transferred and where we might need to order extra—oh, this is so exciting." Her enthusiasm for the project was reassuring. When Heidi had shown her the motor home that Steve had bought for the clinic and their home away from home, Clare had been especially impressed.

"Wow! This guy is really something, girl. Do not mess this up."

And they had hugged and laughed with delight as they talked over the top of one another, new ideas for how they would set up the space spilling forth almost before they could complete a previous thought.

Steve had so much to do in the front office that he and Heidi saw each other only in the evenings at the track as they worked side by side refurbishing the old motor home.

"Anybody here?"

Heidi put down her paintbrush and glanced over to where Steve was installing the cabinet doors she had repainted earlier that day. "You expecting company?" she asked as she ran her hand through her curls in a futile attempt to comb them into some semblance of normalcy.

Steve shrugged. "Come on in," he called.

There was a murmur of female voices outside the door.

"Well, go on," they heard Kent urge.

Suddenly the small area at the entrance to the motor home was filled with the smiling faces of Nana, Patsy, Tanya and Sophia.

"Happy housewarming shower," they shouted in unison as they held up several large boxes wrapped in paper that featured animal prints, tied with "ribbons" made of leashes and decorated with pet toys.

"I'm here for you, buddy," Kent called out from somewhere behind the women. He waited until the women had deposited the gifts on every available surface and then added the pile of smaller boxes he was carrying on top. "You ladies have a real good time now," he said. "Steve and I will be back in a couple of hours."

"An hour," Tanya instructed. "There's work to be done in these boxes."

Kent sighed. "An hour," he agreed. "Come on, cous, before they decide we need to stay."

Steve didn't need to be asked twice.

"This is too much," became Heidi's mantra as she opened the packages to reveal a new showerhead, new faucets for the bath and kitchen, colorful throw pillows with matching valances to brighten the windows.

"Okay, we'll take it all back," Sophia cracked.

"Open that one," Nana urged.

Heidi tore away the paper and lifted the pristine white cover of the box. Inside was a set of dishes, glassware and flatware for eight along with matching dog and cat water and food bowls. "I love it," she cried. "And I love all of you, but it's too much."

"Nonsense," Patsy said. "You'll need your money for setting up the clinic area. Steve said you guys were going to 'make do' with what was already here until you and Steve are married. Now there's no need to 'make do.'"

"We're back-k-k," Kent called. "Is it safe?"

"Depends on your definition," Tanya replied, and the other women laughed. "Get in here, boys. There is work to be done."

"Good thing we brought rations," Steve said as he and Kent came inside laden with several large bottles of soda, bags of snacks and an array of deli items.

In short order, the faucets and showerhead were installed, the dishes washed and placed in the freshly painted cabinets, the entire place vacuumed, dusted and polished and the pillows and rugs carefully placed—rearranged and placed again. Exhausted but pleased, the five women and two men stood crowded together in the doorway and admired their work.

"Welcome to the neighborhood," Nana said as she hugged Heidi.

"Oh, just a minute," Heidi said as she ran to the kitchen area and retrieved a bottle of glue from one of the cabinets. Then as they watched, she took the turtle Nana had given her and held it up.

"Here, Nana?" she asked as she placed the turtle on the dashboard near the driver's seat. Nana nodded and her eyes glistened with tears as she watched Heidi glue the small stone turtle into place.

"Perfect," Steve agreed.

BUT BY THE FOLLOWING MORNING things had moved from the bliss of perfect to the chaos of deeply flawed.

"You had a call this morning," Clare said, her eyes glittering with indignation. "Chester Honeycutt's office."

"Is Macho all right?" Heidi had been so busy running between the mobile unit and the clinic that it had been days since she'd had a chance to catch up on things at the clinic in town. Clare had been handling her appointments.

"This was his assistant—Terry? She didn't call about his dog. She called because apparently Chester and Chuck Marshall have been discussing the possibility of Vittle Farms—or Vitality—funding the mobile clinic. Something about a tour for members of his board?"

Heidi swallowed. "All NARS programs depend on outside funding or donations, Clare," she began.

"I'll take that as your admission that you did know and elected not to share this bit of news with me," Clare interrupted. "Apparently the purpose of this little tour is for them to decide if they want to throw money at us?"

"Well, it seems like it might be a good fit," Heidi said. "I mean, the headquarters for Vittle Farms is practically in the speedway's backyard and—"

"But we're not talking about Vittle Farms. We're talking about Vitality Cosmetics. According to Terry, the board members are in town from Vitality." She waited a beat and then added, her voice no more than a hoarse whisper and her face contorted with rage, "How could you keep this from me?"

"I…I wasn't…"

"Yeah, right," Clare said bitterly as she strode down the hall to her office. She stood by the door obviously waiting for Heidi to follow.

Heidi glanced at the clock. She had no one scheduled for the day, giving her a chance to catch up on things. It was an hour before they would open for business, half an hour before their assistant would report for work. She just hoped that was enough time to work things out.

"Look, Clare," she said as she followed her down the hall. "I am really sorry. I was going to talk to you about it and then—"

Clare slammed the door. "This is not something that the clinic can be associated with. You do get that, don't you?" She'd found her voice and was shouting.

"Calm down," Heidi snapped as she took the chair across from Clare. "As I said, I assumed that it was Vittle Farms we were dealing with. I didn't even know about Vitality until you mentioned it yesterday at the party. I can understand why you might be upset, learning the money might come from Vitality, but—"

"*Might* be upset?" Clare stared at her, openmouthed. "And do you not get that Vittle Farms and Vitality are one and the same now? Do you seriously think we can even consider such an idea?"

Heidi was getting a little tired of Clare's tone—as if Heidi were the bad child. She forced herself to maintain control. "I think we need to hear what Chester is proposing and let him know of our concerns. I think we need to keep in mind that our association with NARS is also a kind of a partnership, one in which they have a voice about the financing of the project. They are the ones driving this, and frankly, I think that—"

"Well, here's what I think—thought." Clare's face was as red as the signature accent color of Kent's car. "I *thought* that you were as dedicated to the cause of animal rights—and the abuse thereof—as I am. Obviously that's not the case."

"That's unfair and you know it, Clare. Besides, you said yourself that the charges against Vitality are rumors. *Unproven* rumors. The least we can do is keep an open mind until we hear what's being proposed."

"And what if the rumors are true?" Clare shouted.

"You don't know that," Heidi shouted back. "Why can't you focus on the good that Vittle Farms has done—the research center for nutrition and dietary health in the biovillage right outside our back door here? Not to mention the fact that the Vittle Farms foundation has donated big bucks to some of the very organizations you are a spokesperson for."

"So we just turn a blind eye to the fact that they now own a company that possibly uses defenseless animals to test the products you apply to that flawless skin of yours."

"Prove it," Heidi said, her own voice ominously quiet in the face of Clare's hysterics.

"I will, but by then it may be too late to prevent you from making possibly the biggest mistake of your career and taking me and this business down with you," Clare growled. "Now, get out of my office."

Heidi didn't stop to remove her lab coat but instead, grabbed her purse and Buster's leash and left by the rear entrance. She held the car door open for Buster, then got behind the wheel of her car. She sat there for several long moments, her head resting on the steering wheel as she tried to think through the scene with Clare.

When she felt Buster's rough tongue on her cheek, she sighed and started the engine. "Come on, Buster," she said. "Want to go to the track and figure this mess out?"

Buster's long tail wagged as he gave her a final swipe of his tongue before settling into position in the backseat, his face halfway out the open window.

Without really thinking about it, Heidi took the local route toward the speedway rather than taking the interstate. She needed time to sort through what had just happened. Clare had turned on her as if their years of friendship had meant nothing. The entire incident felt oddly familiar—as if she had experienced it before, not once but many times, when someone she had thought was her friend, someone she had thought trusted her suddenly and without warning dismissed that friendship and trust as if they had meant nothing the minute Heidi told them her family was moving.

She drove past the signature black rail fencing that marked the boundaries of Vittle Farms corporate headquarters. No buildings were visible from the highway. Instead the scene was pastoral—acres of green grass, bordered by the fencing and backed up by forests of tall pine trees. Several horses were grazing in the distance. The scene was so idyllic that it might have been a painting or magazine cover.

"Why couldn't Chester Honeycutt have bought a company that makes computers or something," she muttered to Buster. "Why does it have to be this one? Everything was going so well."

Buster sighed sympathetically and plopped down across the backseat, his head resting on his paws and one eyebrow cocked as Heidi glanced back at him in the rearview mirror.

CHAPTER TWELVE

WHILE CLARE WAS GOING ballistic with Heidi, Steve was still basking in the glow of their engagement. So when Amy Barber plopped down in the visitors' chair next to his desk and delivered her news, Steve could only see life getting better for Heidi and him.

"Did you see the feature about Kent on the morning news shows?" Amy asked Steve. "Kent's Web site has had a flood of hits already," she continued, not waiting for his response, "and I've been taking calls all morning from reporters looking to do their own feature. And now that Vittle Farms might be throwing some funding at the mobile pet care unit, maybe we could make a tie between Kent and the on-site facility. Kent and Chester presenting Heidi and her partner with a check or something. Heidi all decked out in her lab coat and Kent in his uniform. Will she already have animals to treat or should we plan to stage some? A couple of cute little kitties or, I know, we can have her checking out Sybil's bird. Talk about color."

Steve laughed. "Take a pill, Amy."

"But do you think Heidi would do the PR thing?"

"You have to talk to Heidi about that, and you'll have to see how she feels about staging something. She's pretty much into reality over staging."

"Maybe we could use Clare Wilson in the spots. She's always in front of the camera with her animal rights campaign, and besides—"

A light tap at Steve's office door drew their attention. "Heidi!" Amy said, "timing is everything. We were just talking about you."

Heidi smiled, but Steve knew her too well. The smile was tight and forced. "Do you have a minute?" she asked, her eyes on Steve.

"Sure," Amy replied, not catching the imploring look Heidi was sending Steve. "We were just discussing the funding for the clinic. If that goes through, it could be a great photo op."

"Could be."

Heidi's subdued response, in tandem with the awkward silence that followed, alerted Amy to the situation. She jumped up. "Well, I've got to get back to work. You can't imagine the number of calls I'm getting and—" She glanced from Heidi to Steve and edged toward the door. "I'll talk to you later?" she asked Heidi.

"Sure. Later." Heidi forced another smile and waited for the publicist to leave. Then she closed the door and collapsed onto the chair Amy had just vacated.

"What's happened?"

Heidi told him all about her argument with Clare. "She has a point," she said.

"How can you say that? She's going off half-cocked here without giving Chester or anyone else a chance to present their side of the story. Buying Vitality is a great fit for Vittle Farms. Chester has been looking to expand for several months now and this definitely makes sense—organic foods plus natural cosmetics equals better bottom line, right?"

"I wouldn't know. You're the business major," Heidi said, and knew that the sudden pique of irritation she was feeling was a by-product of her sense of things being totally out of control.

"Whoa! What's really going on here?"

Heidi sighed heavily. "Okay, even Clare will agree that Vitality couldn't claim 'no animals tested in production of this product' if it weren't true. But that doesn't cover them if Vitality uses *ingredients* that have been tested on animals. That's abuse by any definition."

Steve's frown told her he was having some trouble connecting the dots. "You're talking about digging pretty deep into this thing. Isn't it enough that Vitality openly states they do not use animal testing?"

"In their products. That's not the same thing," Heidi argued. "You must see that there is no way that the clinic—or I—can be associated with any company that is in any way connected to a violation of animal rights," she explained.

"You're saying that even if Vittle Farms or Vitality has the most obscure connection to testing, funding for the mobile unit coming from them would be tainted in your eyes—and Clare's?"

"Yes."

"Honey, this is business. Companies take over or merge with other companies all the time. I mean, just look at the list of varied businesses behind some of the major conglomerates. At least this one makes sense. The products have some reasonable connection."

"Yes, but—"

"Okay, what if Vittle Farms is the name behind the mobile unit? Leave Vitality out of it."

"The connection is the issue." Heidi folded her arms and looked at something beyond his shoulder. "They're one and the same."

"Hey, babe, let's take a step back here."

HEIDI WAS FIGHTING HARD to control her emotions partly because she had so wanted her idea of the mobile clinic to work and partly because everything had been going so perfectly for her future with Steve. But ten minutes earlier she had arrived at his door assuming he would immediately grasp the problem and help her solve it. Instead, it appeared to her as if he was looking for ways to ignore it. She looked at him and raised one quizzical eyebrow.

"Take a step back to what?" She glanced around his office. She saw posters of Kent framed on the walls, a life-size cutout of him leaning against one wall, and shelves cluttered with mugs, magnets and all sorts of other promotional items. "Are you worried about how this might affect Kent?"

"No. I'm asking what's Clare's proof."

"Clare doesn't have proof—yet. But the woman has spent years following up on such cases, advising companies who are innocent how to handle such rumors. Surely she knows when something like this might have some validity, even if there's no definitive evidence."

Steve leaned toward her. "That's just not good enough in this case." His eyes begged her to accept what he was saying. He paused and took a long breath. "The wheels are in motion, Heidi. Vittle Farms is prepared to put a major chunk of money behind the mobile unit as part of their launch of Vitality as a corporate partner. They're looking for a sizable return on that investment over the short term. Amy's got plans for building Kent's association with the new company. Dawson is delighted with this new opportunity for Kent to be more in the public eye. I'm not sure there's anything I can do to slow them down—much less stop them."

"But you could try," she said.

Steve shook his head. "I can't. I respect that you and Clare are concerned, but this is business, babe. Don't ask me to make it personal."

Heidi's eyes widened. She slowly stood up and headed for the door.

"Where are you going?"

"You need proof, right?" she replied as she opened the door and started weaving her way through the cubicles to the elevator.

"Heidi!"

Both Amy and Steve called out to her at the same time. Amy

was closer and directly in her path, so Heidi hesitated. Amy handed her several small blue metal containers. "Check these out," she squealed. "Vitality's created this special container for their red lip gloss. We're going to hand them out by the thousands at the race this weekend. Cool, huh?"

Heidi slipped one sample into her bag and laid the rest on the closest desk. "Nice," she mumbled and kept walking.

Amy glanced past Heidi at Steve and then back to Heidi. "Problem?" Heidi heard her ask Steve as the elevator doors slid shut.

Since she had no appointments that afternoon, Heidi left a message at the clinic to say she'd be at the speedway for the rest of the day. She parked near the compound and walked toward the mobile unit. It now sported a temporary sign that read, Mobile Animal Clinic, and featured the distinctive black logo of the NARS on the door, along with Ridgemont Animal Clinic.

Roger Clark was just taping a mock-up paper sign that read, Sponsored by Vittle Farms in smaller white on black printing to the door. Heidi stopped and stared at the sign for a long moment before Roger was aware of her presence.

"Hey, Heidi," he said as he stepped back to admire his handiwork. "I heard that Chester Honeycutt might stop by tomorrow with some of his board members from the foundation. Thought this might be a nice way to drive home the point that funding is a good idea."

"Funding is always a good idea," she agreed, forcing a smile. "Will you excuse me, Roger? I need to make some calls."

"Sure. Catch you later, okay?"

Inside she laid her purse on the small table by the door and her laptop on the dining table. She looked around at the place where Steve had proposed. She had believed that in buying her the motor home, Steve had found a way to show her that he understood that her career was as important to their life together as his was. But she had to face the fact that if it came down to the interests of the Ridgemont Animal Clinic versus Maximus Motorsports, Maximus would win every time as long as Steve worked there.

And why wouldn't he think that way? she thought. She was putting him in a tough position by expecting him to see only her side of this dilemma. Of course, the hoopla surrounding Vittle Farms acquiring Vitality would be good for Kent's career—and what was good for Kent was good for Steve's career.

The only answer she could see was to either clear Vitality's name or find another sponsor. There were other corporations, other possibilities, right? They just needed to think this through.

Relieved to have come up with an idea they could agree on, she scrounged around in her bag and unearthed her cell phone and punched in speed dial for Steve's office.

"You've reached the desk of Steve Grosso at Maximus Motorsports. Leave a message and a number and I'll return your call as soon as possible."

"Hi," she said and drew in a breath. "It's me, apologizing for coming on like the Wicked Witch of the South earlier. I'm at the track and thought maybe we'd have supper here if that's okay. Call me."

"Come on, sport," she murmured as Buster waited patiently just inside the door for her to decide if they were coming or going. Heidi sat down and opened her laptop. "Let's start with finding proof and go from there. After all, Steve has a point. Clare's information could be tainted by her sources."

Pretty damaging, at least circumstantially, she had to admit an hour later after she'd scanned the Internet for reports on Vitality's research and testing processes. The Vitality Web site as well as all ads posted on other sites on the Internet professed that "no product has been tested on animals." Heidi was well aware that the key word in that statement was *product.* What most consumers did not know was that companies could make such a claim even if external suppliers of the ingredients contained in a product indulged in animal testing.

And while she could find no obvious evidence that pointed to Vitality being guilty of such practices, the company had not been included in the Coalition for Consumer Information on Cosmetics—CCIC's list of approved manufacturers. Nor was there any evidence that Vitality had ever committed to a fixed cutoff date for ending on-site testing as well as the use of any ingredient employing animal testing as part of its production—if they were involved in such practices. Heidi rested her chin on her palm and stared at the computer monitor trying to consider her next move. Tracking down Vitality's guilt or innocence was going to be harder—and take a lot more time—than she had imagined.

STEVE RETURNED from yet another meeting to see his message light blinking. He closed the door to his office and played back his messages while he checked his calendar for the remainder of the day. He paused when he heard Heidi's voice. While he would accept her apology, he knew her too well. This issue was far from over and at dinner she would want to keep picking at it. How was he going to convince her that it was too late to turn back the clock on this thing?

In the meeting, Dawson had laid out what he liked to call the big picture—all good news for Maximus. There was no doubt that money had already changed hands in the form of signed agreements—major money when Vittle Farms bought Vitality. The funds that Vittle Farms was offering through its corporate foundation to provide the start-up money for the mobile unit in its first season was also tied to the business of building an image—for Vitality, for Vittle Farms and, as far as Dawson was concerned, for Kent. Unless the evidence was downright shocking, there was nothing Heidi was going to be able to do to convince Dawson—or Kent—that there was a problem.

Steve didn't think Heidi would be too happy if she knew that he'd approached Kent days ago with the suggestion that funding the clinic might be something Vittle Farms would be interested in. Because they hadn't had a chance to discuss it yet, he also doubted Heidi had any real grasp of the amount of expense involved in getting the unit to and from each venue for the rest of the season. And that didn't even begin to address the costs they could incur if the older motor home had a breakdown and needed major repairs. With Kent's encouragement, Steve and Amy had presented their business case for how sponsoring the mobile unit would be good business for both Kent and his primary sponsor. Dawson had talked to Chester, and Chester had agreed to underwrite the clinic. That this was on top of the millions that Vittle Farms paid out annually to be the primary sponsor of Kent's team had been an enormous coup.

"Steve?"

He looked up as Kent entered the office and sat down. Forcing his mind back to the business at hand—the discussion in the meeting about Kent's schedule before and after the Charlotte race—he rummaged around the desk for his notes. "So, you okay with the schedule?"

Kent reached over and took the notepad from him and laid it facedown on the desk. "This isn't about the schedule. You were a space cadet in that meeting. What's going on?"

Steve leaned back in his chair. Kent was more of a brother than a cousin to him. They had grown up together, raced cars together, gotten in and out of any number of life's challenges and scrapes—together.

He unearthed an article he'd found on one of the major animal rights Web sites after Heidi had left, and slid it across the desk. "Take a look at this."

Kent read through the single-page article then laid it back on Steve's desk. "So, VF's going to produce makeup as well as grow corn. Frankly my biggest problem is hoping that Tanya likes this Vitality stuff, because she's going to be expected to use it once we're married."

Steve attempted a laugh but it came out hollow.

"And what else?" Kent asked.

"There's a problem—for Heidi."

"Heidi? She won't have to use the stuff—"

"Read on. Seems these folks are pretty sure that the cosmetics group might use animals to test ingredients for their product."

Kent blinked and slumped into his chair. Everyone in the Grosso family was well aware of Heidi's passion for animal rights. "Uh-oh," he muttered as he scanned the rest of the article.

"Exactly," Steve said, equally miserable.

"Have you talked to Amy about this?"

"Not yet. She's got all these great ideas about how to maximize this for you. I mean, you heard her in the meeting. Your time's not going to be your own for the next several weeks."

Kent frowned. "You're saying Heidi could be a problem?"

"She's not a *problem*. She has concerns and they might be valid concerns," Steve replied stiffly.

"Or might this be Clare Wilson stirring things up?" Kent pushed himself to his feet. "Look, I gotta get over to the shop. Let's not panic on this thing until we have all the facts." He headed for the door. "And for now, don't say anything to Amy or Dawson, okay? Could be the whole thing is nothing but a couple of urban myths circulating in cyberspace and it'll clear itself if we give it time."

"Okay," Steve said, knowing Kent didn't believe a word of what he'd just said. "I'll call you later."

BUSTER'S WELCOMING BARK made Heidi glance out the window next to where she was working in time to see Clare standing outside. She was staring at the sign and frowning. Heidi checked her watch and saw that it was already past five. The clinic was closed for the day.

"Hi," she said as she opened the door and waited for Clare to enter.

"I like what you've done with the place," Clare said, looking around as she absently scratched Buster's head.

Her tone was conciliatory and Heidi was relieved. "Want something to drink? Iced tea? Or I could make some coffee."

"Nothing." Clare continued her visual tour of her surroundings. Heidi saw her gaze settle on the pile of printed pages next to Heidi's computer. She moved closer and read the top copy.

"Homework," Heidi said. "Not that I didn't believe you," she hurried to add. "It's just that if I'm going to make a case for—"

Clare sighed and sat on the love seat. "I am so sorry, Heidi," she whispered, and when she looked up at Heidi her face was lined with the strain of the last several hours. "I wish there were some other way."

Heidi sat next to her friend and patted her back. "Hey, you didn't buy a cosmetics company," she joked. "This isn't your fault."

"But I sure made it seem like it was yours and right on top of Steve proposing. I mean, what kind of friend does something like that?"

Heidi gave her a wry smile. "Well, I'll admit the timing could have been better, but again, that's not your fault."

"It's just that you come up with this incredible idea that frankly could save the business and how do I repay you? By throwing a wet blanket over the entire thing."

"Hey, there's a solution here," Heidi said without much conviction. "We just have to figure it out."

Clare sighed. "I think I already have. I talked to my lawyer. We can rewrite the agreement to separate the businesses—the mobile unit will be yours and the town site mine—different names, no association."

Heidi opened her mouth to protest.

"Hear me out," Clare said. "That way you can accept the funding from Vittle Farms for your start-up costs. We'll issue our own press release so there's no question about an association between the two clinics going forward. We'll—"

"No."

"No? Heidi, be reasonable."

"It doesn't solve anything," Heidi protested.

"It saves our friendship," Clare retorted.

"You think? Tell me how that works when you know that I am every bit as passionate about animal rights as you are? Are you suggesting I sell my soul for the sake of starting my own clinic?" She massaged Clare's back. "You know me better than that, my friend."

"Standing on principle can get pretty lonely sometimes," Clare warned, "and it could cost you a lot more than a career."

CHAPTER THIRTEEN

"GOOD PASTA," Steve muttered that evening as they ate a supper of leftovers from the party at the farm.

Since his arrival at the motor home shortly after Clare had left, conversation between the two of them had been stilted attempts at normalcy.

"I thought I'd work on putting that second coat of paint on the bathroom cabinets after supper," he added a moment later.

"I can do that. It's a tight fit for you in there. You can finish installing the light over the sink."

These snatches of conversation were followed by long stretches of silence—until Steve turned the conversation to the subject they'd avoided all evening.

"I think I have a solution about the problem here," he said as if they were still discussing repairs on the motor home. "For the first year, you could simply manage the mobile unit. In other words, not have it connected to the clinic in town. It could be like you were taking a second job."

"That won't solve anything," Heidi said as she continued picking at her food.

"I'm trying to help," Steve said, his tone tense.

"I know. But not make this ours? I came up with the idea and you just want me to give it away? How about another sponsor altogether?"

"NARS is ready to move on this thing. How will you explain

that to them?" He pushed his plate away and ran his fingers through his hair. "Why won't you at least consider a compromise?" His voice was edged with frustration.

Heidi gave him her full attention, aware that they were on the verge of another argument here. "What compromise? You make me accept Vitality's money by severing ties from that money to the clinic?"

Steve stood and Heidi knew she'd allowed emotion to rule over reason when it came to her choice of words. "I *make* you?" he said. "Oh, that is so rich."

"Okay. Poor choice of words. That's hardly the point."

"What is the point then?"

"Define *compromise*," she said, her voice rising. "Your word, not mine," she reminded him.

"Compromise," he shouted. "As in striking a balance or finding some middle ground. As in give-and-take."

Buster arched one eyebrow in Heidi's direction, read her body language and lumbered over to stand with her.

"Don't lecture me," she replied. "Explain to me in civil terms how your suggestion solves anything."

Steve was appalled. "Are you kidding me? I am offering you an out. I can make this happen—not without some tap dancing around the truth, but I can make it work. You and Clare can use the time to find what you need to clear Vitality's name—or not. I thought that's what you wanted."

"And I understand all of that, but it still puts the VF logo on the door of the unit here—the place we're supposed to live when we travel? Do you think I can just accept their paycheck and forget everything else?"

"Then tell me how you plan to pay for this thing without their financial backing."

"I told you. Find another sponsor."

"By this weekend?"

"Okay, we could do it the same way NARS pays for child care and other services—donations from the driver and owner community."

"Do you have any idea what setting up a program like that entails? What all this is going to cost? Have you actually read the agreement you signed with NARS?" Steve reminded her. "It's contingent on a trial run *this week and next* and securing a first year of funding."

He had her there. Heidi opened her mouth once to dispute the facts he'd laid before her, but came up empty. "I can't make sense of this anymore. I need some air," she snapped, and left the motor home with Buster close on her heels. She had really needed to escape the confines of the small trailer and clear her head so she could think. She took off at a jog down one long lane with Buster at her side. The problem was that she hadn't gone far when it started to rain—hard.

She glanced around for shelter to wait out the downpour.

"Heidi! Over here."

She shook the rain out of her eyes and saw Sybil Marshall waving to her from the front door of her motor home.

"Well, any port in a storm," she muttered to Buster as they made a run for it. "Hi, Mrs. Marshall, what are you doing out here in the middle of the week?"

Sybil laughed. "I might ask you the same. Tie Buster up over there out of the rain so he can dry off some." She motioned to a spot under the large sheltering portico.

"Stay," Heidi instructed as Buster shook himself off.

"Come on inside. I just made some tea."

Heidi kicked off her shoes at the door and stepped inside. "How's Henrietta?"

"Hello," Henrietta replied as soon as the cockatoo spotted Heidi.

"See for yourself," Sybil answered as she set up the tea. "Have a seat."

Heidi perched on the edge of a wicker ottoman.

Sybil set a mug of tea in front of her along with a plate of ginger cookies, then took the chair that matched the ottoman. "You and Steve have a spat?"

Heidi looked up quickly and was about to deny it, when Sybil smiled and gently wiped a drop of water from her cheek with her thumb. "There's more than raindrops on that pretty face of yours," she explained.

Heidi reminded herself that this was not Nana—a woman she was beginning to believe she could trust and confide in without Nana automatically taking Steve's side. This was Sybil Marshall— a woman with a reputation for seeking out the latest gossip, according to Patsy, and sharing it with others.

"It was nothing," she mumbled and hid her dismay behind sipping her tea.

"Oh, my dear, men can be the most exasperating creatures," Sybil declared with a dramatic wave of her manicured nails. "Just when you think you've got a handle on the way they tick, they come along and do or say something that makes you wonder why on earth you ever thought you might know or understand them."

"Oh, Steve is not—"

"Of course he is," Sybil assured her. "Wonderful and loving and head over heels for you—in his way. But he's a man, my dear, and men have this other side to them. In my Chuck's case it's business, maybe Steve's as well. I mean, he's just been in this job a few weeks after all, wants to prove himself to Dawson? Is that it? Did the two of you argue over all the time he's been spending working?"

"He's happy in his work," Heidi attested.

"Of course he is," Sybil said. "But you young folks today lead such complicated lives—his work, your work. Just finding the time to sit down for a meal much less to plan a proper wedding must be a challenge." She set down her tea mug and lifted Heidi's left hand. "What a nice little engagement ring. For a first diamond that's quite impressive." She waved her own ring finger at Heidi. "This is my first—no doubt my last," she confided with a laugh. "I mean, there are some people that like to stack rings on every finger, but give me plain and simple. It's all I need."

Heidi resisted the urge to glance around at the over-the-top decor of the motor home. Instead she fingered her own ring. One thing Sybil said sunk in. Heidi didn't need multiple rings as a testament to Steve's love for her. "Well, this one's really special," she said. "It was his mother's." *And he has entrusted it to me,* she thought, fully appreciating the enormity of that gift for perhaps the first time since Steve had proposed.

And suddenly tears were rolling down her cheeks. Tears that had little to do with Sybil Marshall, although Heidi was vaguely aware that in her version of this visit, Sybil would likely take full credit for bringing the lovebirds back together again.

"Thanks for the tea—and the sympathy, Mrs. Marshall," she said as she got to her feet and edged toward the door. "I think the rain's let up and even so, I want…need to…"

Sybil stood and hugged her. "I told you before. Call me Sybil. Now, you go on back to your man there. He's waiting for you."

"Thanks," Heidi called as she collected Buster and took off.

"Anytime," Sybil called back.

Heidi trotted alongside Buster through the narrow lanes of the makeshift village. Here and there a door was open and she could hear music or laughter coming from inside a motor home. When she turned the corner and saw the smaller trailer with its temporary black-and-white sign, she slowed her step. It was dusk and she could see that the new light was on over the kitchen sink.

Home, she thought as she broke into a run, understanding as she never had before that it wasn't bricks and mortar. It was wherever Steve was—wherever they could be together.

"Honey?" she called as she swung open the door and Buster burst in ahead of her. The sense of emptiness was overwhelming. She saw the sheet of yellow legal paper on the white Corian counter.

Had to go to the shop in Concord. Could be a late one. Get some rest and I'll call you in the morning. We will work this out.
Love you, S

She saw that he had not only installed the light over the sink, but washed and dried the supper dishes as well. She saw the pages she'd printed off the Internet earlier stacked in a neat pile next to her computer. He'd obviously looked at them—and knowing Steve as she did—she was sure he had read them. She just hoped that he had seen something more hopeful in the information she'd uncovered than she had. For one thing was certain, it was going to take a minor miracle and a lot longer than a couple of days to uncover the proof they needed.

BUT THE MORNING brought no miracles. When Heidi reached the clinic, Clare showed her the latest blog chatter among animal rights activists. "Of course, these are some of the more radical players," Clare said. "Nevertheless, they've clearly latched on to the merger between VF and Vitality as a possible venue for action. The question, of course, is what action."

"We need to call Chester," Heidi said. "But tell him what?"

Clare's expression was grim as she continued to study blog entries. "Well, for starters, he might want to rethink this whole purchase of Vitality."

"I'm pretty sure it's a done deal," Heidi said and returned to her office to make the call. Chester's assistant told Heidi that he was in meetings for the morning and politely reminded Heidi that she was scheduled to meet Chester and the members of the board at four at the speedway for the tour of the mobile unit.

"Is there any way I might be able to speak with Mr. Honeycutt first, without the presence of the board members?"

"He has half an hour free at noon," she said.

"I'd like to take that opening at noon," Heidi said.

"Very well. Noon here. You and Mr. Honeycutt. Then four o'clock at the speedway for the tour?"

"Perfect. Thank you." After Heidi hung up, she went in search of Clare.

"So, that's a plus," Clare agreed after Heidi had told her about getting in to see Chester before the tour. "At least it buys you some time."

"Buys *us* some time," Heidi reminded her. "We're in this together, remember?"

Clare frowned. "Not really. You need to stay focused on what's best for you—and Steve. This thing isn't just a simple matter of principle for either of you. It affects everything. Your careers, your personal life, your entire future."

Heidi couldn't help thinking that Clare was overdramatizing the situation. On the other hand, given the effect the situation had already had on their relationship perhaps Clare had a point. There was no doubt that at the moment the only options she had came with significant price tags. If she chose to abandon her principles related to animal rights and disassociated herself from Clare's clinic to manage the mobile pet care unit under the auspices of Vittle Farms' underwriting, what did that say about her as a vet? As a person?

On the other hand, during the long night just past, it had started to dawn on her how effortlessly this entire thing had come together. And even though Steve had never said anything, he had to have had a hand in that beyond the call he'd made to Roger Clark. Her guess was that he'd gotten Kent involved, and

Kent had prodded Dawson to back the idea. If she refused the funding from Vittle Farms and abandoned the idea of the mobile pet care unit in order to cling to her principles, then how would that come back to hurt Steve and his career, not to mention her relationship with Steve's family?

"Uh-oh," Clare said, her voice barely above a whisper as she scrolled through blog entries, scanning them quickly, her eyes widening with alarm.

Heidi almost laughed. How could things possibly get any worse than they already were? "What?" she asked when she saw the look on Clare's face.

"A couple of the more radical animal rights groups have decided that tomorrow's race would be the perfect time to drive home a message. They're calling for a rally—probably picketing Vittle Farms—tomorrow." At the horror she saw on Heidi's face, she raised her hands in self-defense. "I swear I had nothing to do with this."

"But you could stop them," Heidi pleaded.

"It's too late," Clare said. "That train has already left the station—literally. They've rented buses and they'll be here by tomorrow. Several hundred demonstrators if I can believe the e-mail I just got inviting me to speak to the group."

"We have to warn them—Chester, Dawson, Kent," Heidi said. "Amy Barber has come up with this idea to hand out Vitality lip gloss to all female fans this weekend," Heidi said. She ran to her desk and dug through her purse for the sample Amy had handed her—a bright red lip gloss in a blue metallic tube renamed Racin' Red and carrying the No. 427 to match Kent's stock car.

"You have to stop them from coming," Heidi said, handing Clare the sample.

"I can't do that," Clare said. "I won't accept the invitation to speak to the group, but beyond that… You have to appreciate that I have something to lose here as well, Heidi."

"But this is our business. You have to choose."

"I am choosing. I am doing the best I can by not speaking out, but Heidi, until we have proof one way or the other about these rumors, you can't seriously expect me to turn my back on this."

"Then help me get the proof. Let's settle this once and for all."

"It's not that simple and you know it. I saw the research you started. You've barely scratched the surface. It could take weeks—even months—to discover what you need."

She was right, of course. Heidi cast around for some feasible action she could take. "I still have to let Chester know what's happening," she said. "Come with me?"

"Somebody has to mind the store," Clare said with a weak smile, and Heidi understood that her refusal had nothing to do with the clinic and everything to do with protecting her reputation as the chief spokesperson for animal rights. "Go on. You'll be late."

On her way for her meeting with Chester, Heidi called Steve's office. Voice mail. Realizing he was probably at the speedway for last-minute meetings before Saturday's race, she hung up and tried his cell. Voice mail. By now she had reached the entry to Vittle Farms. She turned in.

"I have an appointment to see Chester Honeycutt," she told the receptionist.

"Your name?" the man asked, eyeing her windblown curls and white lab coat stained with the aftermath of her struggle to calm a half-crazed calico cat who was bleeding profusely from a ripped claw earlier that morning. In her haste to get to her meeting with Chester on time, she'd forgotten she was wearing it.

Aware that she must resemble the very fanatics she had come to warn the chief executive officer about, Heidi forced herself to take a deep calming breath and smile. "I'm Dr. Heidi Kramer, the veterinarian." She shrugged out of her lab coat and folded it over one arm.

The receptionist smiled warily, taking in the more presentable black jeans and green-and-white print peasant blouse she wore under the lab coat. "Yes, we heard about the animal clinic you're putting together for NASCAR. There was an item in the employee news—"

"My appointment is for noon. I know I'm a little late—"

The young man pressed a button on the switchboard and adjusted the headset he wore. "Terry? I have Dr. Kramer here to see Mr. Honeycutt." Apparently, Terry had validated the appointment. "Seventh floor," the receptionist said, indicating the elevator across the expanse of the lobby.

On the ride up, Heidi tried to figure out what she was going to say and how she could warn Chester without the CEO assuming that somehow she and Clare were behind tomorrow's protest. The elevator glided to a smooth stop and the doors slid open to reveal Dawson Ritter standing there laughing as Chester pumped his hand and pounded him on the back. Seeing the two high-powered businessmen, Heidi's confidence sagged even further.

"Heidi!" Dawson Ritter was as surprised to see her as she had been to find him standing outside the elevator doors. "Chester, you know Dr. Heidi Kramer, our animal expert and head of the new mobile pet care clinic for the tour."

Chester offered her his hand. "We're old friends—or at least she's the best friend my dog ever had."

"How's Macho doing?" Heidi asked politely, stepping clear of the elevator so Dawson could release it.

"Fine. Never better."

Heidi could see that Dawson Ritter was definitely curious about why she was seeing Chester. The ever-efficient Terry only added to the drama by announcing, "Dr. Kramer wanted to see you prior to this afternoon's tour of the mobile pet care clinic. You had this next half hour free, Mr. Honeycutt."

Oh, gee, thanks for putting me directly in the spotlight, Heidi thought, but knew she had no one to blame but herself. What was she going to say? *I hate to tell you this, Chester, but I'm pretty sure you just spent a gazillion dollars on a company that's going to cause you no end of problems?*

"Yes, well, I thought that perhaps before I met your guests…"

Chester Honeycutt's smile remained fixed, but his eyes studied her closely. "Absolutely. Would you like to step into my office?"

"Thank you," Heidi said as she crossed the reception area to the open double doors of the executive suite. To her surprise both Dawson and Chester followed her.

"No calls, Terry," Chester said just before he closed the doors with a soft click. "Now then, Heidi, what's this all about?" He indicated one of two cloth chairs at his desk and as she sat down, Dawson continued to stand next to the vacant one.

"Heidi?"

Heidi's glance fell on a box filled with the lip gloss samples to be handed out at the race. It seemed as good a place to start as any. "You can't distribute those. At least not this weekend. You see, we're going to need time—Clare and I—"

Both men blew out huffs of relief as Dawson chuckled. "Heidi, it doesn't matter if you're fully up and running with the unit this weekend. It's a trial run. Everyone understands that working out the kinks in these things takes time."

"No," Heidi protested a little too loudly in her zeal to make them understand. This time Dawson sat down and both men gave her their undivided attention.

"Perhaps you should explain precisely why you needed to see me in advance of the tour," Chester said, and she did not miss the way his tone had shifted to something more formal and wary.

Heidi took a moment to regroup. She reminded herself that in many ways she was about to do this man an enormous favor. "You have a problem—with Vitality. There is no proof that their products are free of animal-testing violations, at least when it comes to the ingredients they use," she began.

Both men took a moment to dissect the convoluted sentence. "And there is no proof to the contrary," Honeycutt replied.

"That's true. However, if they have nothing to hide then why have they never applied for certification by the CCIC? It's become pretty standard in the industry."

Honeycutt rocked back in his chair and templed his fingers as he studied her. "Heidi...Dr. Kramer, I can understand that such news might cause you—and your partner—to have some serious concerns and I appreciate that. But let me set your minds at ease. In acquiring any asset, as you may imagine, Vittle Farms does a great deal of due diligence. We are aware of the myths and rumors that have circulated for some time related to Vitality's production and testing processes. Having said that, we are completely satisfied that Vitality is everything they represent themselves to be or we would not have acquired the business."

"But the rumors persist and whether or not there is any truth to them, people take them seriously. Some people take them so seriously that they are organizing a protest." She hadn't meant to just blurt that out. She'd come here to calmly discuss the matter of funding the clinic with Chester—and to warn him about the protest, of course. But the expression on the faces of both men told her what they had heard was her last statement.

"You mean, these people are on their way here now?" Dawson asked.

"Yes. A group of activists have rented buses and called for volunteers to stage something during this race weekend. Best guess is that they plan to picket the VF headquarters, blocking traffic on 29 as people make their way to the race." She picked up one of the lip gloss samples. "Handing these out is like waving a red flag in front of them and could just make things worse."

Chester maintained an aura of calm, although his eyes flickered over to Dawson. "We'll alert security and law enforcement in the area," he said, as if the two of them were developing their plan of action on the spot.

"Press release?" Dawson asked.

"No."

"But—" Heidi protested.

"The minute you give such groups an opening by making a public statement, the worse things get. I know what I'm doing, Heidi." Chester stood, indicating the end of the meeting. "Thank you for the heads-up on this. I'll look forward to seeing you later at the speedway. And Heidi? I prefer we keep this matter between us for now."

That's it? Heidi wanted to scream.

Chester must have read her expression. "I've been in this business long enough to know that the best way to handle such things is to be prepared behind the scenes," he said quietly. "Refusing to give any public indication of concern—to get drawn into the fight—is usually best." He checked his watch.

Heidi dropped the lip gloss back into the bowl on Chester's desk. "But maybe you could postpone giving out the samples?"

Chester smiled. "Business as usual, Heidi. Otherwise the other guys win without really having to try."

Dawson Ritter stood as well and nodded. "Couldn't agree more, Chester," he said. "Heidi, I'll walk out with you." It was not a question but a command.

CHAPTER FOURTEEN

HEIDI COULDN'T HELP noticing that Dawson Ritter was polite but distant on the elevator ride down to the lobby. She was grateful that as they were about to part ways in the visitor parking lot, her cell phone rang, making it possible to leave Steve's boss with an apologetic smile and a wave.

"Where are you?" Steve asked.

"I was just going to ask you the same thing." They were talking like two acquaintances who might get together for coffee. Certainly not like a man and a woman who had recently promised to spend the rest of their lives together.

"Nana called. I told her we might come by the farm for supper, then help her and Milo pack up for the weekend, okay?"

"Sounds like a plan." Heidi hesitated. They hadn't seen or talked to each other since she'd walked out the night before. True to his word, Steve had called earlier that morning, but Heidi had been in the shower and by the time she called back he was in meetings. "Are we okay?" she asked softly.

His laugh was primed with relief. "Oh, honey, sure. It'll take more than a little disagreement to drive me away—if that was the plan."

"That was not the plan and you know it."

"Whew! Had me worried there. I've got to run. How about meeting me at the farm. Dawson's got me in meetings the rest of the day and they could run long and you've got that tour." He hesitated. "You're going through with that, right?"

"Yeah. Four o'clock." She wanted to talk to him about what had happened with Clare. She wanted to let him know that she had tried warning Chester. Of course, Dawson might mention it since he'd sat in on the meeting. But Steve had to go. He blew her a kiss and hung up.

THE TOUR CAME OFF without incident. Four genuinely nice executives—two women and two men and Chester, of course. Roger and Chuck Marshall were there as well. The visitors were properly impressed by everything they saw, obviously having never been quite so up close and personal with the inner workings of NASCAR. It was hard not to appreciate their compliments and pure unadulterated awe at all they were seeing. In any other situation, Heidi would have been delighted that a company represented by such people would be linked to her business. Maybe Steve had a point. Maybe she should consider his idea of her simply managing the clinic—a sort of freelance job like his as a spotter—until she and Clare could clear Vitality's name.

As she bid goodbye to Chester and his guests, Chester took her aside. "Don't worry about a few protesters, Heidi. You've got something really good happening here, and as soon as you get past this race and next week in Dover, we're ready to announce full backing for the rest of this season and all of next."

"You won't announce that this weekend? Or next?"

Chester laughed. "NARS prefers we not be premature about this. They want to be sure you can make the unit work before they go telling the media." Chester patted her back and turned to his guests. He led them across the compound for a tour of the garage and pit area that Heidi had arranged.

A small miracle, Heidi thought as she fished her cell phone out and called Clare with the good news. *Time. They had two whole weeks.*

BY THE TIME she arrived at the farm, Steve was already there. So were several other members of Milo and Nana's extended family. Heidi could hardly miss the fact that the minute she stepped inside the back door, her face wreathed in smiles, all conversation stopped and the others seemed to have a hard time looking at her.

"We need to talk," Steve said, brushing past her and leading the way out into the yard. Steve Grosso rarely lost his temper but there were exceptions to that rule and this was one of them.

"What were you thinking?" he ranted after striding across the yard to a grove of willow trees and then turning on her. "Dawson practically had a coronary when he got back to the office after your little meeting. He chewed me out for what he labeled my 'girlfriend's stunt.' Said you embarrassed him, the team—and yourself. Told me I needed to 'control my woman.'"

In the time they had been dating, Heidi had seen this side of Steve once or twice—always related to something that had happened in a race. This was the first time his temper had been aimed at her. "I thought I should—"

"—question the wisdom of a multimillion-dollar business deal that has nothing to do with you?" Steve ran one hand through his hair and paced back and forth under the willow trees that screened them from view of the house. "Dawson assumed I knew all about your plan to call on Chester. Do you not get that I have just started this job and that for Dawson the jury's still out on me—and the job?"

Heidi bristled at the unfairness of his attack. "Forgive me. I didn't think I needed to clear my business schedule with you— or Dawson. I made an appointment with Chester Honeycutt to discuss something of concern for the mobile pet care unit. I certainly had every right to—"

"You had no right. Not when it affects Kent and the team," he said. "Especially not the day before a major race. You should have talked to me."

"I called," Heidi retorted. "You were in meetings—for a change."

"And when you couldn't reach me, you decided to go off half-cocked on your own? Do you understand the consequences this could have for my job, for our future?"

Your *job*? *What about* my *job*?

"I had an appointment. I went there to warn Chester," Heidi replied, fighting hard to keep her own temper under control. And when Steve stared at her bug-eyed, she added, "At the very least they are going to be picketed—this weekend during the race."

"So there will be protesters along Highway 29. Do you seriously think that's a problem for sixty gazillion fans out for a good time?"

"And at the worst," Heidi continued as if he had not spoken, "there could be a more serious incident. This is coming from the more radical groups and they are capable of much more than just waving a protest sign."

She saw the consequences of this register as Steve paused and stripped the leaves from a branch of the willow. "Clare's behind this, isn't she?"

"Oh, stop blaming Clare just because you don't like her politics. The truth is that Clare was invited to speak to the protesters and she refused."

The sudden silence between them accented the stillness of the air and the bucolic quiet of their setting. Steve stood with his back to her, booted feet planted, shoulders tense, arms folded tightly across his chest. Heidi's head was throbbing with the accumulated tension of the day. She shooed away a droning honeybee hovering around her hair. "I know that your career is important," she said quietly, "for both of us. But it is my career—my business—that was on the line today. That's why I made the appointment to talk to Chester in the first place. Unfortunately by the time I'd told him—and Dawson—about the protest, there was no opening to discuss the main reason I had made the appointment."

"Which was?"

"Funding for the mobile pet care unit," Heidi said, losing patience.

Steve turned to face her but stayed where he was several feet away. "And can't you see that you are making a mountain out of a molehill, Heidi?"

Heidi felt her stomach tighten. "How so?"

Steve's laugh had a sardonic ring to it. "National organic foods company buys national cosmetics company and this affects *local* animal care clinic how?"

Heidi could not believe she was hearing this. She walked the few steps it took to stand toe-to-toe with him. "Try this," she said angrily, "*Local* animal care clinic believes in something and is not willing to compromise those beliefs."

"I do not understand this obsession you have with your job."

"My business," she corrected. "I am really tired of trying to make you understand that this is a part of me—of who I am. I am a veterinarian. My mother gave up a promising—"

"— career for your dad. Got that," Steve said wearily. "You think you had this horrific and unique childhood that has warped you for life. Got that."

Heidi stiffened and turned away from him, twisting the engagement ring round and round her finger as his words hit her.

Steve released a long breath. "Here's what I need you to get, babe. While you insist on seeing everything through the blinders of your past, I'm out here working my backside off to build us a real future." He stepped around so that he was facing her and held out his hand. "So what are we going to do?"

"*You* aren't going to do anything," she said, fighting to maintain her composure for another minute. "It's pretty clear I'm on my own in this and whether you believe it or not, I am taking care of it."

She was thankful that she'd left her purse with keys in the car. The last thing she wanted right now was to face the questioning eyes of any member of the Grosso clan. On her way toward the house Heidi whistled for Buster, who came running and leaped into the backseat as soon as he saw the open car door. When she backed out and made the turn in a spin of gravel, she saw that Steve was still standing under the willow tree.

EVEN THE MOST DIEHARD race fan could not have conjured more picture-perfect weather for race day—clear blue skies, mild temperature and a light breeze. The crowds started gathering early in the morning and continued to build throughout the day until by late afternoon there was an undercurrent of human laughter and conversation every bit as pervasive as the shrill whine of tires on track that later would become the sound track for the festivities.

Heidi was in anything but a festive state of mind when she awoke after spending most of the night stewing over the argument with Steve and one undeniable point—if she couldn't find the proof they needed in the next couple of weeks, what then? Without the backing of a sponsor she and Clare could not afford to run the clinic for NASCAR. They could barely afford the clinic in town. Further, Chuck Marshall had made it crystal clear during the tour that he considered Vittle Farms the only acceptable corporate sponsor for the project.

So, after leaving the farm, she had returned to the mobile pet care unit where she'd left her laptop earlier and continued her search for the evidence they would need. As the evening went from dusk to darkness, she was aware of activity throughout the motor home lot—the laughter of returning drivers and their families, the smell of barbecues, the glow of lights in nearby motor homes. Around eight there had been a knock at her door and Steve's soft voice calling her name. Buster's ears had perked up and he'd raced to the door, but Heidi had kept working. Eventually Steve had given up. Later she had also ignored a second knock, then seen that it was Nana, who headed back to her own motor home. Heidi was surprised at her sudden urge to call out to Nana and invite her in. But she was Steve's family, not hers—not yet. Perhaps not ever.

By two in the morning she was able to locate the main ingredients list for every product that Vitality made and then track down the sources of those ingredients. It was slow going and she often hit dead ends and had to backtrack and take another route. But by four in the morning she had uncovered some solid evidence that at least the key ingredients in Vitality products were untainted as advertised. Encouraged by this progress she had curled up on the sofa with legal pad and pen to map out her next move and promptly fallen asleep.

AT LOOSE ENDS after heading back to his apartment for a sleepless night, Steve arrived at the speedway an hour before he was due at the mandatory spotters' meeting. He released a sigh of relief as he drove past the headquarters for Vittle Farms and saw no signs of protesters. His first thought was to find Heidi and let her know, but when Heidi had left the farm, Nana had advised giving her time. So on his way to the spotters' meeting he bypassed the mobile pet care unit and headed for Milo and Nana's motor home. Nana always had coffee on, plus a way of making sense of things, and he'd already messed this up enough. But just before he started to open the door of Milo's motor home, he overheard a conversation that changed his mind.

"Dawson's rethinking Steve's position," Milo was telling Nana, "and it's all because of that girl butting in where she has no business."

"As I understand it, Heidi was simply trying to warn Chester, and besides, she has every right to voice her concerns where it might affect her business."

"Well, she's made a mess of things, whatever her intentions. Last night Dawson was on a rampage demanding extra security and refusing to say why. Of course, it's hardly a secret that it's because he's expecting some kind of incident. That all leads to talk all around that Vittle Farms is reconsidering their sponsorship."

"Of the mobile clinic?" Nana asked.

"Of Kent," Milo bellowed.

Steve was sure the talk was simply souped-up rumors, but Milo was right about one thing—Heidi's visit to Chester had set this all in motion, whatever her intentions. He had to find a way to make her see that while he understood her concerns, this was neither the time nor the place to keep stirring the pot. Maybe if he spoke with Chuck Marshall, suggested postponing the trial run for the unit until things could calm down a bit.

He glanced at his watch. If he didn't leave for the spotters' meeting right away, they'd be penalized. *After that,* he thought as he strode across the motor home lot and joined the ranks of other spotters and other team members headed for the garage area.

HEIDI CALLED CLARE to report her findings.

"That's good work," Clare said. "Really. Maybe there's a chance—"

"Based on this, surely you could call off the protest group."

There was a pause. "They're already here," she said softly.

Heidi groaned.

"But let me take what you've found to the leaders and see what I can do. Don't give up yet, okay?"

Heidi hung up and stepped outside. She acknowledged the greetings of people she met in the motor home lot as they hurried off to whatever plans they had for the morning. She had lived in the Charlotte area for longer than she had ever lived anywhere in her life. She had gone to vet school here, rented the cottage, taken the job with Clare. And she had met Steve. And now as she stood in the middle of this makeshift neighborhood, she realized that everything she had ever wanted in her life—someone to love, good friends, a real family and a career she was proud of—all of that was hanging in the balance.

Steve was right. While she'd been focused on her past, he had quietly gone about putting together the components of the life she'd dreamed of living. The dream she had packed up and carried along with her to every new school, every new neighborhood of her youth. She had to make this work for both of them.

STEVE WAS LEAVING the spotters' meeting when he saw Kent striding toward him. Kent ignored the whispered comments of recognition from fans who had earned passes to the infield and he did not stop for pictures or autographs.

"What's up?" Steve asked, assuming that once again there had been a blowup in the garage between Kent and Neil.

Kent passed him without so much as a glance and kept walking. "Go check out the car," he muttered angrily.

The garage area was buzzing when Steve reached it. He flashed his pass at security and ran toward the place where it seemed everyone in the area had gathered. Squeezing past the crowd standing four deep, Steve broke into the open.

In the center of the crowd was Kent's race car. The windshield, hood, roof and trunk were splattered with red paint, and on the ground around it were the trampled remains of dozens of blue metallic containers of Racin' Red lip gloss.

"How?" Steve needed no other words as Neil came alongside him and placed a hand on his shoulder.

"They came in like one of the tour groups, had their credentials and everything. Then all of a sudden as we were moving the car, they just swarmed over it. Tobey nearly got himself trampled."

"Where was security?"

"They were on top of it almost instantly. They got them and hauled them off, but the damage was already done."

Steve ran a finger through the red muck on the windshield.

"Apparently the paint's supposed to be the blood of innocent animals," Neil explained. "The sticky stuff is that lip goop."

Steve looked over the car from one end to the other. "Can you get it cleaned up?" he asked.

"We'll have to use the backup," Neil said, shaking his head slowly. "No way the officials will let this go."

"Well, get this one out of here," Steve said and was grateful but hardly surprised that crew members from other teams rallied around to help get the car moved out of the view of curious fans.

"Grosso!"

Steve saw Dawson Ritter bearing down on him. "Meeting in the hauler lounge in fifteen," the owner barked. "In the meantime you find that woman of yours and her rabble-rousing partner and tie them both to a post if you have to." Without missing a step, he turned and followed Neil and the car into the garage.

Steve punched in Heidi's number on his cell. No answer, so he sprinted across the asphalt and into the motor home lot. When he rounded the corner, he heard her laughing. Then he saw her standing next to the portable examination table under the portico of the mobile pet care unit. She was examining a large German shepherd, and standing next to her was a uniformed member of the state police.

"Boomer's a great name for a bomb-sniffing dog," Heidi was saying as she wrapped the dog's front paw with a strip of gauze and tore off a piece of tape with her teeth to hold it in place. "Almost like new," she declared as she helped Boomer off the table and handed his leash to the officer. "Stop by if you see any drainage on the bandage," she advised.

Steve waited until the officer had left before he approached her.

"Heidi?"

SHE HAD BEEN STORING her supplies, her back to him, and she turned at the sound of his voice. At the same time Patsy came around the corner from the opposite direction.

"Did you know about this? Did you know they were planning to sabotage Kent?" she growled through the gritted teeth of a mother lion determined to protect her cub.

Heidi glanced from Patsy to Steve. "What's happened?"

"The protesters got into the garage area," Steve explained, his eyes probing hers. "They vandalized Kent's car by spraying it with paint and smearing lip gloss from the samples on it. He can't drive it."

"He's out of the race?" Heidi's legs felt suddenly as if they were filled with liquid.

"He has to drive the backup car," Patsy told her. "He's prepared for the race in one car and now, just hours before the race, he has to switch."

"I…what can I do?"

Patsy let out a bark of a laugh. "From everything I'm hearing, you've done more than enough."

"Aunt Patsy, please," Steve said. "Heidi, tell me you didn't know about this."

"How can you even think that?" she whispered.

"That's all I need to know. Just do me a favor and go stay with Nana until after the race."

"But—"

He glanced back toward the garage area. "I have a meeting with Dawson. Please do this, okay?"

"Let me go to the meeting with you," she pleaded. "I can explain things to Dawson."

"No. Just stay out of it before you make things worse than they already are." Steve was already sprinting back toward the hauler. Patsy waited for Heidi to go ahead of her and then followed a step behind like a warden walking a perp.

"Sit," Patsy ordered as soon as they were inside Nana's motor home. "I need some espresso," she muttered and headed for the kitchen area.

"I can explain everything that's happened," Heidi told Nana, ignoring Patsy and her commands.

But Patsy interrupted her, recounting the details of the demonstrators vandalizing Kent's car. "How they got the paint in, I'll never know," she groused from the kitchen.

"Water bottles," Heidi said in a voice devoid of emotion. "The opaque ones."

"You knew that?" Patsy shouted, bearing down on her.

"No," Heidi protested. "It's just a guess. It's a tactic that's been used in other situations."

Both Grosso women went silent as they digested the fact that Heidi was well aware of how the act had been accomplished.

"And I understand they had split up into several different tour groups," Patsy said, eyeing Heidi closely as she sipped her espresso.

Heidi nodded, aware but not caring that in their eyes she was condemning herself with every word. "They would have set it up that way so as not to raise suspicion when the group was so large. The ploy also would give them more mobility. While attention was on one group the others could move in."

"You've done this?" Nana was rarely shocked, but this was beyond even her ability to take in stride.

"She knew about it," Patsy snapped.

Heidi glanced up at Patsy and then Nana. "No, I haven't," she protested. "Never. And I didn't know, but I've seen it done, heard about the tactics from—"

"Your partner in crime? From Clare Wilson?"

"She didn't orchestrate this," Heidi said, rushing to Clare's defense. "She would never—" She stood up, her fists clenched at her sides. "Look, I tried to warn them."

"Oh, we heard all about your little meeting with Chester," Patsy said. "Did you give one second's thought to how all of this might be bad for Kent? Forget Kent. What about Steve? You just don't go to the CEO of a major company pouring millions into sponsoring a NASCAR team and start stirring up trouble."

"What would you have had me do instead?" Heidi shouted back, standing her ground. "Ignore the fact that protesters were on the way?"

"Here's an idea. You might have come to the family first and given us the chance to figure this out together," Patsy said in a low voice that was far more intimidating than her shouting. "If you want to be part of this family," she started to add, but then Heidi took a step closer.

"I did what I thought best for everyone. What I wanted was to protect this family—one I hoped I was becoming part of."

She sat down on the sofa. "What I want most of all," she whispered, "is for it to be last week." She felt the sofa cushions sag beside her and then Nana's arm was around her.

"You want an espresso?" she heard Patsy ask after a moment.

CHAPTER FIFTEEN

CONVERSATION STOPPED as soon as Steve walked onto the boardwalk at the top of the speedway just before the race was about to start. He nodded to a couple of fellow spotters, signed in with the official who failed to crack his usual joke and then concentrated on getting set for the race. He focused and refocused his binoculars, using them as a barrier to making eye contact with those around him.

He was well aware that the vandalizing of Kent's car had been the hot topic of conversation before his arrival. He had no doubt that gossip about Heidi and her association with the animal rights movement had also been a subject that had generated laughs and even crude jokes.

He hooked the strap of his binoculars around his neck and put on his headset, adjusting the microphone and testing the signal with the crew down below. He caught Dennis Murphy smirking at him. *Your ass is on the line, golden boy,* Steve could almost hear the man thinking.

Well, it was true. The meeting in the hauler hadn't gone well. Dawson had been furious and Kent had remained silent, stewing over the damage to his car until Neil had stuck his head in the door and announced that the backup was ready. At that, Kent had leaped to his feet, stepped past Steve without a glance and headed for the garage to see for himself.

"You up for spotting this thing?" Dawson had challenged once Kent left.

"Yes, sir," Steve had replied.

"Because that's your own flesh and blood going out there, with a good chance to repeat as NASCAR Sprint Cup Series champ this year, in spite of everything. So if you can't get your head around—"

"I said I'm ready," Steve growled as he stood and faced Dawson eye to eye.

Dawson brushed past Steve and left the hauler.

After Steve had double-checked his equipment, he stood at the railing and ran through a series of stretching exercises that he would repeat several times over the long haul of the six-hundred-mile race.

He watched the last of the prerace pageantry without really seeing or hearing any of it. His mind was on Heidi. The last twenty-four hours had been something of a ten-car pileup played out in excruciating slow motion. In a race, he was used to things happening in a split second that changed everything. In life? Not so much.

"You ready up there?"

Kent's voice brought him back to the moment at hand. It was the first time they'd spoken since the meeting with Dawson. "Yeah."

"How's it feeling?" Steve heard Neil ask and knew the crew chief was still worried about the difference Kent might be experiencing with the backup car.

"I'll be fine. I just want to get going." Kent's reply was terse and not at all reassuring.

"All right, buddy," Neil replied. "Just hang in there."

Under other circumstances it might have been funny that Neil—the hothead—was the one offering words intended to calm and diffuse the tension. But too much had happened in the short time before the race and no one was in the mood for kidding around.

"Okay. Let's have a good race, boys," Kent said, but his voice sounded strained and anything but the normal easygoing this-is-gonna-be-fun tone they were all used to hearing from the driver right before the green flag fell.

Steve made one final adjustment to his headset and stepped to the railing, his eyes scanning the lineup, memorizing their start positions and calculating Kent's best chance for positioning himself in the early part of the race.

Someone jostled his arm and he looked over to see Dennis Murphy squeezing into place next to him. This was an unusual move. Dennis usually spotted from a position several yards farther along the railing. Their eyes met and Dennis grinned then laughed as he murmured something into his microphone.

Too many distractions, Steve thought as he turned his attention back to the track. The simultaneous rumble of forty-three engines bounced around the speedway as all the fans roared their approval from their positions in the stands, the corporate suites and the infield.

The green flag dropped and the pack of cars moved forward almost as a unit. Steve felt his brain shift into race mode.

"Clear," he said. "Go outside." He felt his breathing calm. Gone was the tension of the last several hours, replaced now by the confidence of knowing that at least in this situation, he was calling the shots.

HEIDI STARED BLINDLY at the muted television. Early on there was a crash that eliminated several cars. The caution flag came out and the remaining cars slowed to what seemed more like a crawl while the wreckers cleared the tracks of mangled cars and debris. Then the pace car turned off and the race was on again.

In the silence of the room Heidi imagined Steve's quiet, calm voice as he guided Kent through the pack and into the clear. She thought about the race she had watched with him the night he'd proposed—how proud she had been of him, how amazing he was in his ability to completely concentrate on the job before him. She thought about their last couple of conversations—the hard edge to his voice, the pleading with her to stop messing things up for him—them.

As the race reached its halfway point, she curled more tightly into the corner of the sofa. Uncharacteristically unsettled by the events of the last few days, Nana abandoned her usual race position. Instead she quietly went about packing up leftovers and gathering clothing and personal items she would want in the week between now and next week's race in Dover, while Patsy stared unseeing at the television screen.

There would be no tailgating tonight. The village would be virtually deserted. Out-of-town drivers would head directly from the track to the airport, many of them well on their way home before the last fan left the parking lot. Race cars and tool bays would be loaded onto haulers. Tomorrow the motor homes would be readied for the trip to Dover. And this time next week the "village" in Charlotte would be little more than an empty parking lot.

"I need to let Buster out and feed him," Heidi said.

"I'll do it," Patsy replied.

"I'm not going to make a run for it," Heidi told her. "I just need to feed my dog."

"Some fresh air will be good for you. Help clear your head," Nana said.

"Thank you." Heidi stepped around Patsy and left the motor home.

Outside the noise-free environment of the motor home, she was surrounded by sound. The whine of the race cars as they made turn two and flashed by on the back straightaway. The undercurrent of the more distant cheers from the crowd filling the stands and the more distinct shouts and laughter coming from the infield crowd. The activity in the compound from the joyful shrieks of the children gathered under the twin canopies of the child-care area to the cheers and moans arising from gatherings outside motor homes she passed on her way back to her motor home.

Hers. Theirs. But for how long?

She opened the door and Buster bounded out and straight into the kennel she'd set up for him. Heidi believed in kennel training her dogs. That way, when she took Buster for a walk, his mind was on the exercise and not finding a bathroom. When Buster finished his business, she cleaned up the area and washed it down with the hose. In the time it took to complete these tasks the cars had come round several times. She glanced at the leaderboard and saw the number of remaining laps shift to twenty. In less than half an hour—barring any major mishap—the race would be over.

Then what?

She pulled out a large bag of dry dog food from the storage area under the motor home and poured some into Buster's bowl. While he attacked the food, she filled his water bowl from the hose. Then she sat down on the step to wait for him to finish.

The sun had set but the bright lights of the speedway lit up the infield as if it were high noon. Heidi looked across the expanse past the garage area and up to the suites where no doubt Dawson Ritter sat deciding Steve's fate. And above that, somewhere along the roof was Steve.

As she turned the corner on her way back to Nana's with Buster at her side, she glanced up at the leaderboard. Ten laps to go. She scanned the stack of numbers. Kent was in third place right behind Justin.

At least one thing's going well, Heidi thought.

WITH TEN LAPS TO GO Steve scanned the field. Seven cars were
bunched together running for the lead. Bart Branch had held the
lead for the last half-dozen laps but Kent was in solid position
to make his move. Steve tried not to think about how a win
tonight on top of last week's win would go a long way toward
calming Dawson's ruffled feathers.

"Three wide," he said, letting Kent know he was coming up
on a pack of three cars running side by side.

As the pack headed for turn one, Kent edged closer to the
outside car that was running bumper to bumper behind Justin.
Suddenly the inside car spun out, sending the middle car careening into the wall then back across the track into the infield,
creating a curtain of black smoke so thick that Steve was having
trouble seeing around or through it.

"I can't see ahead," Kent reported.

Steve scanned the track, mentally accounting for each car. In
the split second it took to take in the scene, he saw that Bart
Branch had moved into the clear and was taking a commanding
lead while the three cars Kent had been ready to pass were still
twirling around the track spewing smoke and debris.

Justin. Where was Justin?

"I'm going," Kent barked.

"Stay high," Steve instructed, knowing it was the safest route.
But even as the words left his mouth the familiar orange and brown
of Justin's car emerged from the smoke. "Low," Steve amended a
tenth of a second before he saw Justin cut Kent off high on turn
two. Next to him he heard Dennis Murphy's victorious yelp.

In what seemed like slow motion, fans leaped to their feet as
they watched Kent's car pirouette down the bank of the turn, into
the infield where it rolled once, landing upright but facing the
wrong way.

As everyone held their breaths, the car sat for half a second,
then the engine fired, emitting a plume of black smoke. The

crowd roared as Kent eased it back onto the track and followed the rest of the field behind the pace car until he reached the pit area.

While the crew worked feverishly to repair what damage they could and get Kent back onto the track before the caution was lifted, Steve turned to the official behind him.

"That's reckless driving on the part of Justin Murphy," Steve argued, ignoring Dennis who had followed him over to the official. "Call it."

"You want reckless," Dennis argued. "Your guy couldn't see and went anyway. We were gonna win this thing." He moved toe-to-toe with Steve, so close that his spittle hit Steve's face.

Without thinking, Steve shoved Dennis with his forearm as he turned back to the railing. The next thing he knew, the official was next to him.

"Get your gear and tell your crew, Grosso," he said. "You're finished tonight and suspended for one race."

The last thing Steve saw as he picked up his duffel and headed for the stairs was Dennis laughing as he spoke to Justin through the two-way and watched Steve leave.

HEIDI FELT as much as heard the sudden silence coming from the track. She glanced up and saw the fans on their feet, straining to see something on the track. She watched as the pace car led the field of cars that had made it this far in the race around the track. Mentally she clicked off each car and driver.

Kent. Where was Kent?

She stood rooted to the spot, her heart in her throat. And then she saw his car limping badly as it followed the pack around and into the pit area. She ran the rest of the way back to Nana's motor home and burst through the door, her eyes moving immediately to the television.

"He's all right," Nana said more to Patsy than to Heidi. "See?

There he goes," she added as the cameras followed Kent's car out of the pit area and back onto the track.

"But he's out of it," Patsy said. "He was right up there and…maybe if he'd been driving his best car—" She got up and left.

"I have to find Steve," Heidi told Nana.

Nana restrained her with a firm hand to her arm. "Best to let him find you."

IF STEVE THOUGHT Dawson Ritter couldn't get any angrier than he'd been earlier that day, he was wrong. As soon as the race ended, he cleared the suite and sent for Kent, Neil and Steve.

"Sanchez, get both cars loaded and out of here. Have the team meet you at the shop and tell them to expect to pull an all-nighter."

"Yes, sir," Neil mumbled, rolling his baseball hat nervously in his hands.

"Now!" Dawson bellowed when Neil seemed rooted to the floor. After Neil had scurried out—no doubt relieved to be out of the direct line of fire—Dawson turned to Kent. Steve could not help noticing that neither of them had looked directly at him since he'd arrived in the suite.

"You're going to need a spotter for Dover—this one's gotten himself suspended." Then he wheeled around on Steve. "I thought you were smarter than to let yourself be goaded into a shoving match with some little pipsqueak. That's why I hired you in the first place, to take care of trouble, not to make more of it."

"Hey, Dawson," Kent said, "it's been a long rough day for everybody. Cut the guy some slack. We all know that Steve was right. Justin cut me off."

Dawson prowled up and down the rows of plush seating that overlooked the now-deserted track, chewing on his traditional unlit cigar. "Then there's that girlfriend of yours," Dawson said as if Kent hadn't spoken.

"Her name is Heidi," Steve said quietly.

"Ah yes, *Dr.* Kramer," Dawson growled sarcastically. "I need this? I'm trying to run a business here." He glared at Steve.

"Do you want me to resign?" Steve asked.

"I want to fire your ass," Dawson yelled as a food-service worker who'd come to clean up opened and then immediately closed the outer door. Dawson glanced toward the door and lowered his voice. "But I'll give you one week. Conveniently you've gotten yourself suspended, so a week should be more than enough time for you to sit that woman down and tell her she'd better figure out a way to control that partner of hers."

"I'll talk to her," Steve replied tersely, but he wasn't angry at Heidi. This was Justin Murphy's fault.

"You'll do more than talk to her. You'll make her understand that she's jeopardizing everything. And by everything I do mean your future as well as hers."

Steve stood. "I don't like being threatened, Dawson," he said. "Maybe quitting would be the best move."

Dawson champed down on his cigar as he eyed Steve. "Now who's making threats?" he growled. Then he turned and stared out at the field. "Go on. Get out of here, the two of you," he muttered.

CHAPTER SIXTEEN

AS THE GIANT LIGHTS on the far side of the track shut off, Steve made his way across the track toward the infield. He was drained—physically and emotionally. He stood in the middle of a race track and wondered how it was possible that his entire life had changed so dramatically in just one short week. He understood such things in racing. One minute you were riding high and the next it was as if you couldn't catch a break. But how was it possible that a man and a woman who had been walking hand in hand down the same path suddenly found their lives running in parallel lanes that never seemed destined to merge?

As the last light snapped off, Steve saw Heidi watching him from the edge of the track. Ordinarily he would have held out his arms to her, embraced her and assured her—and himself—that everything would be all right. But after everything that had happened he wasn't so sure he could promise that, so he tightened his grip on his duffel and continued to walk toward her.

"Is Kent all right?" she asked, falling into step with him.

"Yeah."

"I heard about the suspension. I'm sorry."

He felt the full force of the day's frustrations well within him. "Heidi, you had nothing to do with my getting suspended, so don't take that on, okay?"

She said nothing. Just widened the distance between them—

a distance he'd physically created by carrying his duffel in the hand closest to her.

"Are you going home or staying here tonight?" he asked as they approached the motor home lot, still crowded with trailers, although most of them were now vacant.

"I thought maybe we could—"

Steve stopped and looked down at her. "Tomorrow, okay? I just need some time."

"Let me go see Dawson. I can explain. I can—"

"No." It came out sharper than he'd intended.

She ducked her head.

"Honey, I need to take some time to think this through. I'll call you tomorrow," he promised, reaching out to touch her face.

"Sure," she murmured and watched as he walked away from her across the infield to his truck.

EVER SINCE THE DEATH of his wife, Libby, Larry Grosso had developed the habit of spending long nights in his office at the university. There he would work on complex problems, looking for ways to apply the fundamentals of mathematics to finding their solution. One wall of his office was covered in whiteboard from floor to ceiling and that was usually covered in a giant puzzle of equations and mathematical formulas, each written in different-colored neon dry marker in Larry's distinctive precise and neat handwriting.

"Dad?"

Steve saw his father glance up at the large clock over the door.

Steve pulled out a chair and sat down, stretching his long legs out in front of him and his arms overhead. He could not remember ever being so completely exhausted. "You saw the race?"

Larry grinned and sat down, propping his feet on his desk. "Dean coming in third will drive Patsy nuts," he predicted. Steve knew that he was waiting for Steve to continue, knowing this midnight visit was beyond unusual and must have some cause.

"You saw Kent crash."

"Yeah. Tough. He's okay though?"

"Yeah. It was kind of my fault. In all the smoke I lost sight of Justin Murphy. By the time I spotted him, Kent had decided to go, and Justin cut him off."

"Not deliberately?"

"Looked like malice aforethought to me," Steve replied, using a term his father was fond of applying to such situations.

"So help me understand how this is your fault."

Wasn't it obvious? "I lost sight of the No. 448 car—Justin," he repeated. "When Kent decided to go I first told him to stay high when I should have—"

Larry pushed himself away from the desk and turned to the board. He used his bare hand to clear an area and picked up a green marker. "Let me show you something." He drew two stick figures. "You," he said, pointing to the first. "And Kent."

"Flattering likenesses."

"Pay attention. You see Justin's car at the same time you give Kent the signal to go high. Your eye sends that image to the brain. Your brain must form the thought to send a new message to your mouth and you speak to Kent."

"That's the way it happened."

Larry turned his attention to the figure of Kent, connecting a line from Steve's mouth to Kent's ear. "Kent then must hear your instructions, process them through his brain and take appropriate action."

"Okay," Steve said, sitting forward as he tried to understand the point his father was trying to make.

"Eye, brain, mouth," he said, pointing to each feature on the Steve figure, "to ear, brain, action." He waited a beat. "What's the missing factor?"

Steve shrugged.

"Speed," Larry said, sketching a car around Kent. "And time," he added. "By the time you did your part and Kent processed it on his end, the moment had passed." Larry replaced the cap on the dry marker and placed it back in the tray, then dusted off his hands as if he'd been using chalk.

"I'll run that one past Dawson Ritter and see how it flies with him," Steve said, but he was grateful for the logic his father had presented—logic that permitted him to forgive himself for a crash that could have been a lot worse than it had been.

"What else?" Larry asked as he perched on the edge of the desk so that he was closer to his only child.

"Nothing," Steve said and then amended that to, "Everything."

Larry waited.

"I'm not like you, Dad," Steve said miserably, his head in his hands. "All I know is racing. All I ever wanted to do was be part of this world. I thought we had it all worked out. Heidi has really come around about living on the road during the season—even bringing up kids in that life. I mean, once she hit on the idea of the mobile pet care unit, things were clicking on all cylinders for us. We both got to do the jobs we love. Now, it's like overnight it's all coming apart."

Still his father remained silent. The only sound in the room was the hum of the clock's battery. Finally Larry cleared his throat and went to the whiteboard. This time he used a cloth to erase most of the board. Then he handed Steve a blue marker while he picked up a red one. "Take that marker and list everything you think Heidi is dealing with right now while I list everything you're dealing with."

"It'll be the same list," Steve protested.

"In places," Larry agreed as he began writing. "Finished," he announced a few minutes later. "Now switch places and add anything you think I've missed and I'll do the same for Heidi."

"Now what?" Steve said as he looked at the two lists.

Larry drew a circle between the two lists. In the center of the circle he placed a heart. "That's you and Heidi."

"Sweet. Uh, Dad, I really appreciate your listening and all but it's past one and—"

Larry ignored him as he added concentric circles around the heart. "Okay, here's your assignment. I want you to draw a line from each item on your list and Heidi's to one of these circles. The items that are necessary and nonnegotiable for the two of you to be together and happy go in this circle closest to the heart. Items from the lists that are necessary but negotiable go in the middle circle. Items that are simply smoke screens creating chaos and keeping you from building a life together go in the outermost circle. Got it?"

"Okay, but—" Steve watched as his father once again put down his marker and dusted off his hands. Then to Steve's surprise Larry reached for his jacket and briefcase. "Where are you going?"

"Home. I've been up since dawn. Leave your work on the board there and I'll review it and call you." He read the disbelieving expression on Steve's face and handed Steve a textbook that had been buried under piles of papers on his desk. "If you get stuck, check out the next to last chapter," he added in a less flippant tone. "You came here looking for help, son. Here it is." He tapped the board. "Take it or leave it."

"I NEED COFFEE—preferably intravenously," Steve announced the following morning when he showed up on the doorstep of Heidi's cottage at six-thirty.

"Your cousin is the nurse," Heidi grumbled sleepily. "Go ask her for coffee."

Steve held up a cardboard container and a bag that looked suspiciously like it might contain sweet rolls. "Luckily I brought my own," he said. "Can I come in?"

She heard the hesitancy in his voice. "Only if you plan to share," she said. And even though she was wary given their last several conversations, she stepped back and swung the door wide.

Buster lumbered forward and sniffed the bag. Then he immediately assumed the sit position he knew was mandatory for receiving a treat. His tail thumped out an expectant rhythm on the hardwood floor.

"I didn't forget you," Steve told him as he followed Heidi into the kitchen where she was putting out mugs, plates and spoons. Steve pulled a plain bagel from the bag and dropped it at Buster's feet.

"What time did you get up?" Heidi asked as she took a quart of milk from the refrigerator and filled the creamer. "Juice?" she asked before she shut the door.

Steve shook his head. "I haven't been to bed," he replied as he divided out the treats from the bag of bakery and then filled the coffee mugs. "I drove over to Raleigh last night to see Dad."

Heidi handed him a napkin and spread another across her lap. "And?"

He indicated the manila folder he'd laid on the table. "He gave me—us—an assignment."

"Homework?" This had to be a joke, Steve's way of smoothing over what had happened the day before. He was very good at smoothing things over—but not this time.

"Open it." He watched her over the rim of his mug as she slid open the flap and removed the contents.

"I don't have my contacts in yet," she said irritably, although it was evident that she had no idea what to make of the series of circles with notes in each, all centered around a small heart.

Steve reached for her glasses from the shelf next to the sink, unfolded the stems and handed them to her. "Tell me what you see."

"Well, it's very colorful," she commented as she slowly turned the paper around and read the notations. "You say it's a math problem from your dad?"

"Homework," Steve corrected. "He's going to have a look at it later. How do you think I did?"

Heidi laid the paper aside and reached for a cinnamon roll. "How should I know? I don't know what the problem was." *And frankly I would think that you might realize we have far more serious matters to work out than a silly math problem from Larry.*

"That's just it. You—maybe better than anyone—know exactly what the problem is." He slid the paper between them and pointed to the heart. "This is us, and these—" he pointed to three notes around the heart "—are the things that are most important for us to focus on in the short term—at least I think they are."

She squinted at the tiny scribbles in the smallest circle. *Wedding. Home. Ever after.* She blinked up at him. "I get the wedding part," she said.

"Sorry, I had to reduce things down to the bare essentials to fit them in. *Home,* as in setting up a home together and *ever after,* as in getting started on the next fifty or so years of our life together. Do you agree that in spite of everything going on around us—separately and together—these are the three most important things in our lives—necessary and nonnegotiable?"

She thought for a moment about the clinic, her career and his career then realized that whatever happened in those areas, losing Steve and the love they shared would be far more catastrophic. "I don't know," she said softly. "I don't know anything anymore."

Steve hesitated but continued pointing now to the middle circle where he'd written *Career—Heidi. Career—Steve. Extended family.*

"These things are what Dad referred to in one of the math books he wrote—and left conveniently lying open on his desk last night—as necessary but negotiable. There can be a solution without them but it won't work nearly as well as it will with them as part of the equation."

"You lost me at 'necessary but negotiable.'"

"I love you in part because you are so passionate about your work. You, hopefully, love me at least in part because of the way I approach my job."

"Okay."

"In other words we can't be the people we each fell in love with if we try to change who we are at our individual core." Steve grinned. "That's the 'necessary' piece of it."

"And the negotiable?"

"We have choices. We can choose other similar work that is every bit as rewarding or we can do the same work in a different setting or—"

"What about family?" Heidi tapped her finger on the third word. "Why isn't that here in the inner circle."

"Because this is *extended* family. We can make compromises that will keep that family satisfied as long as those compromises don't require us to toy with these things down here."

Heidi studied the chart for a long moment, then she pointed to the outer circle. "I see you put all the real problems out here." She slowly turned the paper, reading the multiple entries aloud. "Sponsorship—Kent. Sponsorship—mobile clinic. Suspension-slash-Dawson. Vitality-slash-Heidi. You sure filled up this space."

Steve covered her fingers with his. "Honey, those aren't the 'real' problems. Want to know what Dad calls that outer circle?"

Heidi nodded, fighting back tears as the enormity of the roller coaster of the last couple of days fully hit her.

"He calls it his 'chaos circle.' His version of the chaos theory, I assume."

Heidi suppressed a hysterical giggle, even as the tears rolled down her cheeks. "I love your dad," she whispered, "but this makes no sense at all."

"We were both looking at this thing from the outer circle in—or at least I was. But if we start here—" Steve placed his finger over the heart at the center of the page.

"We can solve all of this?" Heidi ran her hand over the larger outer circle.

"I think so," Steve said. "Will you come with me to lunch at Nana's?"

Heidi laughed. "I think Milo and your uncle Dean might prefer to serve me for lunch," she joked. "Not to mention Kent and Tanya."

"At least Dawson won't be there. Say yes. We'll deal with the family today over lunch and then face Dawson tomorrow."

"Can I bring Buster for protection?"

"You can bring Buster, but you've got me for protection," he promised her as he fed her the last bite of the cinnamon roll.

THE ATMOSPHERE AT THE FARM was decidedly more subdued and cooler than it had been a week earlier for the party. Nana welcomed them with open arms, but Milo held back, shaking hands with Steve and nodding at Heidi. Dean's greeting was direct and to the point.

"Well, you messed up, Steve, but it's only a one-race suspension. Coulda been worse."

"Did you and Dawson work things out?" Milo asked as he and Dean scowled at Steve.

Heidi was about to come to Steve's defense, when Nana gently took her by the elbow and steered her toward the back door. "I could use your help," she said, giving Dean a look of warning as she, Nana and Patsy left the men on the deck and went inside.

The three women worked in silence, aware of the low hum of the men's conversation. Heidi realized that what was missing was the usual laughter and kidding around that was such a familiar part of any gathering at the farm. What was also missing was the sound of Steve's voice. Milo and Dean seemed to be doing all the talking.

Itching to move back to the deck, but knowing Nana had probably been right to draw her inside, Heidi sought some topic of conversation that would break the strained silence in the house and cover the rumble of conversation on the deck.

"How's Kent?" she asked. *Actually, where's Kent—and Tanya?*

"Fine," Patsy replied tightly, protecting her son from anything else Heidi might be able to do to hurt him.

"He and Tanya drove out to the lake after the race," Nana said. *And Sophia?*

On cue, Sophia came down the stairs rubbing sleep from her eyes and looking as if she needed at least another couple of hours. When she saw Heidi, she stopped.

"Steve's here?" she asked.

Heidi nodded and Sophia turned around and went back upstairs.

"This is going to be a fun day," Patsy said on a breath of pure exasperation. She passed Heidi without looking at her and followed her daughter upstairs.

Nana watched her go. "Sophia had a difficult night," she explained to Heidi. "She came here for some midnight tea and sympathy and stayed over. Her loyalties are very much divided right now."

Heidi stopped pretending to help with preparations for the meal and sat on one of the bar stools next to the center counter. "Everyone's being completely unfair to Steve," she said. "They've no right to be so mad at him."

Nana raised one eyebrow without looking up as she continued stirring batter for biscuits. "We're not mad, just upset," she said, then added, "And it's not just Steve."

Heidi straightened defensively.

"You must see why we're worried, Heidi. I mean, when Clare didn't call off her protest group? They went right ahead and targeted Kent's car. They nearly cost him his place in the race."

"You've got it wrong," Heidi argued. "Clare was the one who told me about the plan to protest. She didn't know they were planning to vandalize Kent's car, but she did try to warn me so I could warn—"

"And you didn't see that her timing was suspect, not speaking up until it was virtually too late? And given her connections, surely there was someone she could have called, someone who could have—"

Steve cleared his throat. Neither woman knew how long he'd been standing in the mudroom listening to their conversation, but he made his presence known now as he crossed the kitchen and stood next to Heidi. "She thought she was doing the right thing. She *was* doing the right thing."

Nana slowly wiped the counter between them. "We're concerned, Steve," she said. "All of us. Not just for Kent's future but for you and Heidi. How will everything that's happened affect the future you've planned together?"

Steve put his arm around Heidi. "Our future will be fine. And Nana?"

Nana looked up and her eyes were brimming with tears.

"They're just jobs," he said, looking now at Heidi. "We both know they can be replaced. But true love—and family—not so much." He glanced back at Nana. "We could use a little support here until everybody settles down."

Nana laughed and swiped at an errant tear with the dish towel as she came around the counter and joined Steve and Heidi in a group hug.

REINFORCEMENTS FOR STEVE and Heidi arrived in the person of Steve's dad. Larry greeted Steve with a hug and a mur-

mured, "Good job on that homework, son." Then he hugged
Heidi as well.

As the family gathered around the table, Larry selected a
place on the other side of Heidi while Nana sat next to Steve, the
four of them forming a half circle that faced Dean, Patsy, Sophia
and Milo. Heidi had the ridiculous vision of the two groups
lining up for a serious game of Red Rover.

"Dig in," Milo growled as he helped himself to three slices of
ham before passing the platter to Patsy. Those were the last
words spoken as everyone passed serving dishes, filled their
plates and concentrated on eating.

"Well, as the kids would say, this is beyond ridiculous," Nana
huffed as she pushed back from the table and went to the phone.
She punched in a speed dial and waited. "Kent? We need you and
Tanya over here so we can figure this mess out." She paused.
"Don't you tell me what sounds overly dramatic, young man"
she warned. "You're the one sulking up there at the lake. How's
that for bad theater?"

Sophia covered her mouth with her napkin, but Heidi could
see by the way the lines of tension and what had appeared to
be a permanent frown disappeared that she was hiding a smile.
She risked a look at Dean and saw him roll his eyes at Larry.
Then Patsy was on her feet. "Let me talk to him," she said.

"Here's your mother," Nana reported, handing over the
phone and returning to the table. "Pass the sweet potatoes,"
she grumbled.

A subdued Kent and Tanya showed up later that afternoon
after the table had been cleared and the dishes stacked in the dish-
washer. While Steve and Heidi handled kitchen duty, Nana had
put Larry in charge of organizing the family confab.

"You're the least involved," she reasoned. "Besides, on this
occasion we could probably benefit from some of that stuff you
teach over there in Raleigh."

"Thanks for the vote of confidence," Larry said. "I think," he added and kissed Nana's cheek.

But he took his assignment to heart and by the time Nana had organized everyone around the cleared dining-room table and set coffee and dessert on the sideboard for people to help themselves, Larry was ready. He handed them all paper and pen.

"Pop quiz," Kent muttered.

"I want you each to make a list," he began.

When Steve realized where his dad was headed with this and saw his uncle Dean's eyes already starting to glaze over, he stood up. "Dad, if you don't mind, I think I can save everybody a lot of time and effort here."

Larry stepped aside, giving Steve the floor. "Look," he began, running his left hand through his hair as he paced back and forth. "Look," he said again as he stopped and faced them all, "I made a mistake, a big one when I failed to account for Justin's position after the spinout."

Sophia slouched down in her chair and folded her arms tightly across her chest. "How did I not see that Justin was going to be the scapegoat here," she muttered.

"If the shoe fits," Kent replied tersely.

"Be quiet, both of you," Patsy ordered. "Go on, Steve."

"And another one when I shoved Dennis in front of an official and got myself suspended." He attempted a wry smile. "I should have shoved him—just *not* in front of an official."

"You should have knocked the little peanut flat," Dean grumbled. "I mean, if you're going to get yourself suspended, why not make it count," he argued when Patsy nudged him.

"All black humor aside," Steve said, "these are two mistakes that have cost us, perhaps in ways that will go way beyond my not being there in Dover."

Sophia sat up straighter. "You're not seriously thinking Dawson will fire you?" She glanced from Steve to Kent and back again.

Steve shrugged. "It's a distinct possibility."

"You had some distractions," Kent said. "It happens."

"Ah yes, distractions." Steve looked at Heidi and so did everyone else. "Well, if I have to lose my job because I was distracted by the best thing that ever happened to me in my life, then so be it."

"That's real sweet," Dean said, "but you weren't distracted by love, you were distracted because this little lady—"

"Uncle Dean, *this little lady* has agreed to marry me and become part of this family. So be careful what you say next," Steve warned, his voice as even and steady as if he were spotting a race.

"Sorry," Dean muttered in Heidi's general direction.

"If Dawson fires Steve," Milo said, bringing them back to the topic at hand, "then Kent will need to adjust to another spotter in the middle of the season."

"Not to mention he might need another sponsor," Tanya reminded them, and the gloom that had already settled over the room deepened. "Dawson called Kent to tell him that Chester is really upset about the picture on the front page of this morning's paper of Kent's car all covered in that mess."

"And let's not forget that Heidi also has something to lose in all of this," Larry added.

"The mobile clinic," Steve translated when Dean and Kent looked blank.

Heidi could see that other than Nana no one else saw this as much of a sacrifice, and that made her furious.

"She'll still have a job in a field she loves," Sophia noted. "Unlike Steve, who'll be out of racing—maybe for good." She glared at Heidi.

Heidi looked from Sophia to the similarly accusing faces of Kent, Tanya, Dean and Patsy. She had heard everything and said nothing—until now.

She was tired of being the Grosso family punching bag.

"You know what? I apologize for any actions I took that might have *inadvertently* turned out to spill over to members of this family. But I refuse to apologize for actions I took because they were right for me and *my* business—decisions my partner and I are wrestling with that have nothing to do with any of you and are frankly none of your business. And now if you'll excuse me, I've had enough."

She was out the door before Steve could navigate his way around the table to stop her. "Thanks for your support," he grumbled to the others as he headed for the door.

"Let her go, son," his father said. "She needs some time to sort things out and right now you're just one more Grosso in the pack of us circling her."

CHAPTER SEVENTEEN

THEY WERE RIGHT, of course—all of them, Heidi thought as she hurried away from the house down the lane and out to the road. Steve stood to lose the job he loved because of her. And no matter what mathematical theory she applied, putting him in a position of sacrificing the work he was practically born to do went against everything she'd ever dreamed of for him—and for herself.

She thought about the cozy little motor home they'd worked so hard to fix up to live in on the road once they were married. Their home in the NASCAR village. Only she didn't belong there—any more than she belonged back there in the big farmhouse. Any more than she had ever really belonged anywhere. The Grossos accepted her because Steve loved her. Period. If she broke it off and left town...

The blast of a truck horn brought her back to the reality of her circumstances. She was standing well into the road and clenching her fists. She stepped aside as the truck blew past her in the opposite direction, then saw the lane leading to the cemetery. She followed it. *At least I'm not likely to step in front of a truck there,* she thought.

She twisted the ring on her finger as she stood facing Libby Grosso's headstone. "I do love him," she said. "More than I can bear sometimes."

Enough to let him go?

She knew the questions were coming from her own jumbled brain, but she continued to speak to Libby. "That's best for him," she said. "He won't think so, but if he loses his job because of me…if we have to start over somewhere else…he's not a saint and he's bound to come to resent that on some level. Look at my mother."

You're going to break the engagement?

"I'm going to break my heart—and his," Heidi admitted. "But it's for the best. Maybe someday…"

STEVE TOOK his father's advice and did not try to go after Heidi. Instead he stood in the doorway watching her until she turned the curve of the lane and he couldn't see her any longer. When he turned, Kent was standing behind him.

"Sorry, buddy," he said. "Guess we were pretty rough on her."

"You think?" Steve retorted sarcastically and pushed past him.

"Okay, we deserve that," Sophia admitted, coming to sit next to him on the sofa as he stared out the window. "All of us. You have every reason to be ticked off."

Kent sat on the other side of him and Tanya pulled an ottoman closer. Patsy had pulled Dean and Larry into the kitchen to help clear away the untouched coffee and dessert. Milo and Nana were also in the kitchen.

"I'll talk to Dawson," Kent offered. "The car's fine. Justin's move in the race? That stuff happens. We've pulled similar things in our day, right? Dawson will have calmed down by now for sure."

"Don't bank on it," Steve said then buried his face in his hands. "She just wanted to help. She didn't start the demonstration, she was trying to stop it. She wants this thing to work. The mobile clinic, us, but she can't go against who she is."

"We get that." Sophia stroked his back. "Want me to go find Heidi?"

Steve shook his head and stood. "I'll go. Thanks," he added as he looked down at the circle of support that had formed around him. "It'll all work out," he added, but even to himself he sounded a lot less sure than he'd been earlier that morning after he'd shown Heidi his father's math theory that had made such perfect sense—until now.

As he followed the lane to the road, Steve caught a glimpse of Heidi through the trees. She was standing on the opposite side of the road waiting for traffic to pass so she could cross. He breathed a sigh of relief that she was coming back on her own and quickened his step. But when she looked up and saw him standing there waiting for her, she froze and seemed unable to decide on her next move.

Steve held out his arms to her. She slowly crossed the empty road, but when she reached him she took his hand instead of falling into his arms as he had hoped.

"You okay?" he asked.

She kept her eyes lowered. "Would you drive me home, please?" was her answer as she started walking toward the house.

Without going back inside she climbed into Steve's truck while he went to let the others know they were leaving. "I don't know," she heard him say as he left the house. Nana was standing at the screen door. She looked at Heidi. Heidi leaned out the window. "Thank you, Nana," she called. "For everything."

"I'll call you later," Steve promised as he started the engine and drove away.

Heidi knew that he was giving her time but that he was also wondering how best to approach her. "After you left, Kent apologized," he said. "Sophia and Tanya came around as well. They'd like to help if they can."

"That's nice," Heidi replied absentmindedly.

Steve shrugged and kept driving toward town. "Mumble jumble?" he asked after several long moments had passed.

"Yeah. More jumble than mumble, I'm afraid."

He took her hand and squeezed it. "We're going to be fine, honey."

Her silence and thin smile were unnerving.

"You need to stop by the clinic for anything?"

Heidi shook her head and stared out the window.

"You know," she said quietly, "it's been a rough couple of days."

"Kent and Tanya were headed back out to the lake. Do you want to go? Change of scene might be good for both of us?"

"No," Heidi said. "But you should go. It would be great for you and Kent to do a little fishing and get back on track."

"Nope. I can fish anytime." Steve pulled into the driveway of the cottage and cut the engine.

"No, don't come in," she said, putting her hand over his. "I just need to catch up on some sleep. You go on to the lake."

"Will you drive out later?"

"We'll see." She leaned over and kissed him, then waved as he backed down the driveway and turned onto the road.

CHAPTER EIGHTEEN

DRIVING OUT TO THE LAKE gave Steve time to really think about how things had gone at the farm earlier. Having grown up in this crazy family, he was well aware that things were fine on that front. It was how he could expect the situation to go when he returned to work on Tuesday after the holiday that had him concerned. Hopefully the extra day away from the office would allow time for the dust to settle. Hopefully he would still have a job.

But even if he did, how did that solve anything? Without the financial backing from Vittle Farms there was no way Heidi and Clare could afford two places. And without the clinic he and Heidi would have no place in the motor home lot, the neighborhood that Nana had introduced Heidi into, the place where she had begun to see a reasonable chance for raising happy well-adjusted children. He'd be back to spotting and trying to find a real job. They'd be back to staying in hotels and no doubt Heidi would be back to skipping races in order to manage the Kannapolis clinic whenever Clare went out on one of her protests. They'd be right back where they'd started.

Mumble jumble, he thought as his cell rang. *Heidi.*

"Quick nap," he said without preamble. "I'm not even to the lake yet." He scanned the road for a place he could turn around.

"Just wanted to let you know I definitely won't be at the lake," Heidi said. "You go on and enjoy the rest of the day with Kent. You two need some time," she added.

He analyzed the tone of her voice. "You sound better," he said.

"Yeah. Just need to get my bearings."

"Fresh start?" he asked.

"Something like that."

They hung up. Steve reached over and turned up the radio. *Fresh start.* Maybe that was the answer. What if they started over somewhere else—Phoenix maybe? He could look for a job at the race track there. Heidi could set up her clinic or work for another one in the city. They'd give up being on the tour, but they'd still have jobs in fields they loved and really settle down. Maybe he'd get back into racing on a smaller scale—build his own car and find a local dirt track to run it. He drummed his fingers on the steering wheel in time to the pulsing rock beat of the music. He turned onto the dirt road that led back through the woods to Kent's lake cottage and floored it.

"DAWSON WILL COOL DOWN," Kent said as he and Steve cast their lines into the lake from the edge of the pier. "Trust me. You've got nothing to worry about. On the other hand, I don't want you to think this is all about me or anything," he joked, "but I'm the one who has to deal with a substitute spotter in Dover next week."

Steve reeled in his line and threw it out again. "Jack Bennett is available. He's one of the best and you've worked with him before."

Kent shrugged. "Yeah. He's okay in a pinch, I guess."

"What if it were more than that?" Steve asked, concentrating on the tip of his rod.

"I told you, stop worrying about Dawson firing you. At least as my spotter. He's not going to switch in midseason, and by the end of the season—"

"What if I were to resign?"

A fish bit and jerked at Kent's line—their first bite all afternoon. "Are you nuts?" he yelled as he reeled and then let the fish run and then reeled some more.

"Dead serious," Steve said as he laid his fishing pole on the pier and picked up the net. "Nice one," he commented as he scooped Kent's catch out of the water.

"Throw him back," Kent said as Steve knelt to remove the hook from the fish's mouth. "I'm fixing ribs on the grill for supper." He sat on the pier and watched as Steve released the fish gently back into the lake. "Tell me you're not seriously thinking about quitting?"

"Resigning," Steve corrected.

"Same thing," Kent argued. "Why?"

Steve ran through the logic behind his decision while Kent listened, openmouthed. "You'd give it all up for her?"

"Wouldn't you give up driving for Tanya?"

"Yeah, but she'd never ask me to do that," Kent pointed out.

"Heidi's not asking me to do this. She doesn't know a thing about it—and I don't want her to know yet because she'll just think it's somehow her fault. So don't go telling Tanya or the family, okay?"

"They'll hear about it as soon as you tell Dawson. The whole world will know about it then."

Steve smiled. Kent's "whole world" was NASCAR, but Steve's whole world was a life with Heidi. "Assuming Dawson doesn't fire me first, I'm going to wait until after Dover to tell him. Same reason. I don't want him thinking it's because of this weekend."

"But it is because of this weekend," Kent argued. "And you're not going to like me saying this, but if Heidi—"

"Then don't say it," Steve warned.

The cousins eyed one another for a long moment, then picked up their rods and turned their attention back to fishing.

"You know I hate driving Dover," Kent muttered.

"Thumpity, thumpity, thump," Steve replied with a grin, imitating the rhythm of the car racing on a concrete rather than an asphalt track. "They don't call it the Monster Mile for nothing."

"You coming up for the race at least?"

"If Dawson can get me into the hospitality suite."

"I'll get you in. I'm not going to put all my trust in a sub-stitute spotter. I don't care how good he is. I want you available by phone, if nothing else—in case."

But Dawson had other plans for Steve.

"Grosso," he growled over the phone an hour later, "get your butt to the airport. Amy Barber will meet you there."

"Because?"

"Because I want you out of town for a while until the dust settles. There's some preliminary work to be done in Orlando and then Chicago. Appearances to set up for Kent. You and Amy can handle it."

"Amy's perfectly capable of—"

"Do not push this," Dawson warned. "Wake up and smell the coffee. I'm giving you a chance here."

"Yes, sir." He hung up and turned back to Kent.

"I heard," Kent said. "Maybe it's best."

"Yeah. Mind if I miss those ribs? I might not get a chance to see Heidi again for a few days."

Kent grinned. "You have got the love bug beyond bad, man," he muttered.

But when Steve reached the cottage, the place was dark and Heidi's car was gone. On the kitchen table was a note—and the engagement ring.

THE FOLLOWING MORNING Heidi called Clare at the clinic.

"Where are you?" Clare demanded.

"I had to get away," Heidi said. "I left you a message. I just need a few days, okay?"

"Not okay. You picked a fine time to take an unscheduled vacation. All hell is breaking loose here and frankly, I don't know what to do."

"I'm sorry. I checked the schedule and—what's happened? Some emergency?"

"You could say that. Chuck Marshall called to find out when you planned to arrive in Dover."

"I don't," Heidi said.

"Well, sweetie, as Chuck pointed out, we have this legal contract."

"So I do the Dover thing. Then what? Vitality and—"

"Vitality and Vittle Foods are no longer on the radar. Apparently we have a new sponsor."

"Who?"

"He wouldn't say. Anonymous donor. What he did say was that they expect you to be in Dover when the mobile pet care unit arrives there."

"But—"

"Then I get a visit from your Nana," Clare continued, her voice dripping with exasperation.

"Steve's Nana," Heidi corrected automatically.

"Could have fooled me. And by the way, you broke the engagement? Are you completely nuts?"

"It's complicated. How's Steve?"

"How would I know? Nana was here to let you know the next meeting of the charity walk committee has been postponed until everyone gets to Dover. She also expects you to be there."

"That was it?" Heidi was stunned. "No mention of Steve or the—that I broke the engagement?"

"No. That news came via Tanya and Sophia, your erstwhile sisters-in-law who came storming in here like the place was on fire about ten minutes after Juliana left."

"They were mad?"

"They were dumbfounded and expected me to make some sense of your lunacy. So what are you going to do?"

"I can't go to Dover. You go. I'll come back and manage the clinic in town."

"Oh, no you don't. You started this thing. You will go to Dover."

"But Steve...I can't see him right now. I just can't."

"You won't. Dawson sent him off on some wild-goose chase. He's called here a gazillion times and when I tried to call you earlier I noticed that you've conveniently let your voice mailbox go to 'full and unavailable' mode. Coward."

Heidi sat in the parking lot of the drive-through restaurant where she'd stopped for breakfast. Just a few yards away cars whizzed by on the interstate. She had been around Steve and racing far too long for it to escape her that she was sitting in the pit area while life was racing along without her. "Okay, I'll go to Dover," she said.

"Oh, gee, what a great idea. Maybe at least this train wreck you seem determined to make of your life won't include the total devastation of a perfectly good business opportunity," Clare said. "Now, have you got a pen? Here's the number for Chuck Marshall. I assume you know how to phone Juliana and Milo?"

"I'll call Chuck," Heidi promised.

"And Juliana?"

"I'll think about it."

The sound Clare made before grinding out the phone number made Heidi smile. "Thanks, my friend," Heidi said and hung up.

What am I waiting for? Steve wondered as the red-eye commercial flight carried him from Orlando to Chicago. *There's only one chance to win Heidi back. We have to start over—somewhere new. Besides, Dawson isn't likely to get the subtlety of my electing not to resign until after the suspension is lifted. Either way he'll think it was just sour grapes, so what's the point of waiting?*

He accepted the plastic cup of coffee the steward offered and stared out into the black of middle of the night as Amy slept.

I'll call Kent first, he thought. *Then finish the Chicago assignment and call Dawson with the results—and the resignation.*

His mind made up, he set the untouched coffee aside, eased his seat back one notch and closed his eyes.

Dover, Delaware, was smaller than most places NASCAR ran. An hour south of Philadelphia and Newark and with Baltimore and Washington within easy driving distance to the east, it was a popular venue, one that sold out for nearly every event. It was also the kickoff point for the series of charity "walks" where fans could not only experience the feel of the track firsthand, but could mingle with drivers, team members and owners all in the name of raising money for charity.

Heidi had barely opened the door to the mobile unit before she saw Nana and a cluster of NASCAR women from the charity committee coming her way. "Heidi? You got my message?"

Heidi nodded, confused by Nana's acting as if everything was normal when for the last forty-eight hours Heidi's world had been whirling around faster than laps on a short track.

"Good. Get Buster settled and meet us over at the media center. We've got a lot of work to do."

The meeting ran long, but Heidi couldn't help being impressed with the women and their zeal to make this the most successful event they'd ever held. As it broke up, several of the women stopped to say how glad they were things had worked out with the mobile unit. They certainly seemed to know more than she did.

"Heidi, walk with me," Nana said, coming up beside her as they left the media center. "Milo wants to see you."

Heidi cringed, but she owed the senior Grossos a lot. So she walked back to the large motor home that for a couple of race weekends she had thought of as her home.

"It's Heidi, Milo," Nana called toward the bedroom. "Make sure you're decent."

"I'm decent," Milo grumbled as he came out of the bedroom buttoning his shirt. "Heidi." He acknowledged her with a nod and a scowl. "Looks like Dawson's gonna keep Steve."

"Yes, sir," Heidi replied cautiously.

"Now we just have to get you to keep Steve," he grumbled.

"Well, sit down. Grab yourself a soda or coffee. The others should be here any minute."

Others?

Milo continued to stare at her, his eyes blazing. "Saw that trailer of yours pull in yesterday. Did you happen to notice there's no corporate logo on the door?"

"Yes, sir."

Nana stepped between Milo and Heidi, tempering his intimidation with her soft voice. "Just wait for the others, Milo."

She was about to ask who they were expecting, when the door opened and Patsy, Dean and Sophia stepped inside.

"Heidi," Dean said, heading straight for the coffeepot.

"Where's Kent and Tanya?" Milo asked.

"They'll be along. Kent got a call."

"We can probably go ahead," Nana said, and everyone nodded as they crowded into the living area and found a seat.

Milo cleared his throat and focused his attention on Heidi. "Got a question for you. Do you love my great-grandson?"

"Yes, sir."

Milo nodded. "Thought so. Then this breaking-it-off-with-him business? That was a mistake?"

Heidi wasn't sure how to answer this and it seemed far too intimate a topic to discuss in front of an audience. But it was an audience she had as the others gave her their complete attention.

"It's complicated," she began.

Milo snorted. "You young folks are so blamed dramatic. Let's cut to the chase."

Nana put a restraining hand on her husband's arm. "What we wanted to say, Heidi, is that we'd like you to reconsider. It took a while but we finally realized that your issues with Vittle Farms and Vitality were just that—your issues."

"So Kent talked to Dawson and Dawson talked to Chester and Chester talked to Chuck Marshall—" Dean drew in a breath and continued "and long story short, Vittle Farms is no longer funding the mobile unit—at least not this year. You're in the clear."

"I…Clare and I appreciate that," Heidi said, trying hard to gauge what was really going on here. "Clare tells me a new sponsor has come forward—anonymously."

"That a problem?" Milo asked.

"Only if the new sponsor has ties to animal abuse," she said firmly.

"Well, let me think now," Milo mused, stroking his chin. "I don't think I've ever whipped my Tennessee walking horses and, Dean, you don't put lipstick on your dogs, do you? Now, maybe we have to take a look at Kent's fishing, but—"

"It's you?" Heidi could not believe what she was hearing. "You all are the new sponsor?"

Milo shrugged. "Anonymous, remember?" But he grinned.

Nana wrapped an arm around Heidi's shoulders. "Our Steve loves you, Heidi, and we've come to love you as well. We've gotten so used to being around folks who are used to how we operate that we just naturally assumed you would do all the adjusting when it came to becoming part of this loony bunch."

Patsy laughed. "We're a little slow on the uptake but we finish fast," she assured Heidi.

"I don't know what to say," Heidi murmured.

"Say you'll take back that ring," Dean ordered.

"I—"

The door to the motor home was wrenched open so hard that it banged against the sidewall as Kent burst in with Tanya close behind him. "Steve's going to resign," she announced. "He called Kent from Chicago. He's quitting before the season's even half over," she added with disgust.

Heidi noticed that Kent had trouble meeting her eyes as Tanya delivered this news. But Tanya had no problem facing her. "You have to stop this," she ordered.

Heidi reached for her cell phone. "I'll call him. He can't resign. Not when everything has changed."

They all seemed to be holding their breaths as she punched in Steve's speed-dial code. She frowned and clicked the phone shut. "Not in service," she said.

Tanya addressed her as if there had been no interruption to her story. "Kent tried to talk some sense into him, offering him options like continuing as spotter if you two are set on moving to Phoenix. And frankly, he owes Kent at least that much."

"Moving to Phoenix?" Heidi blinked in disbelief. "We're not moving. You must have misunderstood. We've talked about getting married in Phoenix, but—"

"Steve told me he wanted the two of you to get a fresh start," Kent said. "He mentioned it when we were fishing, but I just thought it was idle talk, the aftermath of his missed call at Charlotte. Steve can be pretty hard on himself when he thinks he's made a mistake."

"But resigning, leaving everyone in the lurch?" Tanya muttered.

"Let's just all calm down here," Milo ordered. "It's starting to sound like a henhouse in here and this rooster needs a minute to think, so shush, all of you."

Everyone exchanged looks and then retreated into the silence of their individual thoughts. Milo stood at the kitchen sink staring out at the compound.

"Where's Steve now?"

"He's stuck on the tarmac in Chicago, tornado warnings or some such," Kent reported.

"But he's on his way here?" Milo asked.

"Eventually," Kent answered. "I told Dawson I wanted him available even if he can't spot the race."

Milo headed for the door.

"Where are you going?" Nana demanded, following him.

"Never you mind. Kent, Dean, come on."

Left alone, the four women circled warily around each other under the guise of helping Nana make a fresh pot of coffee, and put out more snacks.

"He's just doing this because he loves me," Heidi said finally.

Patsy released an exasperated sigh. "Well, duh," she muttered, effectively sending Heidi back into silence. Then she laughed. "You know, sometimes I think I prefer an old-fashioned man like Dean. It would never in a gazillion years occur to him to create a multilife pileup just because of me."

Nana smiled. "These modern young men do tend to be a little more sensitive."

Tanya giggled. "Don't let Kent hear you accusing him of 'being in touch with his feminine side' or any such thing, Nana. He's his idea of an alpha hero—not to mention my alpha hero."

"So what are we going to do?" Heidi ventured, getting into the rhythm of this group of women who moved easily from high drama to humor without so much as blinking an eye.

"Let's wait for Milo," Nana suggested. "Not that I don't think he might be making things worse instead of better, but we need to have the full picture of what we're dealing with before we come up with a strategy for fixing it."

The other three women agreed and when Milo returned half an hour later he found the four of them sitting, yakking about what they were going to wear for the charity do.

STEVE MIGHT HAVE expected that Milo would weigh in on the disapproving side of his decision to resign, but he'd hardly expected to hear that objection via phone as he sat on the runway of O'Hare airport. He had one more stop to make before he got to Dover the following day—if he got to Dover. The way things were going, he might never get off this plane.

"I thought you were the world's best spotter, but you are blowing this race to the altar big-time," Milo announced without bothering with a greeting or with identifying himself—as if that gravelly voice could belong to anyone else. "What makes you think Heidi even wants to move to Phoenix? You don't even know if you can get her to marry you in the first place. And you got us all worked up about convincing her that the tour was 'home' and now you want to just up and move west without so much as discussing the matter?"

"I—"

"You will put yourself in Neutral until you get here and see what's really what. How do you know what's happened? You've been out gallivanting all over the blamed country while the rest of us—" Milo stopped in midsentence and Steve could hear the murmur of another voice. Kent. "Oh. Right," Steve heard Milo say before he took his hand away from the receiver and continued his rant. "Now what time are you getting here?"

"I don't know, sir. We're still on the runway." The term of respect seemed called for if Steve had any hope of calming Milo.

"Don't you 'sir' me, you overgrown whippersnapper. I know when I'm being pacified and it won't work. You make that call to Dawson and I swear on Juliana's lasagna I'll make you regret you ever thought about pulling such a stunt. You got that?"

"Got it."

"Good. Now here's your cousin. Heaven only knows how he keeps racking up the points when you and that gal of yours keep getting in his way, but he needs to make up some lost ground this weekend and not you or anybody else is going to stop that. Understood?"

"I—"

"Hey, Steve," Kent said, his voice a welcome calm following Milo's storm. "Sorry about that. I was upset by your call and Tanya was right there and I had to tell her. Then she insisted we run over to Nana's and—"

"Got the picture," Steve replied. "I have to get off. We're getting the signal to go. See you in a couple of hours."

THE CHARITY appearance of several drivers along with their wives, kids and pets was scheduled for Saturday afternoon. The setting had been moved from Souvenir Alley to the area outside the speedway.

"That way we get folks as they're headed to their seats," Nana explained.

Patsy had suggested that all the Grosso—or "almost" Grosso—women wear matching black jeans with bright yellow T-shirts she'd picked up earlier that day. Tanya came up with the idea of handing out treats for kids to give the pets.

Heidi was moved by these signals that they had completely welcomed her into the fold of the family. Whatever happened, she understood these women—and Clare—were friendships she would have for life. She and Nana had just finished changing, when Roger Clark knocked on the door of the motor home.

"Heidi? All set? Chuck wants to introduce you and the mobile pet unit at the kickoff."

Why? Heidi couldn't help wondering.

Heidi followed Roger around the corner to where a flatbed truck had been set up near the mobile unit and where Chuck Marshall was waiting. The head of NARS smiled at Heidi. "Well, Doc, looks like we might get this thing off the ground after all."

"Yes, sir," she replied nervously. "Thank you for—"

"Heidi?"

Chester Honeycutt was standing just outside the clinic door. He was, frankly, the last person Heidi would have expected to see anywhere near the mobile unit. To her further shock he handed her a nosegay of roses.

"Just wanted to add my congratulations. Clare Wilson stopped by my office the other day. She showed me the research you've done so far and explained that it was good news for Vitality, and she pushed for us to get that certification."

"You won't regret it," Heidi replied.

"I spoke to the board and they agreed that we needed to do whatever necessary to avoid any further…incidents."

"I'm sorry it didn't work out. You know, with the mobile unit. I never—"

She never finished the thought since Kent had taken the microphone and was addressing the media, fans and members of the NASCAR community who had gathered around. He wore his uniform and every journalist moved a step closer, determined not to miss a word of whatever the popular driver might have to say, especially after a week of speculation had him changing spotters.

STEVE WAS SURPRISED to see Dawson's driver waiting for him as he exited the security area at the airport. "Something up?" he asked, checking his cell for messages even though he'd already checked it as soon as the plane touched down.

"Boss just wants you in his suite as soon as I can get you there," the driver explained.

Steve groaned and followed the man to the town car.

Dawson's driver turned on the radio as he navigated the car smoothly onto the New Jersey Turnpike. Steve knew that the radio would automatically be turned to the closed-circuit NASCAR broadcast station. It was Dawson's car after all. He sat up straighter when he heard Kent's voice. He practically jumped out of the car when he heard Kent say they were standing in front of NARS's newest service for drivers and their teams and families—a mobile pet care unit.

As they waited for Chuck to take the microphone, the announcers filled in their usual speculative chatter: "…accused Vittle Farms…animal testing…well-known activist and spokesperson…vandalized car…"

Steve turned up the volume as Chuck cleared his throat once and then again. The shrill whistle of the microphone as he started to speak had him starting over. Steve glanced at the driver, who kept his eyes on the road.

"Ladies and gentlemen, this seems exactly the right moment to introduce this expansion of programs NARS is pleased to offer the NASCAR community. I am further pleased to announce that Dr. Heidi Kramer, the veterinarian who will manage the clinic, is here with us today. Dr. Kramer, would you do the honor of unveiling the sign?"

Steve's heart was hammering. *She had caved, given in to the pressure of his family, agreed to go against everything she believed in. Why? Because she thought it would help him.* Steve was as sure of that as anything. He envisioned Heidi stepping forward to remove whatever was covering the sign on the motor home—*their* motor home. Her business. The career she—like her mother—had now sacrificed for the man she loved.

"Can't you make this thing go any faster?" he growled.

The car had barely braked and the engine was still running when Steve jumped out and headed for the mobile unit at a run. In the background he could hear the master of ceremonies reading a long list of people who had helped organize the appearance of members of the NASCAR family and their pets to raise money for charity.

"Steve!"

Kent was coming off the flatbed that blocked Steve's view of the mobile unit, a couple of reporters still trailing along.

"Where's Heidi?" Steve asked.

"Over there."

"She can't do this," Steve said. "She's going against everything that she believes in."

Kent grinned. "I want to show you something, okay?" He draped an arm across Steve's shoulders and walked him around so that they were standing in front of the motor home. "Notice anything missing?"

Steve didn't like games when a race was on the line and definitely not when his future was on the line. "Just tell me," he said, glancing around, trying to spot Heidi.

"Let's see," Kent said with maddening calm. "Sign reads Mobile Pet Care Unit up there in big letters. And there's the NARS logo there."

"Yeah. I see it," Steve said impatiently.

"Do you?"

Steve blinked, then looked at Kent. "No sponsor name. What happened?"

Kent shrugged. "Got another sponsor—anonymous—but rumor has it that it's all in the family." He grinned as he watched the light dawn. "You got that ring with you?"

"I do," Steve said, unbuttoning his shirt pocket.

"That 'I do' part comes later, man. Do I have to teach you everything?" Kent sighed. "Come on, let's go get you two engaged—again."

THE FANS WERE delighted with this rare opportunity to get up close and personal with not only their favorite driver, but family members and pets, as well. Money poured into the bright yellow containers available near every ticket gate. Heidi took a moment to take it all in. Now there was no question that she would be at every race. Living in the 'hood, as Sophia might say. She had a business to run and, if she was lucky, a wedding to plan. The only question now was, would Steve still want her?

"Hey, lady, need someone to walk your dog?"

Heidi wheeled around and then flung herself into Steve's arms as Buster danced around the two of them and the thousands of fans kept streaming toward the entry gates. "You made it," she squealed with delight.

"I'm so sorry about everything," they said in unison and laughed.

"Did you hear?" Heidi asked. "Do you know?"

"Yeah. I also heard the whole unveiling thing. Dawson's driver just happened to flip on the radio on the drive down from Newark." He kissed her and then regarded her with narrowed eyes. "I don't suppose you had anything to do with that."

"Milo," she murmured as she kissed him back. "The man is a total romantic." Then she pulled away. "You can't be here. You're suspended."

He came in for another kiss. "I know a guy who knows a guy," he said as his lips closed on hers.

She pushed against his chest. "Now you listen to me, Steven Grosso. You have no idea what hoops your family has had to jump through to soothe ruffled feathers. You get yourself suspended again and—"

"Okay. Okay." He picked up Buster's leash.

Heidi glanced down and saw that Buster was carrying a small beribboned box Saint Bernard–keg style under his chin. "What's this?"

"Something I've decided to think you temporarily misplaced?"

Heidi untied the ribbon and opened the box, her eyes welling with tears of happiness. Steve removed the ring and slid it onto her finger. "I hope I never have to do this again, lady," he said as he knelt before her, holding her hands in his. "The knees are not what they used to be."

"Just ask," she whispered.

"Will you marry me and be my wife and the mother of my children? Will you be my NASCAR woman?" he said.

Heidi pulled him to his feet and flung her arms around him. "Yes, yes, yes," she said, punctuating each with a kiss.

Just then Dennis Murphy strolled past with a woman on each arm. "Hey, Grosso, see you later. Oh, right, you got smacked with a suspension. Rumor has it that you're planning to quit just like the sore loser that you and that driver you spot for are. Been nice knowing you—not!"

Steve let the man get several yards away and then yelled, "Hey, Dennis."

Dennis was laughing with his lady friends, certain that he'd gotten to Steve.

"Have a good race tonight. I'll see you next week, up top at Pocono." He waited a beat. "You see, I'm not going anywhere but on to the next race."

Dennis's grin turned to a scowl as he stalked off.

"So all that business about you resigning—that was just a rumor?" Heidi said, her blue eyes wide and innocent. "We— meaning the Grosso clan, that is, of which I am at least an honorary member—heard you were headed for Phoenix."

"You like Phoenix," he reminded her.

"Yeah. In November, just like I enjoy Dover in June. I just don't plan to get married or make a home with you in either place, you got that, Spotterman?"

"Ten-four," he replied. "Hey," he said softly, pulling her close. "Have I mentioned how much I love you?"

"Actions speak louder than words," she replied with a grin.

"No problem," he murmured, and he kissed her and kept on kissing her until they had begun to draw a crowd.

"Get a room," one man shouted, and several others joined in with similar teasing as they paused to enjoy the spectacle of two beautiful young people, obviously in love and oblivious to the world around them.

Heidi could feel Steve's lips curling into a smile as he kissed her. Laughter bubbled up inside her at the sheer lunacy of making out in the middle of thousands of race fans.

"He might have a point," she said to Steve, indicating the man who had made the comment.

"We've got better than a room," Steve said as he pulled her closer. "We've got a home—two of them—a cottage in the middle of a field of flowers just outside of town and a little home away from home right over there."

"Ah, those are just shelters from the storms," she said as she ran her fingers through his hair and pulled him closer. "Our real home has always been right here—in each other's arms."

"Whither thou goest?" he whispered.

Heidi nodded. "I will go," she said as Steve lifted her high in the air.

"Put me down," Heidi demanded, but she was laughing.

"Nope," Steve said as he turned to the crowd. "Folks," he shouted, "we'd like to thank you for your generosity in support of this charity event and now this wonderful woman and I invite you to join us in celebrating our engagement."

The crowd went nuts. Several fans grabbed cans of seltzer water from the refreshment table, shook them hard, opened the pull tabs and let the bubbly water spew like champagne. Steve hoisted Heidi higher in the air and she pumped one fist in the air as she had seen winning drivers do.

"Kiss her again," Tanya called. She and Kent had moved to the front of the crowd gathered around them and Tanya was aiming her camera to capture the moment.

"No problem," Steve replied as he lowered Heidi back to the ground and murmured, "Hey, what are you doing New Year's Eve?"

Heidi frowned. "Gee, I don't know. Sounds like a good day for a wedding to me."

Steve grinned. "I was hoping you'd say that."

"Well, we don't have all day," Milo growled as he hobbled through the crowd and put his arm around Juliana. "Get on with it."

"Yes, sir," Steve said and kissed Heidi lightly on the lips.

"You call that a kiss?" Milo shouted. "Watch and learn." Then he grabbed Juliana and planted a kiss on her to the delight of everyone.

"Yeah, cous, watch and learn," Kent shouted and bent Tanya over his arm as he kissed her.

"Oh, stop showing off," Patsy said, covering her laughter with one hand and holding on to Buster's leash with the other. Then she shrieked as Dean came up behind her and started making loud sucking noises as he kissed her neck.

Heidi looked from couple to couple and then at Steve. Her blue eyes were wide. "Is everything a competition with this gang?"

"Yep," he replied. "Want to try that slingshot move and beat the lot of them?"

Heidi giggled. "Your call."

"Be ready," he whispered. Then in one smooth move he swept her up into his arms and walked away from all of them, toward their motor home. Heidi wrapped her arms tightly around his neck as he covered her lips with his and they continued kissing as the crowd hooted and cheered.

*For more thrill-a-minute romances set against
the exciting backdrop of the NASCAR world, don't miss:
PEAK PERFORMANCE by Helen Brenna,
available in May.
For a sneak peek, just turn the page!*

THANKS FOR THE COMPANY, Rachel. I haven't danced in a long time."

"Me, neither."

"Not a date," Payton said as if he were reminding himself and not her.

She stepped away, and he touched her hand. Barely, but that was all the invitation she needed. She turned back around and walked into his arms. And stayed there. A minute. Maybe two. In a hold too intimate to be called a hug.

He leaned his forehead against hers. "What are we doing, Rachel?"

She wished she knew. "Could be this is all about you wanting an interview."

"Maybe the night started out that way." Slowly, he shook his head. "Right now an interview is the furthest thing from my mind."

"In that case, we're having fun." She offered the best answer she had. "Enjoying each other's company. Is there a problem with that?"

"Absolutely not. As long as we both know where we stand."

"We stand as friends. This is casual. No ties, no expectations, no commitments. No claims. We might sleep together. We might not. It's too soon to tell."

"I've never met a woman who could live with that. You think you can?"

"I'm sure. Can you?"

"Yes, ma'am." Already, he was sounding a bit Southern, but the intensity of his gaze was anything but polite. "Give me the contract and I'll sign it right now. Tonight. Then we can take care of that sleeping together part you mentioned."

"Too soon on a first date, isn't it?"

"I thought we agreed this wasn't a date."

She leaned in, bent her nose against his, brushed her mouth over his. He brushed back. She tasted her own lip gloss on him. Red raspberry, sweet and a little tangy.

"I suppose that wasn't a kiss," he murmured.

"Not by a long shot."

But it had been the most moving not-a-kiss on such a comfortable not-a-date she'd ever experienced. She nearly changed her mind and walked down with him to the lake. A definite no-no.

Instead, she looked into his eyes, tilted her head and opened her mouth over his. He was as sturdy as a wall, and she melted into him, running her tongue along his with motions that were as much a dance as the moves they'd made at the club earlier. He moved to wrap his arms around her, but she drew away.

"*That* was a kiss." She ran up the steps and into her house, closing the door firmly behind her. As flavors went, Payton Reese was proving to be sweet as could be.

"The more I see, the more I feel the need."

—**Aviva Presser,** real-life heroine

*Aviva Presser is a Harlequin More Than Words
award winner and the founder of **Bears Without Borders.***

Discover your inner heroine!

MTW07AP1

REQUEST YOUR FREE BOOKS!

2 FREE NOVELS PLUS 2 FREE GIFTS!

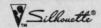

SPECIAL EDITION®

Life, Love and Family!